Praise for Lesley Kelly

THE HEALTH OF STRANGERS

'An intriguing tale of crime in a post viral Edinburgh, told with panache.'   -Lin Anderson

'It's well paced with strong storylines, a frighteningly plausible plot and entertaining banter between its main characters throughout.'   *-Portobello Book Blog*

'The characters are brilliant. Their dialogue is spot on and the relationship between Bernard and Mona is great. A truly fantastic read!'   *-The Crime Warp*

'Lesley Kelly has a knack of leaving you wanting more...'
-Love Books Group

'A crime thriller in a dystopian and ravaged Edinburgh with a great cast and the pages which virtually turned themselves. I bloody loved it.'   *-Grab This Book*

'*The Health of Strangers* moves along at a cracking pace and the unsettling sense you get of an all-too-believable Edinburgh of the near future, or perhaps an alternative Edinburgh of today, helps draw you into what, at its heart, is a really well constructed and extremely entertaining thriller.'   *-Undiscovered Scotland*

'*The Health of Strangers* is as humorous and quirky as it is insightful and observant.'   -*Lothian Life*

'A great read... I'm looking forward to catching up with the characters in book 2.'   -**Sandra**, *Beauty Balm Blog*

A FINE HOUSE IN TRINITY

'Written with brio, *A Fine House in Trinity* is fast, edgy and funny, a sure-fire hit with the tartan noir set. A standout debut, if there is justice in the world this book will find its audience.'   -**Michael J. Malone**

'The storyline is strong, the characters believable and the tempo fast-moving.'   -*Scots Magazine*

'This is a romp of a novel which is both entertaining and amusing ... the funniest crime novel I've read since Fidelis Morgan's The Murder Quadrille and a first class debut.'   -*Crime Fiction Lover*

'Razor sharp Scottish wit is suffused throughout and this makes *A Fine House in Trinity* a very sweet shot of noir crime fiction. This cleverly constructed romp around Leith will have readers grinning from ear to ear and some of the turns of phrase deserve a standing ovation in themselves.'   -*The Reading Corner*

'A welcome addition to the Tartan Noir scene, providing as it does a more light-hearted approach to solving a crime. Lesley Kelly is a fine writer, entertaining us throughout. The near-300 pages are deceptive, as this is a book perfect for romping through in one sitting.'   -*Crime Worm*

Lesley Kelly has worked in the public and voluntary sectors for the past twenty years, dabbling in poetry and stand-up comedy along the way. She has won several writing competitions, including the Scotsman's Short Story award in 2008. Her debut novel, *A Fine House in Trinity* was long-listed for the William Mclvanney award in 2016. She can be followed on Twitter (@lkauthor) where she tweets about writing, Edinburgh and whatever else takes her fancy.

Also by Lesley Kelly

A Fine House in Trinity
The Health of Strangers

SONGS
BY
DEAD GIRLS

A *HEALTH OF STRANGERS* THRILLER

LESLEY KELLY

SANDSTONEPRESS
HIGHLAND | SCOTLAND

First published in Great Britain by
Sandstone Press Ltd
Dochcarty Road
Dingwall
Ross-shire
IV15 9UG
Scotland

www.sandstonepress.com

The publisher acknowledges subsidy from Creative Scotland
towards publication of this volume.

ISBN: 978-1-912240-08-1
ISBNe: 978-1-912240-09-8

Cover design by Blacksheep, London
Typeset by Iolaire Typography Ltd, Newtonmore
Printed and bound by Totem, Poland

To all the hardworking Annemaries in the voluntary sector – the world would be a much worse place without you

CONTENTS

CONFIDENTIAL MEMO: HEALTH AND SAFETY

To: Team Leaders, Edinburgh Health Enforce-
      ment Teams: North, South, East and West
From: Police Scotland
Subject: Drug Dealing in Edinburgh

As you are aware, the growth in demand for both narcotics and non-prescription Viral prophylactics is currently making the drugs market very lucrative.

We wish to draw the HET's attention to the recent death (from the Virus) of Angus McNiven. Mr McNiven has been of interest to us for a number of years with regard to organised crime, particularly in relation to the importation of illegal substances.

His death has greatly destabilised the situation on the East Coast, with new suppliers looking to move into the territory. Existing suppliers are extremely twitchy, and the new players appear willing to use extreme force to establish themselves.

We are aware that the HET's role in seeking people who have missed their monthly Health Check continually brings you into contact with people living 'chaotic' lifestyles, of which drugs may often play a part.

IT IS IMPERATIVE THAT HET OFFICERS EXERCISE EXTREME CAUTION WHEN GOING ABOUT THEIR DUTIES UNTIL THE SITUATION STABILISES.

We suggest that you raise this memo with staff at your next team meeting, and that all staff members are briefed to be exceedingly cautious. Anyone requiring further information contact Ian Jacobsen, East of Scotland HET liaison officer.

MONDAY

NAUSEA

I

It was a horrible noise, the kind of unnatural high-pitched squeal that Bernard often found punctuating his nightmares. The fact that he was currently wide awake didn't make the noise any less excruciating. It took all his self-control not to stick his fingers in his ears. Mona, the creator of the ungodly noise, pulled the remaining bits of shrink-wrap off the stab-proof vest, provoking yet more shrill squeaks.

Bernard shivered. '*Beware of all enterprises that require new clothes.*'

'What?' Despite her question, Mona's profile radiated a certain degree of indifference which made it difficult for him to work out if she did actually want to know more. He decided to venture further down the path.

'It's a quote from Henry David Thoreau. You know – the nature writer? Advocated simple living? Spent years in a forest?' The look of annoyance on his partner's face clarified that she wasn't interested in updating her knowledge of woods-based philosophers at this point in time. 'Never mind. Can I have a look at it?'

She passed the vest over to him. It was a solid torso-shaped affair, rigid, although lighter than he was expecting, with a strange rubbery feel.

'I don't know what you're complaining about.' Mona's blonde bob covered her face as she set about unwrapping the second vest. 'This is about keeping us safe. Remember that HET officer in Aberdeen who tried to retrieve a Health Defaulter from a crack den and got a knife in the balls for his troubles?'

'Not exactly the body parts that will be covered by these.'

She tutted. 'Oh, well, put in a special request for a reinforced rubber codpiece.'

A fug of depression settled around his shoulders. He'd been in the car with his partner for all of ten minutes and already she was annoyed with him. It wasn't unusual for them to spend the best part of a working day trapped in a car together. As members of the North Edinburgh Health Enforcement Team it was their job to find people who'd missed their monthly Health Check, a front-line attempt to stop the spread of the Virus. This involved a lot of driving, knocking on doors, being lied to, sitting in wait, and eventually catching up with the Defaulter. On the days when he had inadvertently irritated Mona, eight hours of close contact with her could feel considerably longer.

He tried to avert this looming disaster with some humour. 'Not sure it's really an area worth protecting. It's not like it's in use.'

'Spare me, please.' She continued with her peeling, then suddenly looked up, with a slightly more conciliatory expression on her face. 'No chance of getting back with your wife then?'

Glad as he was that Mona was no longer scowling at him, he didn't feel inclined to enter into that particular area of discussion. 'Not looking for one. Anyway, shall we suit up?' He slipped his jacket off, then tried to fit his arm into the appropriate opening. The rigidity of the

4

vests and the limited dimensions of the car made this no easy task, and he accidentally elbowed Mona.

'Sorry. It would be easier to put them on if we got out of the car.'

'No. I don't want them to notice us and do a runner.'

They were parked on a quiet side street in Morningside, one of the most affluent areas of Edinburgh. The property currently attracting their attention was a terraced sandstone building, with a large sloping garden leading up to it. The grass had not been cut for some time.

'Not a bad residence for someone without a job,' said Bernard.

'I suspect the wages of sin are paying for it.'

'What makes you say that?'

'Number one,' Mona held up a finger. 'This is a nice bit of town, and that's, what, a three, maybe four-bed house. You're looking at the best part of half a million. Who is paying the mortgage on that?'

'Our Defaulter could have a very rich daddy? Or she could just be renting?'

'Even the rents in this bit of town are eye-watering. And I have another point. Number two.' She was now holding two fingers up. 'This is a fabulously expensive house, and look at the state of the garden. Every other lawn in the street looks like the grass was trimmed into place with nail scissors, yet this place looks like waste ground. And have they washed the windows any time in the last few years?'

'You sound like my grandmother.'

'Grandma could probably do a very good job of knowing a wrong 'un when she sees one. And my third and most important point is, we're here, so there must be something dodgy going on.'

'Not necessarily.'

'Ha! In all the months we've been doing this, how many people have defaulted on their Health Check for reasons that were not to do with overconsumption of drink or drugs, or who were not in some way participating in illegal activity?'

He thought for a second. 'Occasionally they turn out to be dead?'

'Usually due to the overconsumption of drink or drugs. Anyway, turn round, Bernard, and I'll get the straps.'

He obediently presented his back to her. 'What do we know about today's Defaulter?'

'Alessandra Barr, twenty-five, missed her Health Check three days ago. And I don't want to be judgemental or anything, but take a look at her picture.'

She held up their Defaulter List, and Bernard stared at a slightly blurred photograph of a gaunt young woman. She had badly dyed blonde hair, which sat awkwardly with her dark colouring.

'Has she got two black eyes?' Bernard ran his finger across the photograph.

'Yep. The day she turned up to get her Green Card photo taken, she had a face full of bruises. I'm going to go out on a limb and say she's not a soccer mom.' She opened her door. 'Shall we?'

Bernard tried to ignore the knot of fear in his stomach. Unlike Mona, he didn't have the confidence that police college and years of law enforcement experience instilled. He'd previously worked in health promotion, where the day-to-day work of encouraging breastfeeding and smoking cessation had left him woefully underprepared for the realities of working at the HET. Most of the Defaulters they chased were less than delighted to see

6

them, and he had spent many work hours being sworn at, spat at, and occasionally punched. He wondered if he'd ever get through the day without this ever-present feeling of doom.

'Mona!'

She stopped with her hand on the garden gate. 'What?'

'What's our plan here?'

'We knock on the door, ask whoever answers if we can see Alessandra. If they say no we insist that we come in, using the powers bestowed on us by the Health Defaulters Act, blah, blah, blah. The usual.'

'But what if she makes a run for it?'

'Then you stop her.'

'What with?'

Mona raised her hands in the air and wiggled them. 'These.' She started walking again. 'Because rightly or wrongly, they're the only weapons that the HET have seen fit to supply us with.'

She pressed the bell, which made no sound.

'Try knocking.'

'Thanks, I wouldn't have thought of that.' Mona hammered on the wood. The sound echoed through the house, but didn't appear to rouse any occupants.

Bernard left the path and peered through the crack in the curtains. 'I don't see anyone, though it's not that easy without the lights on.'

Mona knocked for a second time, and again was met with silence. She turned the handle, and the door opened. 'Result! Come on.'

Bernard stepped over the threshold, both aware and annoyed that his heart was beating ridiculously fast. Amongst his many secret fears was that on one of these jaunts he was actually going to have a cardiac arrest. His only hope was that the heart failure would be instantly fatal, and wouldn't involve him having to face the ridicule of the HET team from a hospital bed. He tried to calm his nerves by focusing on the surroundings. The hallway was dark, with the only light coming from the open door behind them. It was uncarpeted, but not in a trendy, stripped-back wood kind of way, more in the mode of 'we haven't been living here long enough to cover the floor'. Or maybe, as in Mona's theory, the overconsumption of illegal substances had made investing in carpet a low priority. There were a number of doorways leading off the hall, and, from what he could see in the gloom, a rather magnificent staircase straight ahead of them.

Mona turned to her right and shoved open a door. He made to follow her.

'What are you doing?' she hissed.

'Coming with you?'

She pointed at him, then at the door opposite, indicating he should check that room. He mouthed an irritable 'OK', and turned his back on her before she could see the look of fear on his face. He much preferred being two steps behind her. Bernard would have taken a blow to the head or a knife in the vest quite happily just so long as Mona was making all the decisions. Backup he could do. Pole position was a different matter.

He reached for the handle and tried to remember what he'd been taught in his month-long induction to the HET. He seemed to recall that there had been a whole day about 'Encountering Hostility and How to Respond'. He paused with the door slightly open, and tried to remember the key phrases.

Be confident. Breathe. Show respect. Moderate your tone. Keep your distance. Know your exits.

He wiped the sweat from his hand, and threw the door wide. There was no response, so he flicked the light switch. To his relief the room was empty, although there was a lingering smell of cannabis in the air suggesting that it had been in use not so very long ago. In common with the hallway, the room did not benefit from any floor covering. Furniture was sparse, with the large and gracious room hosting only a dilapidated sofa, a coffee table, and a TV of a size and depth that predated the birth of the flat screen. The absence of furnishing meant a limit to places where someone could hide, although there was a door in the corner of the room, potentially a cupboard. He walked swiftly across the room and pulled it open to find it led on to another room. He caught his breath as he saw a figure coming toward him.

'Hey.'

Mona.

She reached past him and turned on the light, illuminating the kitchen. Once upon a time, the fittings were probably state of the art, but it was difficult to tell from the layer of grime which covered the work surfaces. Unwashed dishes were stacked on every unit.

'If your grandmother didn't like dirty windows, Bernard, she'd have a fit looking at this place.'

He pulled a face. 'How can anyone live like this?'

'Beats me. Puts the state of the Guv's office into perspective, though. Anyway, there's no one here; let's try the upper floor.'

At the top of the stairs they separated again, Bernard to the left and Mona to the right. He opened the first door he came to, which as he expected was a bedroom. The curtains were drawn, but enough sunshine was sneaking through the cracks to allow him to see that

9

the room was actually somewhat better furnished than downstairs. There was a rug on the floor, for starters, two ancient double wardrobes, and an incongruously ornate dressing table. There was also a double bed, upon which, he realised with a start, there was a large, person-shaped lump. A lump that was lying extremely still. Whether he was looking at a live body or a dead one was not clear, and a sudden hope it was a corpse flitted through his mind, to be followed immediately by a chaser of remorse. However unpleasant some of the Defaulters were, they were still his fellow human beings, and he didn't wish any of them dead.

He did, however, wish that he wasn't on his own. He looked round but Mona had vanished into another room. He could go after her, explain what he'd found, and confirm to her – if it was ever in doubt – that he really couldn't hack it. Or he could stay here and try to pretend that he wasn't in imminent need of a defibrillator. He took a deep breath and turned back toward the divan.

'Hello.'

His voice was high-pitched and squeaky, rather like shrink-wrap peeled off plastic. *Be confident. Breathe.*

With a conscious effort he lowered his voice. 'Excuse me.' *Show respect.*

The lump in the bed didn't move. He took a step toward it, and could see a mass of long brown hair spread across the pillow. He felt a certain amount of relief that this was a woman. In his experience, women weren't any less likely to throw a punch at you, but for the most part they tended to do less damage. It didn't appear to be Alessandra, however, unless she'd radically changed her look since her photograph was taken.

'Excuse me.' His voice was getting louder, and snippier. He caught himself. *Moderate your tone.*

His tone of voice, inappropriate or otherwise, wasn't provoking a response. After a careful consideration of the duvet he was pretty sure that it was going up and down, blowing his corpse theory out of the water. This was a warm body, who might not take well to being woken by a strange man in her house. He shot a glance over his shoulder. Perhaps under the circumstances Mona would be less threatening than him? Tempting as this was, it was a cop-out. With a sigh and a quick check how many steps it was back to the door – *know your exits* – he walked over to the bed and shook the woman gently by the shoulder.

The body rolled toward him, revealing broad shoulders, a hairy chest and three days of stubble. 'Who the fuck are you?' The man sat up, and grabbed his arm.

Bernard tried to wriggle free. 'We're from the Health Enforcement Team. If you let go of me I can show you some ID. We're looking for Alessandra Barr...'

The man was looking at him with a strange expression on his face. His grip on Bernard's arm slackened.

'Are you OK?'

The man responded by opening his mouth and vomiting profusely down Bernard's front.

He snatched his arm back. 'For goodness' sake!'

Mona appeared in the doorway, and surveyed the scene.

'Oh, Bernard.' She stared at his ruined vest. 'This is the reason we keep our distance.'

'I wonder if I could have a quick word with you about your neighbours?' Mona held up her HET ID to the crack in the door. It opened further and a middle-aged woman appeared, squinting into the July sunshine.

'Are you from the police? Is this about my complaint?' The accent was plummy, redolent of Edinburgh public school and a career in financial services.

'No. We're the Health Enforcement Team – we look for people who've missed their monthly Health Check.'

A brief look of disappointment crossed her face, but she quickly recovered. 'Well, if they are in trouble about that as well it doesn't surprise me.' The door opened yet further, and Mona had a flash of a much grander hallway than the one she'd seen next door. 'They're up to all sorts over there. If you want to hear about it, you'd better come in.'

She looked over at the HET car. Bernard, minus his vest, was standing guard. The young man they'd encountered, although singularly unapologetic for his recent retching, had not given them any trouble. He'd dressed, accompanied them outside, and allowed himself to be safely locked in the back seat of their car. Surely her partner couldn't get into any trouble if she left him for a few minutes? But then Bernard had confounded her expectations before. 'Any chance we could just run through it quickly here?'

Ten minutes later she hurried back down the path to her partner. 'Did you turn up anything?'

'His name's Stephen McNiven, and he's got a fully up-to-date Green Card ...' He lifted it up to show her.

'McNiven? That name rings a bell.' Had she arrested him before? 'Sorry, I interrupted you. Go on.'

'I was just going to say I ran a database check and he's not a Health Check Defaulter, and he's not wanted by

Police Scotland. Did you find out anything useful from next door?'

'I'm not sure how useful it was, but I can say definitively that he won't be winning any good neighbour awards. Not if the lady in number 29 is telling the truth, anyway. Lots of people coming and going, she said. She seemed to be particularly offended by the female visitors in, as she put it, "high heels and skirts that barely cover their backsides". Occasional screaming and shouting late at night, in response to which she always calls the police, who invariably "do nothing". She really wasn't a fan of Mr McNiven.'

'I kind of see where she's coming from,' said Bernard, pointing at his sodden vest, which was airing well away from the car.

She tried not to smile. 'Shall we see if he wants to chat?'

McNiven did not look up as they climbed in. Mona turned on the intercom.

'Are you all right back there? Not feeling nauseous anymore?'

He ignored them and turned his attention from staring at the floor to staring out of the window. Mona took the opportunity to give him the once-over. Mid-twenties, she'd say. The clothes he'd scrambled to put on earlier were clearly expensive designer gear, although the look was undermined by the few remaining bits of vomit in his hair. Designer gear, disreputable visitors day and night – the scenario screamed out dealer.

And yet … this was an unusual area of Edinburgh for a dealer to set himself up in. A ground-floor seller would struggle to pay the rent on this size of place, and from the look of Mr McNiven he was no kingpin. And, as his next-door neighbour had just proved, people round here were on the phone to the police at the first sign of anti-social behaviour. McNiven could just as easily be some spoiled trust-fund kid, living it large with no thought for the neighbours. She decided to tread carefully, in case he turned out to be the son of a high court judge, or someone else with the wherewithal to sue the HET.

'So, do you go by Stephen or Stevie? I'm going to guess you are a Stevie.'

He sighed, theatrically. 'Are you going to arrest me, or what?'

'We're not the police. We don't arrest people. We can, however, detain them while they assist us with our investigations into the whereabouts of people who have missed their Health Checks. The two processes are not dissimilar, and your chance of experiencing either one depends entirely on how helpful you are intending to be.'

He stared at her blankly, and she tried to work out if he was bluffing, or really didn't know why they were here.

'Alessandra Barr.'

He shook his head. 'Don't know her.'

'OK. Let's start with what you do know. Who else lives in the house with you?'

'I don't live there. I just met some bird last night and went home with her.'

Mona loved it when their cover stories were this idiotic. She filed it away in her memory to tell to the others when they got back. 'And she got up early to go to work and just left you there, a complete stranger, alone in her house?'

He shrugged.

'Well, no offence, Stevie, but that strikes me as pretty

14

implausible. And you know what else makes me think you are lying?'

'Nope.'

'Your next-door neighbour. Did you not just watch me talk to her for the past ten minutes?'

He shrugged.

'The lady who lives in the house next to yours, sorry, I mean the house that you found yourself in this morning, well, she was very vocal about a man with long brown hair that lives at this address. Apparently she's had several run-ins over loud music, visitors at all times of the night, and the numerous undesirable types staying here. Think if I went back in to get her she'd be able to identify you?'

He snorted. 'Yeah, the old bat would love that. All right, I live here. Don't know any Alexandra whatsit though.'

'Take a look at this picture.' Mona held it up to the Perspex window between the front and back seats. 'Do you recognise her?'

He glanced at it, and quickly looked away. 'Nope.'

'Take a proper look.'

He made a show of leaning forward on his seat and staring at the photograph. 'I don't know her.' He spoke the words slowly and aggressively. 'And judging by the state of her, I'm glad I don't. Can I go now?'

Mona turned to Bernard, to see if he had anything to add to the discussion. He returned her look with one of slight panic, which she took as a no.

'Just one last question – what do you do for a living?'

'This and that.'

Mona pressed the button to unlock the rear doors. Their passenger jumped at the noise, and looked at them uncertainly, as if they might be setting some kind of trap for him.

'You can get out. You're free to go.'

Mona stepped out of the car, and waited for Stevie McNiven to emerge. She passed him a HET business card. 'But if you do remember seeing anyone looking like Alessandra Barr, do be sure to give us a ring.'

'Course I will.' He took the card and shoved it in the back pocket of his jeans, which appeared to be Armani. Whatever the 'this and that' profession was, it was obviously profitable. With a final smirk, he sauntered off, looking back at them as he strolled up the path to his house. His neighbour was still standing on her front step, her body language radiating disapproval. Mona wondered if her annoyance was with McNiven, or more likely, with the HET for letting him back out of the car. McNiven ground to a halt, and gave the long-suffering homeowner next door a mock salute. She disappeared back into the house, shaking her head.

'Do you reckon he knows Alessandra Barr then?' asked Bernard.

'Of course he did.' She started the car. 'He looked away far too quickly. Let's get back to the office and try and find out some more about Mr McNiven.'

2

'What is that smell?'

Maitland's head appeared round the side of his computer, nostrils twitching as he made a show of sniffing the air. Bernard braced himself for an onslaught of abuse. Maitland got to his feet, pulling his lanky 6´3″ to its full height, and stood towering over him. 'Bernard, are you responsible for stinking out the office?'

'My stab-proof vest had a nasty accident.' He held the offending article aloft.

Maitland moved hurriedly backwards. 'Oh, that's what they're for! Catching Bernard's vomit when he gets so scared he pukes!'

'Maitland!' said Carole, the fourth member of their team. 'Be nice.'

Mona appeared with a handful of plastic bags which she spread out on the floor next to Bernard's desk.

'Thank God.' He dropped the vest, delighted to offload it. 'I was puked *upon*, actually.'

'By your Defaulter?' asked Carole.

'No. Some guy that was at the house when we went looking for her.'

'Did you bring him in?'

'No.' Maitland looked sceptical, and Bernard felt immediately defensive. 'We had no grounds to. He denied all knowledge of knowing any Alessandra Barr.

His Green Card checked out OK, and Police Scotland weren't looking for him for anything.'

'Where's the Guv?' asked Mona.

'In his office.' In one corner of the main room an MDF structure created an internal office for their team leader, John Paterson. This gave their boss a private, although not very soundproofed space, particularly as Paterson was seldom given to communicating in anything less than a bark.

'In his office *with the door shut*?'

'I know!' said Carole. 'It's not like him at all.' Their team leader valued the two-way communication afforded to him by an open door. He could yell at his staff without having to get up, and could eavesdrop on their conversations with minimal effort.

Maitland took up the story. 'He was fine first thing, then about nine thirty he shut the door and we've not seen him since. We didn't hear him taking any phone calls, so we reckon it must have been an e-mail that's upset him.'

'Trouble, do you think?' Mona looked thoughtful. 'I wonder if we should tell him that we're back?'

'Tell him about Bernard puking on himself.' Maitland chuckled. 'That'll cheer him up.'

'I did not puke. It was ...' he tailed off as Paterson flung open the door to his office.

'Maitland, I need you in here.'

'Just me?' asked Maitland, surprised.

'Yup.' Paterson wasn't catching anyone's eye. There was a slight shiftiness about his manner. In anyone else Bernard would have said he detected an air of embarrassment, but he couldn't conceive of an issue that would provoke that kind of emotion in his rhino-hided boss.

18

Maitland's usual smugness had been replaced by an expression of mild alarm. 'Just me? Am I in trouble?'

'It's, well, it's a ... sensitive issue.'

'So, he *is* in trouble?' asked Bernard, hopefully.

Paterson sighed. 'I might as well tell you all as I'll need to speak to you as part of the investigation.'

'Investigation?' Maitland imbued the word with all the horror he could muster. Bernard suspected that the tone was justified. Investigations ended careers, halting promotion prospects in their tracks. Even if they got the all-clear, chances were some mud stuck. Investigations were bad news, and Bernard couldn't be happier that Maitland was in the middle of one, although he was racking his brains to work out what his colleague could have done.

'There's been a complaint about Maitland's behaviour on the Weber and Greenwood cases a couple of months back.'

Maitland's jaw dropped. 'But it was Bernard and Mona that arsed that up.'

'I don't disagree.'

Bernard glanced at Mona. There was a tiny flicker of hurt on her face which quickly disappeared. She turned back to her computer, he suspected to avoid catching his eye.

He was inclined to agree with Maitland, himself. Colette Greenwood, a divinity student, and Heidi Weber, the daughter of a German MP, had both been Defaulters. They'd been young, pretty and totally in thrall to a religious cult with a dangerous interest in prophylactic drugs. Mona and Bernard had messed the case up, and Heidi had been found dead. It was only the desire of the German government not to have any further light shone on the case that had let them keep their jobs. Bernard was pretty sure that Paterson had been engaged on some wheeling-dealing on their behalf, but whatever had gone on behind the scenes, the end result seemed to have caused irreparable damage to the Guv and Mona's relationship. He couldn't honestly remember a civil word passing between the two of them in the past couple of months.

'Anyway, Maitland, as I said it's sensitive so in my office, now.'

He still didn't move. 'If this is an investigation, am I not entitled to have someone with me?'

Paterson considered this. From the look of indecision on his face Bernard deduced his boss was not as familiar as he should be with the staffing information that all the HET team members had been given as part of their Induction Guide. He, on the other hand, had taken the precaution of memorising several essential nuggets, in case he was ever subject to a grievance, disciplinary or any other deeply unpleasant HR procedure. He swithered for a second, then opened his mouth.

'Under Section 73 of the staff handbook you're entitled to be accompanied by a union rep ...'

Maitland's expression remained in panic mode. 'I'm not in the union.'

'Or another member of staff.'

Carole laughed. 'Oh, Maitland. If only you knew a staff member with an encyclopaedic knowledge of rules and regulations who could help you out.'

He turned to him. 'Bernard ...?'

'Right,' said Paterson, turning on his heel. 'Can you and Perry Mason there finally get in here?'

'I didn't say I'd do it,' said Bernard to his boss's retreating back.

'Come on, don't be a dick.' Maitland bounded over to Bernard's desk, nearly tripping over the desecrated vest in his haste.

'No, sorry.' He pressed his computer's on button. 'Not doing anything for that kind of attitude.'

'OK, I apologise.' He crouched down and lowered his voice. 'Please help me out here, mate.'

'Going to have to be considerably more begging than that.'

'OK.' He stood back up, and sighed. 'If you do this, I'll owe you one.'

'A favour to be redeemed from Maitland?' He considered the offer for a moment. 'That's worth having. OK, I'm in.'

They trooped into Paterson's office. He didn't look up, seemingly entranced by the documents spread in front of him.

'So, a complaint has been made that you, Maitland, were, ehm ...' there was some rearranging of the papers on Paterson's desk, ' ...em, having sexual relations with one of the witnesses on the Greenwood case.'

Maitland's face contorted. 'This is bloody Emma, isn't it? My ex?'

'All complainants are given anonymity during the investigation.'

'It is her though, isn't it?'

Paterson shrugged, which Maitland took as a yes. 'Not bad enough that she dumps me, she also has to make trouble.'

'Speaking as a divorcé, making trouble for the errant male does seem to feature pretty highly on a scorned woman's to-do list. I could have been sacked three times over if people had believed everything my first wife said

21

about me when I left her, so I'm not unsympathetic.'

'Ehm, anonymity, Mr Paterson?' said Bernard.

'Not that I'm confirming it was your ex. Anyway, so, you *weren't* sleeping with,' he checked the name, 'Kate Wilson during the investigation?'

Bernard laughed, incurring glares from both Maitland and Paterson. Usually his team leader's wrath would be enough to swiftly rid him of any feelings of happiness, but this was just too good. He doubled over and chortled.

'Something funny?'

'Well, firstly, Mr Paterson,' he fought to get his breathing under control, 'Kate is a Christian of the variety that doesn't believe in sex before marriage, and secondly, she's a good-looking woman with more sense than to look at Maitland.'

His colleague glowered at him, before his features morphed into an expression closer to coyness. 'Actually...'

Silence filled the office.

'Actually, what?' asked Paterson.

'We're dating.'

Paterson slumped back in his chair. 'There are boundaries, Maitland...'

'But it started after the investigation ended!'

'OK.' He thought for a second. 'That's a very relevant point. And you're not...' Paterson made a vague gesture with his hand. Bernard could contain himself no longer and started to giggle again.

Maitland elbowed him in the ribs. 'No.'

'So, just to clarify, Bernard, did you notice any inappropriate behaviour of a sexual nature by Maitland toward anyone involved in the Greenwood case?'

'Just his usual level of inappropriate sexual innuendo.

22

And some misplaced homophobia in my direction.'

'I'll put that as a no, then. Mona! Carole!' They appeared suspiciously quickly at the door. 'Did you notice any inappropriate behaviour of a sexual nature by Maitland toward anyone involved in the Greenwood case?'

'Like what, Mr Paterson?' asked Carole.

'If you have to ask, Carole, I'm going to take that as a "no".'

'Mona?'

She grinned. 'No, Guv.'

Paterson continued scribbling on his notes. 'OK, as far as I'm concerned that's the investigation concluded, bar submitting the paperwork.' He pointed at the door. 'Now, out of my office.'

'I expect you want to know what all that was about?' asked Bernard, pulling the door shut behind him.

'No. We could hear pretty much every word,' said Mona, grinning. 'I particularly liked the bit about Maitland having a new girlfriend but not getting laid.'

'Same as Bernard, then, except for the girlfriend bit.' The colour was returning to Maitland's cheeks. 'Anyway, doesn't anyone have work to do, people to find, etc., etc.?'

'Not sure we're quite finished taking the piss, but it'll keep.'

3

'Mona, get your coat.'

She looked up to see Paterson standing in the doorway of his office, shrugging on his mackintosh. 'We've been summoned to SHEP.'

'We have?' Mona grabbed her jacket and bent down to pick up her bag. By the time she was upright, Paterson had vanished. She could hear him thundering along the corridor outside; he might have requested her company, but he wasn't giving off any vibes that suggested he was happy to be spending time with her.

'Bernard – can you handle the IT visit without me?'

'No problem. Good luck at SHEP.'

He looked slightly concerned about her trip.

'It'll be fine,' she said confidently. 'Probably just ...' she tailed off as she realised she couldn't think of a single positive reason for the summons. A call from the Scottish Health Enforcement Partnership usually meant only one thing. Someone, somewhere had cocked up, and Cameron Stuttle, the SHEP chief executive, was looking for someone, somewhere to shout at. That someone, with tedious regularity, tended to be Paterson. And both Mona and Paterson knew that there was still some outstanding business from the Weber/Greenwood cases that Stuttle hadn't dealt with yet. Perhaps today was the day.

A thought struck her, a horrific thought that had her reaching for her seat and grabbing the mouse of her computer. Had Amanda made contact with SHEP? She hesitated, torn between checking her e-mail and catching up with her boss. *Oh, God, Amanda.* Heidi Weber's friend, if friend was the right word for someone who used your credit card to buy drugs to sell. And who filmed everyone and everything on her phone, including some pictures of Mona that she would rather no one ever saw. Her last contact from Amanda had been an e-mail asking for her help. She hadn't responded, and while there had been silence ever since, she would bet every pound she possessed that she hadn't heard the last from her.

Paterson was waiting for her at the bottom of the stairs, impatiently tapping his foot.

'Any idea why our presence has been requested, Guv?'

He ignored her question, and as she followed him out to the car park she felt the familiar pull of disappointment that he still wasn't talking to her. Paterson continued to rebuff her attempts to start a conversation while he signed out a pool car, retrieved it and sat in traffic for ten minutes on Lothian Road.

'Roads are bad today, Guv, aren't they?'

In response to her conversational gambit, Paterson turned on the radio.

'Oh for God's sake!' Mona's anger bubbled over and she snapped the radio back off. 'Guv, are you ever planning to speak to me again?'

'Don't take that tone with me.'

'What tone?'

'You know, that "poor me, my boss is being so unreasonable" tone.'

'Well...'

'I'm not being unreasonable! If I'd had my way, you'd have been off my team two months ago. But your pal Stuttle won't hear of it.'

This was news to Mona, on both counts. She'd assumed that Paterson had fought Stuttle to keep her, not the other way round.

'So I may be stuck with you, but I haven't forgotten what you did, and I certainly haven't forgiven it.'

She stared out of the window. 'I don't think what I did was that bad,' she said, quietly.

Almost immediately she regretted her words, as Paterson nearly swerved the car into the oncoming traffic. He recovered the wheel, and took a deep breath. 'Not that bad? Really? Are you suffering from a bout of amnesia or something? You went over my head!'

She considered intervening, but decided it was futile. She contented herself with a heavy sigh, and some passive-aggressive window-staring.

Paterson wasn't done. 'By some miracle, we managed to get through the whole Weber and Greenwood thing without anyone becoming cult members, getting arrested, or getting killed. And don't forget, that was a real possibility with Bernard. He took quite a beating, one that could have been avoided if any of my staff had bothered to involve me in what was going on.'

It was becoming quite uncomfortable listening, due to the high truth content in what Paterson was saying. Bernard *had* taken a beating, and had been behaving like a nervous kitten ever since.

'But we get through all that, and due to a bit of behind-the-scenes pressure from the German govern-ment, everyone keeps their jobs. I make it clear to you both that we've made it out by the skin of our teeth, and that this case is now firmly a hundred per cent closed. And what do you do? You immediately send Cameron Bloody Stuttle an e-mail, don't you?'

The truth quota was making her itchy again. It was all true. She'd been sent video footage, taken by Amanda, that implicated a senior German diplomat in Heidi Weber's death. She'd forwarded it on to the head of the Strategic Health Enforcement Partnership on the, apparently naïve, assumption he would act on it.

'And what did Stuttle do with it?'

She drew her fingernails across the back of her hand. Perhaps if she could make the itch a real one she could scratch, her discomfort would disappear. 'He sat on it, Guv.'

'He sat on it. And why was that?'

Another relevant question, but not one she had an answer to. When she'd joined the HET, she'd felt pretty confident that she knew how the world worked. She had five years of police work under her belt, including a couple spent in CID, which she reckoned gave her an excellent insight into the criminal mind. She'd developed enough of an understanding of organisational culture to be considered, at one time at least, a potential candidate for a fast-track promotion. But the longer she worked for the HET the more she realised there was one area that she really didn't understand. Try as she might, she just didn't get the politics of it all: the alliances, the mis-briefings, the whole *information is power* thing. And Cameron Stuttle, as she was coming to realise, was a Grade A, first-class, no bones about it, political operator.

'Because I think there are a number of possibilities, Mona. Maybe Stuttle wasn't keen to rock the boat at that

27

precise moment – after all the HET had just about got out of the whole mess with our heads still attached. Or maybe he thought that your little video would be useful to add to his stack of evidence about important people who've been naughty boys, so he can whop it out next time the German government are being a bit awkward. Or maybe, just maybe, he thought it would be useful to have in his vault of data on HET officers who've cocked up, so he can use it to bully us into something.' He shook his head. 'Jesus, Mona, you were the one person on the team that I thought had some common sense.'

She redoubled her efforts at scratching her hand.

'And of course it gave Stuttle a fascinating insight into the way my team works. He must be laughing his arse off at the lack of respect you have for me.'

'That's not true.'

Paterson brought the car to such an abrupt halt she was able to verify the effectiveness of the seat belts. He began reversing into a parking space, and she realised they were near the City Chambers, where SHEP had their offices.

'He asked for you specifically, today. Not just any old HET officer; he didn't say bring Bernard, or Maitland, or whoever happens to be in the office. No, he was quite specific that he wanted to see Mona Whyte. He's probably got something in mind to help fast-track your way out of the HET. Probably trying you out for a permanent job at SHEP, doing his dirty work. After all, he's seen your potential.' With that parting shot he got out of the car, slamming the door behind him. Within seconds he reappeared. 'Sort out the meter.'

She rooted around her bag for change. If the Guv was right about Stuttle fast-tracking her out of the HET she might take him up on it. When she'd gone over Paterson's head, she assumed that one of the outcomes would be her sacking, or at least an insistence on her immediate resignation. She'd drafted a letter that noted, not entirely accurately, how much she had enjoyed working at the HET, but had felt compelled blah blah blah. But with Stuttle sitting on the information she'd given him, she'd been left in limbo, neither whistle-blower nor trusted colleague.

Edinburgh's City Chambers were opulent, even by the high standards set by the rest of the city centre. Located on the High Street, the Chambers had originally been built in the eighteenth century as the Royal Exchange, where the city's merchants could meet to trade in grand surroundings designed by John and Robert Adam. Sadly, the merchants themselves were creatures of habit, and saw no need to relocate from their usual spot by the Mercat Cross. The building lay empty, until bowing to the inevitable, the council taking it over as offices, some of which they now sub-let to SHEP.

The Chambers were in Edinburgh's Old Town, the steep and cobbled streets that ran from the castle to Holyrood Palace. The steepness should not be under-stated; from the High Street the City Chambers was an imposing but not unusual four floors high. If you exited by the lower level back door on Cockburn Street, you could look back to see that the building was a full thir-teen storeys in height.

Mona stood at the bottom of Cockburn Street, and looked in vain for Paterson. He'd probably tried to shake her off, which seemed rather pointless as they were both attending the same meeting. She assumed that he'd gone to the front entrance, but there were numerous narrow lanes that linked this street to the High Street and he could have taken any of them. She resigned herself to not catching up with him, and set off up Warriston's Close.

When she did finally locate him it was in the wood-panelled surroundings of the SHEP waiting room, where he was slumped in a Chesterfield armchair.

She gave it one last try. 'So, you've no idea what this is about, Guv?'

To emphasise that he was ignoring her, Paterson picked up a copy of *Hello!*, and began flicking through it.

'John.' Cameron Stuttle appeared, and pointed at the magazine. 'More challenging reading material than usual, I see. Keeping those aging brain cells working?'

Paterson flung the publication in the general direction of a table. 'Let's get this over with.'

'I see he's in a good mood today, Mona.' Stuttle smiled at her. 'Anyway, come in. I need to ask a favour.'

As she followed him into his office, Mona reflected that between Maitland and Stuttle it appeared that nobody in health enforcement knew how to ask for a favour properly.

'So.' Stuttle settled himself behind his large oak desk, folded his arms on its top, and looked at them both. 'I need your help.'

The Guv was staring at his feet. He didn't seem about to respond, so she ventured a tentative, 'OK?'

'A person of importance is in danger of missing his Health Check.'

This made Paterson sit up. 'Who?'

'Alexander Bircham-Fowler.'

'As in Professor Bircham-Fowler, Scotland's leading authority on the Virus?' asked Mona.

'Yup. And I cannot stress enough how confidential this discussion is.'

'No way.' The Guv shook his head. 'Bircham-Fowler wouldn't miss a Health Check. He's one of the key backers of the policy. It would be hugely damaging to his credibility.'

'Indeed. The professor has always been a strong supporter of the HETs, so we would very much like to see him delivered safely into a Health Check, on or before midday on Thursday the 7th of July, when his next Check is due.'

'How do you know he's going to miss one?'

'Oh, come on, John. You know how these things work.' Stuttle smiled. 'We've got someone in his office, who says he's done a runner. Disappeared off from work, missed meetings. Totally out of character.'

'You've got a spy in a university?'

'Grow up. The professor's too important to all this to, you know, leave him unattended.'

The Guv was looking grumpier by the minute. 'And what exactly do you mean by "all this"?'

'You know what I mean.' He let out a long hiss of exasperation. 'Everything. Virus policy.'

'And your career prospects. And you keeping your big office on the Royal Mile.'

Irritation tipped over into anger. 'That is *not* what I mean. Listen, both of you. Things are getting difficult. We've had the best part of two years of consensus on Virus policy, but that's starting to break down. There's a fair few people out there who would love to see the professor discredited, as a first move toward disbanding the HETs.'

Paterson made a noise somewhere between a snort

31

and a tut, which conveyed that he didn't see this as the end of the world.

'But it's not just about the HETs. Bircham-Fowler is due to give a speech at the Parliament on Friday, and word has it that the content of it is making him very unpopular in certain circles.'

'Unpopular enough for Bircham-Fowler to come to harm?'

'We live in interesting times, John. Politicians are much more able to justify things to themselves – and to the electorate – now that we are living in an officially recognised State of Emergency.'

'So, where do we come into this? We only chase Defaulters, not people who might possibly be vaguely considering not turning up to a Health Check.'

'I'm well aware of that, but I'd like some discreet questions asked. And I'd rather not do it myself.'

'But you're happy for us to do something that we have no legal right to do. If he's a missing person, get the police to find him.' To underline his point, Paterson folded his arms and sat back in his chair.

'There are certain people at Police Scotland that we would rather not alert to his potential absence. And anyway, as I said, you two owe me a favour.'

'In exactly what way do Mona and I owe you a favour?'

'I could have thrown the book at you over that whole Weber case fiasco.'

Paterson snorted. 'And you would have, if you'd been allowed to. Your hands were tied.'

'Well, put it this way. The bonds have loosened somewhat, and I'm not averse to making your life miserable.'

The two of them glared at each other, and the silence

32

stretched on uncomfortably. Mona decided to nudge the conversation on. 'What exactly do you want us to do?'

'Thank you, Mona, for showing an interest.'

Paterson shot her a filthy look. 'Showing some self-interest, more like.'

Stuttle ignored him. 'I want you to pay the professor a visit – make up some semi-official excuse to be there – and see if any of his colleagues can shed light on where he is. Then report back to me.'

'OK.' Paterson got to his feet. 'Seeing as I appear to have no choice. But one visit and that's us done there.'

Stuttle smiled, the kind of tooth-baring grin that a lion might give before it ate its prey. 'I'd be eternally grateful, John. Nice to see you again, Mona.'

The Guv took off at such a rate that Mona had to run to catch up with him. His pace slowed as he walked along the High Street. She kept a couple of paces behind him, and nearly crashed into him when he stopped abruptly.

'Are you spying on me for SHEP?'

'Guv! Of course not!'

'Are you sure?' His eyes narrowed, and he stepped slightly closer to her than she would have liked. She had an overwhelming urge to push him away, but settled for edging her bag in between them. 'This isn't your attempt to get a promotion fast-tracked, reporting back on me to Stuttle?'

'Absolutely not! I can't believe that you'd think that.'

Paterson stared at her for a moment, then turned on his heel and marched off in the direction of the car. She watched him go. 'For one thing, Guv,' she said quietly to herself, 'you're not that important.'

4

The HET's IT section was located in the basement of Police Scotland HQ, known to everyone as Fettes. It was next door to the famous public school of the same name, but was at the opposite end of the architectural spectrum. While the school had so many turrets and ramparts it wouldn't have appeared out of place in a Disney theme park, the police HQ looked as if the architect had delivered on a one-line brief: keep it functional.

Bernard pushed open the door to the IT lab, and was met with a silence so complete that he wondered if anyone was in. After a second of lingering in the doorway he saw that the two technicians were bent silently over their screens, each with a huge pile of files next to them.

'Hello?'

'Bernard!' Marcus leapt up, his hand outstretched and a wide grin on his face. The thing that Bernard liked the most about the senior IT officer was that he was his only colleague who could be reliably depended upon to be pleased to see him. He gave Bernard a firm, if slightly sweaty handshake. 'How are you?'

Bryce, the other technician, gave him a wave. In nearly a year of acquaintance, Bernard had never actually heard him speak. He assumed that he *could* speak, but just chose not to. Or at least opted not to express himself when there was anyone other than Marcus around to hear him. Perhaps he chattered non-stop when there were no outsiders in the room. Then again, left to their own devices, perhaps the IT section communicated entirely by semaphore.

'I'm good. You two look busy.'

'We are. SHEP appears to have confused us with data entry clerks and sent us an entire box room of files for digital archiving. I have never been more pleased to see a HET officer needing assistance.' He turned to his colleague. 'And I know what you are going to say, Bryce—'

Bernard wondered how.

'—but it's definitely my turn for a break, so I'm claiming this one. What can I do to help?'

'We have a Health Check Defaulter with a possible false address, and a hostile Defaulter witness. I'd like you to do some background checks on both of them.'

'And you have the appropriate paperwork, signed by someone far more important than you?'

Bernard produced a sheet of paper from his bag, and held it aloft. 'I have a printout decorated with the finest electronic signature I could download for my team leader?'

'Close enough.' Marcus returned to his computer. 'OK, give me names, and what you want to know.'

'Alessandra Valentina Barr, date of birth, etc. as per the paperwork. Can you tell me any addresses you have for her?'

'I assume you've checked the phone book and census already?'

'Actually, no.'

Marcus tutted. 'I expect that slipshod approach from your colleagues, but ...' He tapped the keyboard rapidly, then looked up. 'Nope, no sign of her.'

35

'National Insurance records?'

Tap, tap, tap on the keyboard again. 'No, nothing there either. Are you absolutely sure about the date of birth, spelling of her name, etc.?'

'It's all from her Green Card info.'

He snorted. 'So all of it is open to question then. Right, let's start at the beginning. We'll check the register of births.'

Further tapping. 'Got her! Alessandra Valentina Barr, born 12th of April 1991, Glasgow.'

'So, she does exist. What about bank accounts?'

Bernard grabbed a chair, and sat watching Marcus type. After a good ten minutes of keyboard clattering, he looked up.

'Nothing under that name.'

'Is she a benefits claimant?'

Marcus sighed. 'This is going to take a while. Go, find coffee somewhere, and come back in quarter of an hour or so?'

'Can you check out a Stephen McNiven, while you're at it?' He passed over McNiven's details.

'The hostile Defaulter witness, I assume?'

'Correct.'

Bernard did as he was told, and wandered off to the cafeteria. He returned exactly fifteen minutes later with three doughnuts and hope in his heart. 'Any joy?'

'Ooh, thanks.' Marcus bit a chunk of doughnut, and threw one across the room to Bryce. 'Nice.' He pointed at the screen. 'I did them both while you were gone. Mr McNiven has a Green Card, NI number, a bank account currently showing an overdraft, and a chequered employment history in the fast-food industry.'

'Interesting,' said Bernard. Unless McDonald's paid an

awful lot more than he'd assumed, Stephen McNiven's designer gear was obviously being funded by another source.

'Now, Alessandra. Intriguing, this one. Birth certificate, Green Card, and Medical Card.'

'Any medical conditions?'

'Oh, no. Can't tell you that. The powers invested in us by the hastily written Health Defaulters Act mean we can poke around at will in people's employment and benefit history, their mobile phone records and their bank account, but stops short of letting us nose around in their medical files. Which is ironic, seeing as it is their health that we are particularly concerned about.'

'OK.'

'What we don't have for Ms Barr is anything that indicates a work history, a claimant history, or a stake in the formal banking industry.'

'So how is she supporting herself?'

'Bernard! Are you really so innocent that you need a humble IT technician to spell it out?'

He smiled at the look of mock horror on Marcus's face. 'She's a prostitute?'

'Or a member of any other profession that operates on an entirely paper money basis. Professional shoplifter, gambler, cash-in-hand plumber ... but I'd go with your first thought.'

'So why bother with a Green Card when she has none of the other things?'

'Because people like yourself or Police Scotland have the right to stop and ask to see your Green Card. In her probable line of work, that's a risk.'

Bernard stood up to go.

'And a couple of other odd things to consider. Couldn't

find any evidence of a passport, and she's only had a Green Card for six months.'

'Fits in with her not having an arrest record – yet.'

'So you'll be off to track down your missing prostitute now? I assume you'll be starting with the red light district in Leith?'

'Probably.'

'Will you be taking Mona for backup?' Marcus's tone was casual. Bernard tried not to smile; he'd never had a whole conversation with Marcus without him mentioning her.

'Probably.'

'Nice woman. Not slow to get you into trouble though.'

Marcus had also suffered from the fallout of the Weber case, after he'd allowed himself to be bullied by Mona into assisting her access some e-mails she had no right to see. The severe dressing-down he'd received didn't appear to have ended Marcus's unrequited crush.

'True. Thanks, guys.'

5

'Maybe we should have phoned ahead to the university, found out the best way to get there?'

As before, Paterson didn't answer her, and, as before, this made her blood boil. It heightened the irritability she was already feeling due to the Guv's Y chromosome rendering him incapable of asking for directions. For the last twenty minutes they seemed to have been driving round in circles, somewhere just outside the city bypass. The sun was out now, and Paterson seemed to have some objection to either turning on the air conditioning or opening a window. She fanned herself, and made one last attempt. 'I've got a satnav thing on my phone we could use?'

'Save it. We're here.'

He turned into what appeared to be an industrial estate. A substantial barrier prevented them entering. Paterson pulled up to it and spoke into the machine, and in reply a crackly voice promised to 'be there in a minute'. While they waited, Mona read the large brown sign which mapped out the estate; the university seemed to use about half of the units, with the other occupants being largely scientific and technical firms.

A man in a university-issued polo shirt jogged in the direction of the car. 'Green Cards, please.' He thrust a handheld device through Paterson's open window, and each of them held their cards against it in turn. The machine beeped twice, satisfied that neither of them presented a public health risk. 'Where are you looking for, pal?'

'The Department of …?' he stopped and looked at Mona, realising he didn't actually know the correct name.

'Two minutes, Guv.' Mona searched the Internet on her phone. 'The Virology and Pandemics Unit, please.'

He nodded. 'Turn to your left, and it's about five minutes' drive. It's a blue, glass-fronted building. You can't miss it.'

They drove slowly in the direction the porter had indicated, passing building after building, all new combinations of metal and tinted glass. There was not a single person, student or otherwise, to be seen.

'Not exactly dreaming spires, is it, Guv?'

He grunted.

'What are we going to say when we get there? Have you thought of a good reason for our visit?'

'I'm going to say, "We're from the HET, where's Professor Bircham-Fowler?"'

'But aren't they just going to say, "He's not here"?'

He shrugged. 'And that is what we will report back to SHEP, then we get on with doing the work that we legally have jurisdiction to do.'

'Blue building, Guv.' She pointed, and Paterson turned into the small car park.

The door to the building was made largely of reinforced tinted glass. It was also firmly locked. Mona looked around for a buzzer or an intercom, but there didn't appear to be either. 'How do you think we get in?'

'There must be something.' Paterson held up a hand to block out the sun, and peered through the glass. 'There doesn't seem to be a reception.'

Mona stepped back and looked up at the building. The opaque windows made it impossible to tell if anyone could see them. 'I don't think they get many visitors. Shall I see if I can find a phone number?'

'Yes, but hurry up.'

She resisted the temptation to snap at him. It wasn't her fault that they were on this wild goose chase, although she was pretty sure he didn't see it like that. She concentrated on the screen.

'No phone number, Guv, only an e-mail address. Do you want me to send a message?'

Paterson peered into the building again. 'I think someone's coming.'

A young man in jeans and T-shirt appeared on the other side of the door. He waved to them through the glass. 'I saw you from the window. This building is not open to the public.'

Paterson held his ID up against the glass. 'We're here to see Professor Bircham-Fowler.'

The student peered at the HET badge, and decided that their credentials passed muster. The door buzzed and he held it open for them. 'I've not seen him today. I don't think he's in.'

Mona stepped into the cool of the foyer; it felt great to be out of the heat. 'In that case we want his secretary. Where would we find her?'

The student burst out laughing. 'Maggie? Best of luck!' He pointed at a couple of leather chairs. 'Take a seat and I'll ask her to come down.' He disappeared up a set of metal stairs, still chuckling to himself.

'Well, that was weird, Guv, don't you think?'

Paterson didn't respond, and she threw herself on to one of the chairs, with as loud a sigh of irritation as she

41

dared. She didn't have long to fume, as almost immediately they heard the sound of someone clattering down the stairs. A pair of legs in sensible shoes appeared at the top of the stairs. As the shoes descended, a royal blue A-line skirt appeared, followed by a blouse with a pussy-bow. Finally, a head appeared with light brown hair, combed into a side wave, and a face that looked extremely similar to a previous female prime minister of the UK. It occurred to Mona that it was very unlikely that this woman's given name was actually going to be Margaret.

'Guv!'

It was too late. Paterson was already on his feet, with his right hand extended. 'You must be Maggie.'

She glared at him. 'No, I must not. I am Theresa Kilsyth, assistant to Professor Bircham-Fowler. I believe you are looking for me?'

'Actually, we're looking for the professor. Is he here?'

'No.'

'Where is he?'

Mona winced at the Guv's tone. He knew this was sensitive; he should be treading a bit more carefully. Theresa Kilsyth was looking even less impressed.

'He is not here, as I have already stated. Now if you will excuse me …'

'No, I'm afraid that's not good enough, Miss Kilsyth…'

'Mrs.'

'Why is he not at work, *Mrs* Kilsyth?'

'That is a personal issue.'

'What kind of personal issue?'

'The kind that is personal.'

Mona stifled the urge to laugh at the look on her boss's face. His tone and imposing physical presence tended to get people scurrying to do his bidding. Now he was being stonewalled by someone very small, and apparently unmoveable. She decided to jump in.

'We're very sorry to inconvenience you, Mrs Kilsyth, but we will need to see the professor's office, and take a look at his computer.'

Mrs Kilsyth raised two eyebrows at this. 'On what grounds?'

'On HET business,' said Paterson, irritably, showing his ID again.

'Do you have a warrant?'

Neither of them said anything.

'I thought not. As Professor Bircham-Fowler has not missed a Health Check, you have no legal right of access to his office, his computer files, or anything else.'

'You certainly know a lot about the law, Mrs Kilsyth.'

'Working for the professor in the current climate, I've had to acquaint myself with a lot of rules and regulations.'

There was a clattering of feet and a number of young people came thudding down the stairs. They looked curiously at the three of them.

'Outside, everyone,' said Mrs Kilsyth to the group. 'This is not a student common room.'

The students grinned but hovered watching them.

'I have some more questions about Professor Bircham-Fowler,' said Paterson, in a loud enough tone for everyone in the room to hear.

There was a small ripple of interest in this from the group.

Mrs Kilsyth looked furious. 'Very well,' she said, accepting defeat. 'You'd better come upstairs.

The professor's office was surprisingly tidy. From what Mona had seen of him on TV she'd expected something more mad professor-ish, with piles of papers everywhere, and possibly a test tube or two bubbling away.

'It looks very well organised in here,' she said.

'That's my doing,' said Mrs Kilsyth, gesturing that she should sit down. She conspicuously ignored the Guv. 'The place would be a tip if it was left up to Sandy.'

There was a picture of a girl on the professor's desk. She looked about seven or eight, with long brown hair tied up in pigtails.

'Pretty girl,' said Mona. 'The professor's granddaughter?'

Mrs Kilsyth was looking in the opposite direction. 'What does he think he is doing?'

Paterson was attempting to turn on the professor's computer. Mrs Kilsyth marched round to the other side of the desk, and Mona thought for a minute that she was going to slap the Guv's hands out of the way.

'As I said downstairs, you do not have the right to do this.'

'Mrs Kilsyth, we are on the same side. It is in the interest of everyone in this room that Professor Bircham-Fowler makes his Health Check. Think what it would do to his reputation if he misses it.'

She stared at him. Mona could see her struggling to decide what to do. After a second, she waved a hand dismissively in the direction of the computer. 'You'll not find anything on it. Anything important is password protected, and I take it upon myself to delete the browser history on it every evening.'

'That's very security conscious.'

'Yes, it is, Mr Paterson. Unfortunately, I feel the need to take those kinds of measures.'

'Why?'

44

She gave a tight-lipped smile. 'As I am sure you are both aware, there are people in this office spying on him.'

'Well, we wouldn't know anything about that.' Paterson didn't sound convincing.

'Of course you wouldn't. Anyway, I think it's time for you to go now.' Mrs Kilsyth opened the office door. 'I'll see you out.'

Paterson reluctantly stepped away from the computer, and they both allowed themselves to be shooed in the direction of the main entrance.

'Thank you for your time, Mrs Kilsyth.' Mona held out her business card. 'If you think of anything we would be delighted to speak to you. We are concerned about the professor, truly.'

She took the card. 'Yes, well, I know where you are if I need you.' She turned on her heel and they heard the clatter of her shoes retreating back up the stairs.

'I'm sure she had something she was debating whether to tell us, Guv.'

He grunted, and set off toward the car.

Mona slid into the passenger seat. Without taking his eyes from the road, Paterson spoke. 'Mrs Kilsyth was quite something, wasn't she?'

'I quite liked her, Guv.'

Something approaching a smile played across Paterson's face. 'So did I.'

Mona's mobile beeped.

'Is that Bernard?' asked Paterson.

'Yep.' She read the message. 'As I suspected, he thinks our Defaulter is a prostitute.'

'Time to visit Annemarie?'

'Absolutely, Guv.'

6

Annemarie was a Leith legend. She'd run a project supporting working girls for as long as anyone could remember, and had managed to tread a fine line between supporting her clients, and working, occasionally co-operatively, with the police. If Alessandra Barr had been plying her trade on Salamander Street, Annemarie would know about it. Bernard had never met her, but Maitland had spent half an hour regaling him with stories about her robust attitude to working with law enforcement, and consequently his stomach was churning as his hand hovered over the buzzer.

'Are you sure she'll be happy to talk to us?'

Mona reached past him and gave the buzzer a good long press. 'Only one way to find out.'

After a couple of seconds, a small, stout woman with greying short back and sides appeared. She opened the door a crack, and surveyed them. She looked at Mona. 'I know you, don't I?'

'I was CID, now in the Health Enforcement Team.' She held her ID aloft. 'Can we come in?'

'You can, he can't.' She pointed at him, and he jumped. 'No offence, son, but it's a women-only space.'

'Oh, OK, no problem.'

'Tell you what, I'll come out there. Just let me grab my fags.'

Mona whispered to him. 'Do *not* say anything to her about the dangers of smoking.'

'I wasn't going to,' he lied.

Annemarie reappeared with her cigarettes and a large set of keys.

'Quite some security setup you've got here, Annemarie.'

'I know, hen. I've worked here for thirty years, and when I started the women could just walk in off the street. Then someone's pimp tried to stab one of the girls on the premises so we got the intercom. Then you lot came along and we had to get a Green Card machine.' She laughed, which turned into a cough. Bernard wondered if he should have a quiet word about smoking cessation after all, then caught Mona's eye. He smiled, guiltily.

Annemarie was breathing again. 'It's a wonder any lassies come in at all. Anyway, what can I do for you?'

'We're looking for a woman who has missed her Health Check. We think she's possibly working as a prostitute, and we wondered if you'd seen her.'

'She got a name?'

'Alessandra Barr.'

Annemarie let out a long puff. 'Don't know her.'

Bernard tried not to wave the smoke away. 'She might be using a different name?'

'No, I'd know her real name. They used to be able to call themselves anything and we were happy with that, but these days you lot would close us down if we didn't know the names and health status of everyone that comes in here. Doesn't make it easy to help vulnerable people, but what can you do?'

Mona unfolded a photocopy. 'Would you look at her picture?'

Annemarie peered at it. 'Two black eyes? Poor cow.'

'You don't remember anyone coming in with two black eyes?' asked Bernard.

The two women exchanged an amused glance, and Bernard kicked himself for his naivety.

'That photo could be half of the lassies we have in here on a bad day. You tried looking in one of the refuges for her?' Two women appeared round the corner of the building, one tall and one short, both with cigarette packets in their hands. 'Here – ask a couple of the lassies.'

'Ladies.' Mona nodded to them. 'Can I ask if you recognise this woman?'

They huddled in to look at the picture.

'Look at the state of her.' The smaller girl shook her head. 'Can't say I know her.'

Bernard watched the other girl. She'd glanced at the picture then stepped away.

'What about you, miss? Do you know her?'

The tall girl shook her head.

'OK,' said Mona. 'Thanks for your time, everyone. We'll check out the refuges as you suggested.' She held out a card to Annemarie. 'You'll get in touch if you hear anything?'

She nodded, and put the card into her pocket without looking at it.

As they left Bernard looked back over his shoulder. The tall girl was busy texting on her phone. She looked up and saw him watching her, and swiftly turned her back on him. He wondered if the text was related to their visit. Was she texting Alessandra to warn her they were looking for her? Or was she warning someone else?

7

'Mona?'

She pressed the print button, downloading a copy of the contacts page from the Edinburgh Women's Refuge website, then looked up to see Marguerite, the ever-cheerful admin assistant, standing in the doorway to the office. She was beaming from ear to ear. Mona wondered what had induced this idiotic level of happiness. It couldn't be falling in love; she knew from many unfortunate encounters in the Ladies toilet that Marguerite had a long-term boyfriend called Kevin, who if she was to be believed, had a poor employment record and a wandering eye (although for some reason she remained annoyed that he hadn't yet proposed to her and showed no immediate signs of preparing to). But if not love, then what? Purchase of puppy? Maitland for once telling a joke that was genuinely amusing, rather than sexist?

'There's a woman downstairs asking for you.' She giggled. 'She wouldn't give her name but you'll never guess who she looks *exactly* like?'

Had Theresa Kilsyth paid them a visit? So *that* was what was amusing her – though Mona felt a little surprised that Marguerite could correctly identify a politician who had been out of power since before she was born. 'Is it by any chance Mrs Thatcher?'

Marguerite's face fell. 'Oh, how did you know?'

'Lucky guess. I'm amazed you know what Mrs T looked like.'

'Oh yeah, my dad was a big fan. He met her during the Falklands War – you know he did a tour of duty there? In fact, he got his photograph taken with her. It's up in our living room, next to the one of him meeting Jim Davidson.'

'OK.' Mona couldn't help but think that Kevin's marital reluctance might be a little bit to do with his new in-laws. 'Anyway, can you tell her I'll be down in a minute.'

She stuck her head into Paterson's office. 'Guv, I think Theresa Kilsyth is here to see us.'

'Who?' he asked, not looking up.

'Maggie Thatcher from earlier.'

'Crap.' He threw his pen down on the desk. 'I'd hoped we were done with all this nonsense. Well, go and get her. Let's see what she wants.'

'Hello again, Mrs Kilsyth.'

Theresa Kilsyth stopped dead when she caught sight of Paterson. 'I came in to see this young woman, not you.'

He shrugged. 'Well, you got us both as a package. What can we do for you?'

'Can we close the door?'

Mona obliged. Even after it was shut Mrs Kilsyth seemed reluctant to start speaking. She pulled her handbag on to her lap, and sat hugging it to her. Eventually, she sighed. 'I have decided, possibly against my better judgement, to trust you. As you have identified, Sandy is missing, and as you have also realised, in serious danger of not attending his Health Check. Which, of course, would mean the end of his career.'

'Has he been under a lot of stress?' asked Mona.

'My dear, his life is non-stop stress. How could it be otherwise? He generally copes with it very well. No, this is nothing to do with work.'

'So, you know where he is?'

'Not exactly.' She hesitated, then produced a large brown envelope from her bag. 'Shortly after you left today, this arrived for him.' She passed it across the desk.

'Private and Confidential?' Paterson read the front of the envelope.

'Do you want to find Sandy or not?'

Paterson smiled, then flicked open the flap and slid the contents out. Mona looked over his shoulder at the contents. It was a black-and-white photocopy of a photograph, taken at night. A pretty girl in a sleeping bag was seated on the ground, leaning against a concrete wall. In the background, a river was visible. The girl was wearing a hat and gloves, and the whole scene had a wintry feel to it. Another sleeping bag was next to her but all that could be seen of the person occupying it was another gloved hand.

'Turn it over,' instructed Mrs Kilsyth.

There was writing on the back which Paterson read aloud. '"I wouldn't let my daughter live like this."' He looked up. 'I don't understand. Care to enlighten me?'

'I'm very worried about him. Sandy was married, quite briefly, in his thirties. He had a daughter, but the marriage didn't last. Although I can't say I was surprised when his wife left him; he's really not an easy man to live with. Even in his thirties he was a complete workaholic. Anyway, the divorce was what you might call acrimonious, and his wife moved down to England somewhere, to be near her parents. And over the course of the years

51

he lost touch with his daughter, which I know caused him a great deal of pain.'

Mona remembered the photograph of the young girl on his desk.

'But over the last couple of years, since the Virus came along, I know he's been trying quite actively to find her. We all know that young people are a high-risk category for the Virus, Sandy better than anyone, and not knowing if his daughter is alive or dead is taking a dreadful toll on him. And then, the day before yesterday, one of these big brown envelopes arrives.'

'What was in it? The same as this one?'

'I don't know – it was marked P&C, so I just passed it straight to him. But I do know he went a little bit crazy after it arrived, storming around his office swearing, which is totally unlike him. Then he left early, which is even more unusual. I've never known him leave the office before 7pm.'

'Any idea where he went?'

'I checked his web browser, and the last site he looked at was for flights to London.'

'Why London?'

She picked up the photocopy. 'It's been a year or two since I was down there myself, but I'd say that that photograph is of the South Bank. That's the Thames in the background.'

'Would the professor know that?'

'Probably. We were both down there for a long weekend before all the Virus nonsense kicked off. We went to a couple of things at the National.'

There was a delicate pause. 'You're a couple?'

'Sandy is a colleague and a dear friend. We are not a couple, an item, lovers, however you care to phrase it. But I care for him deeply, and I do not want to see the press eat him alive because he has missed a Health Check.'

Mona peered at the envelope. 'I think the postmark says Mount Pleasant – is that London?' Nobody responded. 'I'll check it out.' She pulled out her phone.

'So, your theory is that the professor is in London somewhere, probably near the National Theatre, looking for his daughter who may be sleeping rough?'

She nodded. 'That would be my guess, yes.'

'Have you tried contacting him?'

'His phone is switched off.'

'So, what's the daughter's name? Mona can liaise with the Met, see if she's been arrested for anything.'

'I don't know her name. If we knew that we'd have found her by now. When she was seven years old her name was Maria Bircham-Fowler, but I think her mother probably remarried, and she may well have taken her stepfather's name. To say nothing of the fact that now she's nudging thirty she may well be married herself.'

'Mrs Kilsyth, do you think anyone else will know that the professor has gone to London?'

She shot him glance. 'Like who? Your spy? Someone else in the office who's spying on him?'

'I'm not any happier about this than you are.' Paterson looked aggrieved. 'But yes, our spy or anyone else's.'

'I'm pretty sure that no one else saw the contents of either envelope, and I cleared the browser immediately, but I'm no technician. If someone knew what they were doing with technology, who knows? And of course, whoever sent him the letter will probably guess that he'll be on the next train. So what happens now?'

'I phone SHEP,' said Paterson, 'and I assume they will dispatch some people to London to find the professor.'

'We need to find him soon. And we need to make sure all this is done discreetly.'

'I can assure you that SHEP is just as concerned about the situation as you are, Mrs Kilsyth.'

She stood up.

'I'll show you out.' Mona ushered her back out of the office and down to reception.

Mrs Kilsyth paused at the front door. 'So you think I'm right about that being the South Bank?'

'I'm not as familiar with London as you are, but looks like it. And Mount Pleasant is a London sorting office, so it does all tie in.' She touched Mrs Kilsyth's arm. 'Try not to worry. He's lucky to have a friend like you looking out for him.'

'Unfortunately, my dear, I think he's going to need more than friendship to get him out of this.'

Mona sat at her desk, idly doodling the word 'London'. She'd been to the Big Smoke precisely three times in her life: once on a training course, when she'd seen little except the inside of the airport and the conference centre, and twice to visit a woman she had befriended. *Kat.* She'd had high hopes of the friendship turning into something more intimate, but a few fumbles aside, this hadn't happened. Her trips to London had introduced her not just to women-only pubs, but also to the world of after-hours bars, and clubs, and the dangers of the night bus home. She was glad she'd had a guide to show her round. Late-night London was a tough old place; she hoped the professor was equal to navigating its challenges.

54

'Mona.' The Guv nodded her in the direction of his office, closing the door firmly behind her. 'I spoke to Stuttle.'

'And is he sending someone to find the professor?'

'Yes.'

Paterson looked surprisingly annoyed about this. Mona wondered why – surely he was expecting that this would be how SHEP would play it? Unless ... a sudden, unpleasant thought crossed her mind.

'Is he sending us?'

'Yes.'

'Really?'

'*Yes!* And the even better news is that this is still unofficial. He wants us to take a day's annual leave each to do it.'

Mona's jaw dropped. 'He can't make us do that!'

'No, he can't *make* us do it. But I'll say yes because he'll make my life hell if I don't, and you'll say yes because it'll help speed your climb up the greasy pole.'

'Give it up, Guv.' Her boss's cynicism about her motives was getting wearing. 'I'll say yes because it's important Professor Bircham-Fowler is found.'

'Well, whatever, it looks like we're off to London.'

'For how long?'

'There and back in a day, if I can possibly swing it. Two days tops. I'm not hanging around there any longer than I absolutely have to. So, go home and I'll text you when I know what our travel arrangements are. And make sure you travel light. We don't want to be hauling bags round London.' He stood up. 'I suppose I better tell that lot out there.'

He opened the door, and was met with the kind of silence that indicated that until very recently the people in the room had been talking about what was going on in Paterson's office.

'Listen up, you three. Mona and I are both taking a day or two's annual leave, starting immediately.'

'You're going on holiday together?' asked Maitland.

'I don't have to explain my plans to you, Mr Stevenson.'

Carole caught Mona's eye and she looked back in a manner that she hoped communicated the futility of asking Paterson anything at the moment. She wasn't sure how much she was at liberty to share with her colleagues, but she'd definitely be making it clear to them that the Guv hadn't invited her for a dirty weekend at a country hotel. As it turned out, her colleagues had other things on their mind.

'So who's in charge while you are gone, Mr Paterson?' asked Bernard.

Maitland snorted. 'I can't believe you even had to ask that, Bern. It's got to be me, obviously, Guv. You need a bit of police common sense to run this place properly.'

Bernard's expression registered fury, mixed with a hint of resignation. Mona thought he'd made a fair assessment of his chances. The 'police common sense' slant was bound to play well with Paterson. Personally, she wasn't sure that either of them could be trusted to manage anything more complicated than finding their way to the canteen and back.

'Oh God.' Paterson looked round at the options before him. 'Well, Carole has obviously got more common sense than the two of you put together, and Bernard is the brains of the operation. But, though it pains me to say it, Maitland probably has the best idea ...'

'Mr Paterson, you can't be serious. Maitland doesn't

56

have the skills for what is largely an administrative role ...'

Mona winced. This wasn't the best angle to take with the Guv, who preferred to see himself as still firmly in the front line of law enforcement, ignoring all the evidence to the contrary, not least his expanding waistline.

'Sorry, Bernard, but my mind is made up.' He pointed at Maitland. 'And you – don't make me regret this.'

Bernard picked up his coat, zipped it all the way to the top, and walked briskly out of the office, without a word to anyone.

'Don't go,' shouted Maitland, smirking. 'I want to discuss your work plan for tomorrow.' He took off after him, intent, no doubt, on further gloating.

'I'm regretting this already,' said Paterson.

Mona patted her remaining colleague on the shoulder. 'Best of luck, Carole.'

8

'It'll be a firm but fair regime, Bernie. I won't put up with any slacking, though.'

Bernard spun round to face him. 'Maitland, if you don't leave me in peace, I'll ...'

His tormentor raised an eyebrow. 'You'll what?'

'Oh, I don't know – I'll contact HR or something.'

Maitland burst out laughing. Bernard turned on his heel and half-walked, half-ran into the Meadows. As he hurried into the expanse of green parkland, he heard Maitland shout something unintelligible after him. He kept walking without giving Maitland the satisfaction of looking back at him.

Paterson was insane, literally certifiable, if he thought that Maitland could handle the responsibility of running the team. Despite what Paterson chose to tell himself, the job of team leader was 90 per cent paperwork, with the occasional foray into politics. Maitland's inability to correctly fill in the simplest of forms was legendary. For goodness' sake, this was the man who needed help every month to fill in his own timesheet. He'd never yet submitted an expenses claim that actually added up correctly. Well, Hell mend them both. He wouldn't be digging Maitland out of any holes.

Checking his watch, he debated whether it was too early to go back to his new flatshare. *Flatshare*. Even the word felt strange and new. Another part of the brave new world he'd been thrust into since his separation, the inevitable end of a process set in motion by the death of his son. He'd been married for almost ten years by the time the Virus took Jamie. A decade of happiness, of a stability that he'd taken completely for granted. He loved Carrie, she loved him, and he thought the two of them would be together for ever. But then two had all too briefly become three. The grief had been unbearable, the pain changing both of them, and their relationship from that day onward. So, now here he was, thirty-five, separated, and living in the spare room of a ground-floor flat owned by a beautician.

Megan, his landlady, had taken a bit of persuading that she wanted to live with a man. He could see her point. Maitland was a man. Mr Paterson was a man. Neither of them would make ideal lodgers, given their propensity to fart, tell inappropriate jokes, and eat food that did not belong to them. So he'd worked hard to persuade her that he was not a laddish sort, drawing on examples from his sporting past (as a professional badminton player) and his previous work (in health promotion). But the part of his argument that had proved the most persuasive was the emphasis he'd put on his long working hours.

'So, you probably wouldn't be in all that much of an evening?'

'No, no,' he had lied. 'When we get going on a case, we work round the clock.'

Turning up at 6pm might show this statement to have been a gentle massaging of the truth. That being said, Megan did seem to have warmed to him over the week that he'd been living there. She'd been welcoming enough that he'd felt able to not spend every evening alone in his room, and was beginning to feel almost comfortable sitting on the green leather sofa in her living room watching TV. Still, six o'clock was pushing it a bit.

He side-tracked to a bench. The Meadows were busy, full of joggers, amateur jugglers and people lolling about on the grass enjoying the early evening sunshine. He pulled out his phone and stared at it for a moment, trying to think of a reason that would justify him phoning his wife. Maybe he didn't need a reason. They were still married, and he remained concerned about her health and happiness. As, presumably, she did about his, making her his best bet for someone who would listen to him whinge about work. So without any further soul-searching he opened the phone's address book, and pressed his wife's name. It rang twice, then she answered.

'It's me. Bernard.'

There was laughter at the other end of the line. 'I know who it is. How are things?'

'Terrible. Mr Paterson's on leave for a couple of days and he's putting Maitland in charge.'

'Maitland?' Carrie laughed again, a gentle sound full of empathy. 'You'll hate that.'

'Yeah.' He smiled. It felt good to speak to someone who knew him so well. 'Anyway, you sound happy.'

'I am, actually.' She sounded surprised, as if this was a revelation to her. 'Happy*ish*, at least.'

Bernard watched a group of people in sportswear unroll yoga mats while he considered if his wife's happiness was a good or a bad thing. Obviously, he wanted the woman he loved to be happy, but it hurt like hell that she seemed to be happier without him.

60

'Anyway,' he said, irritated by the tentative tone of his voice, 'do you want to meet up at the weekend, you know, for a drink or a film or something?'

There was a long silence from the phone.

'Bernard...'

'Just as friends, no pressure?'

'Bernard, we're supposed to be moving on. Nothing's changed. I still want another baby and you don't want to bring a child into a world full of the Virus so ...'

'I miss you.'

The phone took a depressingly long time to reply.

'I miss you too, but you are making this even harder.' Carrie sighed. 'It would be better if you didn't phone me again. At least not for a while. Goodbye, Bernard.'

She hung up, over his protests. *Moving on.* In a few years he'd be forty. Was it time for a mid-life crisis? Could he just put everything behind him, his marriage, his dead son, his failed career as a badminton player and move on to something new? He could move to a different town, a different continent even. He could take his health promotion skills to a developing country, where he could be sure he'd really be making a difference. Except he couldn't go anywhere. He was a HET member, and in the current climate it would be nigh on impossible to resign. Every single member of the HET team had had the Virus and survived, meaning that they were now immune to it. Immune workers were at a premium, and he was not going to be allowed to go anywhere.

His new home was a main-door flat with a pocket hanky-sized garden to the front. The lights were on in the kitchen, and he could see Megan pottering about. She had her long hair tied up in a bun, and a red and

61

white striped apron on. She caught sight of him as he walked up the path and waved.

'How was your day?' Her voice drifted through to him.

He closed the door behind him, wondering how to answer this. He couldn't face explaining Maitland from first principles, so he opted for, 'OK, I suppose.' A wave of cooking aromas hit him. 'Wow. Something smells good.'

Megan appeared in the hallway, her apron covered in flour. 'I'm making fish pie – it's a new recipe I've not tried before so I don't know how it'll turn out. If you're feeling adventurous you're welcome to have some?'

Bernard was a little bit overcome by the offer. He couldn't remember the last time someone had cooked for him. Carrie had pretty much given up on eating, never mind cooking, since their bereavement. 'That would be lovely. Really lovely.'

'And, Bernard, I was thinking about being a little naughty.' She smiled.

For the second time, his emotional core took a punch. Unless he was very much mistaken, the conversation was taking a flirtatious turn. It had been a long time since a woman had cooked for him. The last time a woman had flirted with him, there may have been an ark floating past the window. He slowly lowered his bag to the ground and waited to see what transgressive activity she was planning.

'I know it's only a Monday night, but I was thinking about cracking open a bottle of wine. What do you think?'

Bernard felt several emotions, the chief of which was relief. 'Ehm, OK?' He followed Megan into the kitchen, and watched her expertly open a bottle of Shiraz. A strand of her hair had fallen across her face. She tucked it back behind her ear, and smiled.

'I wasn't sure how it would be living with a man, but I think this is working out just fine, don't you think?'

He took the glass of red. 'Ehm, yeah. Great.'

9

'Hi, Mum.'

'Oh, Mona, it's you.' Her mother looked pleased to see her. 'I expect you're here to find out what Dr McCallum had to say today.'

Mona felt a pang of guilt as she followed her mother into the house. She'd completely forgotten about the appointment. 'Yes, of course. What did he say?'

'Come on through and sit down.' Her mother waited until she was settled before she spoke again. 'It's not the best of news, I'm afraid. The cancer is spreading. You need to be prepared.'

Mona stared at her mother.

Her mother looked slightly exasperated. 'You do understand what I'm trying to tell you?'

'You are going to die.' A lump was forming in the back of her throat. Growing up she had never been particularly close to her mother; she'd been a daddy's girl through and through, to the extent of following him into the police. But since her father's death, and particularly over the past few months, they'd grown closer. The thought of losing her mother, her only remaining relative, filled her with dread.

'We're all going to die, Mona. But in my case it won't be that long. I'm sure you're not entirely surprised.'

'I knew it was a possibility, but still…'

Her mother sat next to her on the sofa, and took her hand. 'Mona, I want you settled before I'm gone. I know I'm not going to get a son-in-law, and a couple of grandchildren, because that is not your inclination, and that is fine by me. But I'd like to think that you were at least in some kind of relationship, not going home to an empty flat every night.'

'It's complicated.'

'Is it? It doesn't seem that complicated to me. You need to go out and socialise, and find someone you like and settle down. That is simple enough in my opinion. And it seems to me that the first step is that you actually tell people you are a lesbian.'

'I'm not sure if I'm ready to, Mum.'

'Mona, you're twenty-nine years of age. When exactly are you going to be ready? Because you'll never meet a nice girl if nobody knows you're available.'

Mona smiled. 'Shall I stick the kettle on?'

'Indeed you will not. This is my house and while I've still got breath in my body I'll be the hostess.'

In spite of the brave words, Mona's mother struggled a little to get back out of the chair. Mona took her arm and helped her through to the kitchen. 'I just wanted to tell you, Mum, that I'll be away for a few days with work, but you can get me on my mobile.'

Her mother pulled a face. 'I hate those things. Write your number out for me and leave it by the phone. And don't waste your time worrying about me, because I'll be fine.' She took Mona's hand again, and held it to her face. 'You're the one that I worry about. Promise me you'll think about what I said.'

She nodded. 'I will.'

TUESDAY

EARACHE

I

'Guv, this is getting boring.'

Mona had been in her boss's company since their 6.30am rendezvous at the BA desk in the departure hall of Edinburgh Airport. They were now ten minutes away from landing at Gatwick, and during that time Paterson had said three whole sentences to her. She'd been counting: three sentences, thirteen words.

You're late.

That's our flight being called.

Not that row, the next one.

At this rate, the sentence count for the whole trip wouldn't require her to take off her socks and unleash the little piggies. It was unbearable.

'Guv?'

Paterson didn't answer, continuing to stare out the window at the clouds that surrounded them.

'Can we at least discuss what we're going to do when we get there?'

He turned fractionally in her direction. 'We're meeting a contact I've got from the Met.'

'I thought this was supposed to be hush-hush?'

Paterson glared at her. 'Considering neither of us knows the geography or politics of the area, what else do you suggest?'

The *Fasten Your Seat Belts* light flashed, and they buckled up as instructed.

'Anyway, he owes me a favour. He's not going to say anything.'

'So, where are we meeting him?'

'In the airport. He said to look out for him outside the Costa in the exit hall.'

The plane touched down, and without waiting for the seat belt signs to go off the two of them were on their feet and retrieving their hand luggage. They walked purposefully through the terminal, then ground to a halt while they looked for the meeting place. Mona spotted it first. There were a number of people loitering outside the coffee shop, but Mona knew immediately who her money would be on to be Paterson's acquaintance. A tall, well-built man in his late twenties was eyeing people walking past with an air that suggested he was ready to spring into action at any moment. A cop, if ever she had seen one. He caught sight of Paterson, and waved them over. Paterson and the man grunted a greeting at each other. Whatever favour had been called in, it looked pretty grudgingly fulfilled.

'This is Mona.'

The man stuck out his hand, and smiled. 'Greg. Let's get a coffee and we can talk.'

Paterson plonked himself at the nearest available table. She dropped her rucksack onto a seat.

'What'll it be, Mona?' Greg pointed to the counter. 'Tea, coffee, breakfast roll?'

'Just a black Americano for me, please.'

'And what about you, Dad?'

Paterson was busily engaged in fiddling with the menu. 'The same.'

70

Mona waited until Greg was out of earshot. '*Dad*? Greg is your son?'

'Yes, he's my eldest.' Paterson kept his eyes on the menu. 'And as you've probably picked up, he's not desperately delighted to be helping me out. I wouldn't have asked him, but like I said, we're travelling blind here.'

Mona's desire to ask more questions was cut short by Greg's return with the coffees. 'Well, I've asked around as discreetly as I could, but from what I can make out he's not been arrested or ended up in hospital.'

'That's good, I suppose?' said Mona.

'Good for him, definitely,' said Paterson, 'but it leaves us with a lot of London to search.'

'Maybe not as much as you think. You said your man was looking for a rough sleeper? Well, the homeless tend to cluster around certain areas. Your best bet is to head to the South Bank and start from there.'

'Wasn't there a big push to get rough sleepers off the streets of London?' asked Mona.

He smiled. 'There was, particularly to get the more touristy bits of London cleared. But keeping people off the streets takes a big investment of resources, and since the Virus came along it's really eaten into those kinds of budgets. And in some ways, it's easier for our equivalent of your team to have people sleeping in certain locations, because it allows for health interventions to take place. They can card them, and take their blood if they know where they are.'

'And is it unusual for a woman to be sleeping rough?'

'More unusual than for the men, because women are usually better at having somewhere they can go to. If they've got kids the council has to house them, even if it's just in a B&B. But for a single woman, with no friends or relatives to fall back on, they end up on the South Bank like everyone else.'

Mona pulled a face. 'Not a safe place for a young woman, I would imagine.'

'No, it's really not, so I'm not surprised that your man dropped everything and headed down here. Like I say, the South Bank is probably your best bet. But, if you don't bump into your professor, speak to Elijah from the Rough Sleepers project.' He handed Mona a sheet of paper with an address. 'He knows everyone and everything that's going on in that bit of the world. If there's been a mad professor type poking around, he'll know.'

'Thanks.'

He held out another sheet of paper. 'I've also written you a note of how you get to the South Bank from here by Tube. And you need to download an A–Z of London app to your phone if you haven't done so already.'

Paterson didn't take it, and looked vaguely offended at the offer. 'I'm sure I can negotiate the London Underground without help.'

'I'm not,' said Mona, and reached out for the directions. 'Again, thank you.'

Greg got to his feet. 'Well, I'd better be off. Mona, nice to meet you. Dad, you've got my number if you need me.'

Paterson grunted something that wasn't quite a thank you.

It was nearly two hours before they reached the South Bank, including ten minutes spent travelling in the wrong direction on the District Line. Paterson had used this as an opportunity to make a snide comment about Greg's instructions, although Mona couldn't help but notice that he wasn't actually contributing anything himself to navigating the London transport environment. She just about managed to keep her temper, and was delighted to emerge, at long last, into the sunshine at Embankment Station.

'I don't think I could bear travelling that kind of distance every day, Guv.' Mona pulled at her shirt, which was sticking to her back. 'Even without this heat it would be a killer.' She turned her phone around in her hands to try to orientate herself. She looked up to see Paterson scowling at her.

'Could you look any more like a tourist?'

'Is that a bad look for us, Guv, really? Given the sensitivity?'

Paterson thought for a minute. 'Fair point.'

Mona smiled. She might well look like a tourist, but the Guv would still look like a cop if he was dressed in a Bermuda shirt and shorts.

'So we need to get ourselves on to the other side of the Thames, then according to the notes Greg gave us, if we walk along as far as the National Theatre, we should encounter some rough sleepers.'

Paterson sighed. 'Lead on then.'

Mona walked along the narrow pedestrian walkway at the side of Hungerford Bridge. She had to shield her eyes from the sun, and cursed herself for not bringing sunglasses. One of the downsides of a Scottish upbringing was you forgot the possibility that somewhere else in the world the sun might be shining brightly. Squinting aside, it was fun looking out at London. Maybe she'd come back for a holiday, see the place properly. Make her mother proud by going to a gay bar.

From the look on Paterson's face, he was less enamoured with the sightseeing. He was pulling at his collar in a manner that suggested that the weather had been added to the list of things he was furious about. They reached the end of the bridge and turned onto the South Bank. Mona's eyes flicked between her surroundings and the directions she'd been given. 'This looks similar to where the photograph was taken, Guv.'

'It does. They really like their concrete down here, don't they?'

The sharp corners of the National Theatre appeared. 'I think they call the architectural style "brutalism".'

'Don't get all Bernard on me, for God's sake.'

A couple of men were sitting at the side of the walkway, with signs in front of them that outlined the circumstances that had brought them here. A couple of tourists stopped for a moment, conversed with the men, then threw coins into the hats in front of them. Mona guessed the tourists must either be immune to the Virus, or have an adventurous approach to risk, to get so close to two people with unknown health status. Maybe they were superstitiously repaying their good fortune by giving alms to every beggar they encountered.

Time to start asking questions. She stopped to put her phone away, and as she did so, some activity further along the walkway caught her eye.

'Guv?'

'What?' He stood next to her, squinting as she had been to protect his eyes.

'Look!' She pointed. 'I think we've been beaten to it.'

2

'I still don't see why Mr Paterson left you in charge.'

Maitland was installed behind Paterson's desk, with a layer of paperwork spread across it. He stretched both his arms wide, and folded them behind his head. 'Because the boss and I are on the same wavelength. Him and me, we share a vision for this place. We know who the bad guys are, we know what the difficulties are, and he knows that, unlike you, I'll rise to the challenge. '

This was an annoyingly good description of Paterson's assessment of the situation. It was, to Bernard's mind, also highly unfair. He had risen to many challenges in his time. And as the challenge in question was the efficient and timely filing of paperwork he knew he was more than man enough for the job. 'You've got no understanding of administration. How are you going to prioritise this lot?'

Maitland swept the papers up into a pile. Bernard caught a glimpse of something that looked important.

'There was a memo in there marked "Urgent".'

'Everything in here is marked urgent,' said Maitland. 'If a memo went out marked anything less than murderously crucial it wouldn't get read.'

'Yeah, but it said something about drugs.'

'We're in the middle of a pandemic! Almost every memo mentions them. I know what I am doing here,

Bernard.' Maitland sighed. 'Every bit of paper is important, and I will read it all when I get some peace. That's after I've read the ton of papers for the Parliamentary Committee.' He poked a large pile of papers.

'*The Parliamentary Committee?*' Bernard's jaw began a slow, involuntary movement toward the ground. 'You're representing the HETs at the Parliamentary Committee?'

'Yeah, it'll be fine.' He flashed Bernard a happy, confident smile.

'You are going to stand up in front of a group of politicians and talk about the work of the HET?'

'Yes.'

'A group of politicians, half of whom are making a career out of savaging the HET's role in Virus prevention?'

'Yes.' Maitland was starting to sound defensive. 'The Guv manages it, and he's not exactly a public speaker.'

'Except Mr Paterson messed it up so badly last time Stuttle had to step in to stop him getting sacked. The politicians are going to eat you alive!'

'Carole!' Maitland leaned sideways and looked past Bernard, out into the main office.

'Yeah?' She appeared in the doorway.

'Can you get Bernard out of my office and doing something useful?'

'Like what?'

'Help him find his Defaulter. Or in fact, help him do anything that doesn't involve him being here.'

'Right, fine.' Bernard turned on his heel. 'Come on, Carole.'

'Where are we going?'

Bernard realised with a start that his colleague was

speaking to him. Since he'd left the office he'd been replaying the conversation with Maitland continuously in his head, and each time he thought it over he became more convinced that Paterson had had a temporary bout of insanity when he'd left the Paperwork Clown in charge. 'Sorry, what was that?'

'I said, where are we going?' Carole was smiling at him. 'I'm totally happy to help out, but, you know, some vague idea of what we're up to would be useful?'

'Sorry, I should have said.' Bernard slowed the car down. It wasn't Carole's fault that Maitland was an idiot. 'We're heading to Colinton. I want to check out the address that Stephen McNiven's Green Card is registered to.'

She nodded. 'OK, good plan. Just one question.'

'Uh-huh?'

'Who is Stephen McNiven?'

'The guy who vomited on me yesterday.'

'Ah, him.' Carole smiled, and stared out the window. 'And are we tracking him down to deliver some vigilante-style justice?'

'Yes, I'm about to deliver a dry-cleaning bill that will have him quaking in his boots.' Bernard smiled. He liked the occasions when he worked with Carole. She radiated good-natured calmness, and he inevitably found himself cheered up in her company. Her only fault that he could see was the fact that she got on well with Maitland. 'He claimed that he didn't know our Defaulter but I don't believe him. We think our Defaulter might be working as a prostitute, and I'd like to know more about Mr McNiven's line of work.'

'You think he's living off her immoral earnings?'

'He was pretty evasive about what he did for a living, so in short, yes.'

They drove on in silence for a few minutes, until Bernard found his rage bubbling up again. 'I can't believe Mr Paterson left Maitland in charge. You know he's got to do the Parliamentary Committee?'

There was no response.

'There's no way he's not going to mess that up.' He glanced over at her. She was still staring out of the window. 'Carole?' He tried again, more loudly. 'Carole?'

'What?' She jumped. 'Sorry, Bernard, I was miles away.'

'Am I ranting too much about Maitland?'

'No.' She smiled. 'Well, maybe a little. Maitland will probably be fine.'

He was absolutely delighted to hear the note of uncertainty in her defence of her partner. 'When you say "probably"...'

She cut across him. 'Bernard, can I talk to you about something? Something private?'

'Of course.' He slowed down even further to look at her, and was loudly honked by the car behind. He gave a hasty wave over his shoulder and speeded up again. 'What's up?'

'Things aren't going so well at home.'

'Oh no.' *Marriage trouble?* He'd only met Carole's husband once when he'd picked her up from work. He remembered him being very thin, very amiable, and with a handshake so strong it had taken a couple of hours for Bernard to regain feeling in his fingers. 'What's up?'

'You know how my eldest was ill a couple of months ago?'

Bernard reached deep into his brain for a name. 'Michael, is it?'

'Yes.' She lapsed back into silence, staring out of the

window. 'It was absolutely terrifying when he caught the Virus.'

Young people were the most in danger of dying from the disease; it was one of the Virus's most terrifying quirks. The Virus played havoc with the immune system of those it infected, stimulating them to the point where the body just couldn't cope. Those with the strongest immune systems – the young and fit – were most at risk, as their bodies turned in on themselves, killing them in an attempt to fight the viral threat. There wasn't a parent of teenagers in the country who hadn't lost sleep to that particular fact.

'But now ...' Carole sighed. 'Michael's immune, of course, except he thinks that "immune" actually means bloody immortal. He's gone completely off the rails. Coming in at all hours, smelling of alcohol and weed.'

'You think he's going to illegal meet-ups?'

'I think so. I mean, I'm not entirely unsympathetic to his point of view. When I was his age I was going to discos along with hundreds of other people my own age. Then in amongst all that emergency legislation the government rammed through there's the thing about no more than twenty non-immune people in any social gathering – I mean, can you imagine being a teenager and not meeting up with a big group of friends?'

Bernard considered this. His youth had been spent almost entirely on the badminton court. He doubted that his entire teenage network extended to twenty people. 'Well, yes, but I'm probably not typical.'

'He's going to get himself into trouble.'

'If it's any consolation I think the country's entire teenage population sees that particular statute as largely advisory. You know who you should talk to?'

79

'Who?'

'Marcus. He told me at great length one day all the code words and emojis that the UK's youth are using on social media to denote when and where meet-ups are taking place. Frankly, Carole, the digital natives are running rings around us oldies.'

'I know. And it's great that I don't have to worry about him catching the Virus, but not all his friends are immune, so now I've got irate parents phoning me up complaining he's a bad influence.'

'Oh, I'm sorry. I…' He stopped, unable to think of the right thing to say. He'd no experience of the challenges of parenting a teenager. 'If there's anything I can do?'

'Thanks. It was good just to talk to someone and get it off my chest. Jimmy and I can't seem to speak about it without fighting.' She gave herself a little shake. 'Anyway, enough of me moaning…'

'You weren't moaning, you were talking something through.'

'Either way, let's talk about something else. What do we know about this McNiven guy?'

'To be honest, we don't really know much about him at all, apart from the fact that he was at the house that our Defaulter was supposed to be living in. And he used to work at McDonald's.'

'We know one other thing about him. On the basis of your previous meeting with him, he appears to have a delicate stomach.'

'Yup, that is certainly true.'

'You'll be standing well back this time.'

'I'm not too bothered.' Bernard shrugged. 'I've borrowed Maitland's vest.'

'Bernard!'

He grinned. 'We're here.' He pulled the car over to the side of the road. 'This is the address his Green Card is registered to.'

They were stopped outside the gates of a grey-stone detached house. Set well back from the road, it was surrounded on all sides by a sturdy six-foot-high wall. In common with McNiven's residence from the day before, the expensive villa had a large and untidy garden to the fore.

'It's a nice house,' said Carole. 'In fact, a very nice house.'

'I'd go as far as to say it's a prime piece of real estate. And so was the house where we encountered McNiven yesterday. Both Colinton and Morningside are considerably nicer than our usual stomping grounds, wouldn't you agree?'

'There's someone in.' She leaned forward. 'Upstairs window. A woman I think.'

A figure was watching them from the upstairs bay window, half hidden by the curtain. Bernard saw a glimpse of long dark hair.

'Actually, I'm pretty sure that's the man that we're looking for. Let's see if he lets us in.'

They walked up the driveway to the house, the gravel crunching under their feet.

'What a waste of a garden,' said Carole. 'I'd kill for a plot this size! And look at the state of that poor rose bush.'

Bernard was only half-listening, worrying about the kind of reception they could expect. McNiven had been asleep when they had disturbed him before, naked and vulnerable. Now he was forewarned of their approach, he might not be so willing to play along with the HET.

There could be violence, violence that neither he nor Carole were ideally placed to manage.

'Right, OK. Here we are.' He paused on the doorstep, and found himself reluctant to knock.

Carole seemed to sense, and share, his discomfort. 'What do we do if he doesn't open up?'

Right now, he was viewing an abortive attempt at entry as the best possible option. 'I'm pretty sure if Mona was here she'd be checking out the back door in case he's making a break for it.'

'Yeah, Maitland would be too.'

The two of them looked at the side of the house. A metal gate was in place to stop anyone accessing the rear of the property. Unfortunately, the gate was wide open.

'Bernard, this might make me a bad person, but I don't think I get paid enough to risk getting beaten up.'

He nodded, and felt a tiny wave of self-loathing wash over him. It was easier for Carole. No one really expected her to have the ability to deal with violent customers. But by the simple virtue of him being a man, his colleagues seemed to assume that he would be able to handle himself in a fight. In reality, nothing in his life had prepared him for that. Being a professional badminton player had given him agility, flexibility, and a turn of speed that occasionally came in useful. What it hadn't given him were any skills he could realistically use in a fight.

He braced his shoulders, and rang the bell. A faint electronic 'Für Elise' played inside the house. The music ended, and silence took its place. Bernard peered through the small glass window in the middle of the door. If he counted to ten and no one came, they could give up and go back to the office. Their heads might not be held high, but at least they would still be attached to their bodies.

82

Mona would be back soon, and he could try accessing the house again with her. Although the occupants would be well warned by then ... Self-loathing and self-preservation fought for supremacy in his mind, before being replaced by fear at the sound of approaching footsteps.

To his surprise, it was a young woman who opened the door. She was what Bernard thought of as an identikit girl: skinny, wearing jeans and a vest top, she had long blonde hair with the roots showing her original darker colour, a tan which was verging toward orange, dark eye make-up, and a large and elaborate tattoo on her left arm. He'd see ten girls who looked similar on the bus home.

'Can we speak to Stephen McNiven? We're from the HET.' He showed her his ID card.

'He's not in.' There was a hint of aggression, or possibly defensiveness, in her voice. In Bernard's experience the two were quite closely related.

'Are you sure?' asked Carole. 'Because we're certain we saw him at the window.'

'I said, he's not here.' The back door – they should have had it covered. Maybe he wouldn't tell Maitland about this. It would only give him another excuse to make his life hellish.

'But Mr McNiven does live here?'

She shrugged, and gave the tiniest of nods.

'And can I ask who you are?'

She lifted her tattooed arm and rested it on the door-jamb, attitude dripping from every pore. 'I'm Alessandra Barr.'

Bernard and Carole exchanged a look of surprise. 'We've been looking for you.'

'I know. Stevie told me.' She kept her eyes fixed on

Bernard. 'Do I have to come to one of those check things?'

'Yes, you do. Have you got your Green Card?'

'Hang on.' She turned back into the hallway, leaving the door open behind her. Bernard followed her in. Now they had actually found her, he was taking no chances. Although he was slightly apprehensive about walking into Stevie McNiven wielding a baseball bat. Alessandra reappeared almost immediately, and the two of them almost collided.

'Watch it!'

'Sorry.'

'Here's my card.'

He took it from her, and looked from the card to her and back again. The picture on the card matched the one on the file, of a blonde girl with two black eyes. She caught his eye, and looked defensive. 'I had a fight with my boyfriend the day before my picture was taken.'

'Is Stephen McNiven your boyfriend?'

She shook her head. He waited for her to elaborate, but she said nothing.

'Come on, let's get this Health Check over with.'

She nodded, and stepped out of the house.

3

'Looking for someone?'

The tiny figure pivoted slowly in the direction of Paterson's voice. Mrs Kilsyth's face registered surprise, then slight embarrassment. After a second her features regrouped into an expression of extreme irritation. She gave a cursory wave in their direction and turned back to the two old men with whom she'd been conversing.

'What is she playing at?' Paterson matched Mrs Kilsyth's look of irritation, and raised it to furious.

'The same as us I expect.'

'And is she planning to just ignore us standing here?'

'I don't think so, Guv.' She sincerely hoped that she wasn't. She could do without a set-to between the two of them, watched by half the homeless people in London. To her relief, Mrs Kilsyth seemed to be saying her good-byes to the men.

As she walked away, one of them shouted after her in a broad Glaswegian accent. 'I think I know the man you want, doll. Come back and we can talk about it.' He cackled. 'You can buy us a cup of tea first.'

'Looks like you've got a hot lead there, Mrs Kilsyth.'

She glared at Paterson. 'At least I'm trying.'

'Trying to do what? Get yourself mugged?'

'What choice did I have? After speaking to you yesterday I didn't have much faith that you were actually going to do anything. And as the old adage says, if you want something doing, do it yourself.'

'Well you had no need to come all the way down here. I spoke to our HQ and they've sent us to retrieve the professor.'

She looked up and down the length of the Embankment, as if searching for something. 'Just the two of you?'

'Yes just the two of us! What did you expect? We are trying to be inconspicuous here. Would you prefer it if we had an army of police officers scouring the alleyways of London, and leaking to the press while they do it?'

She considered this for a moment. 'I suppose.'

'Have you found out anything useful?' asked Mona.

'I've been showing Sandy's picture to the many gentlemen of the road I have encountered, and several of them are of the opinion they could take me to him right now if I paid them suitable expenses.'

Paterson smiled. 'And yet you're still here.'

'Call me cynical, Mr Paterson, but I'm not sure they're telling the truth. Nobody has said anything sensible, such as they saw him here last night.'

'Well, you can leave the hunting to us now.'

'I don't think so!' She folded her arms. 'I'm staying right here to make sure that you do actually look for him.'

'And you know a lot about mounting a search do you?' Paterson indicated the homeless men who were watching their discussions. 'Another half hour here and you'd have been minus both your purse and your innocence.'

'You're a few years late to be protecting that, Mr Paterson. Now I may not be trained in the ins and outs of witness recovery, but I've been around your kind of institution long enough to spot a token effort when I see one.'

'It's not token, it's discreet.'

She raised an eyebrow.

'Believe me, we are every bit as keen as you to find the professor.' It was Paterson's turn to fold his arms. 'And anyway, I only have your word for it that you are genuinely interested in Professor Bircham-Fowler's well-being. For all I know *you're* spying on him, for persons and reasons unknown.'

'Then I've been embedded for a bloody long time!' She waved a hand at him, dismissing him back in the direction of Hungerford Bridge. 'Right, have it your way. You continue your investigation and I'll continue mine.'

'Guv,' said Mona, a note of concern in her voice. Having Theresa continuing her own search would be disastrous. While she had more faith in Mrs Kilsyth's ability to look after herself than Paterson did, there was huge potential for her to get into trouble. She could get mugged or attacked, and end up attracting the attention of the police. Or, if she wandered around long enough she was sure to bump into the London equivalent of the HET, who would be busy trying to contain the public health problem presented by a large number of people with uncertain health statuses bedding down together for the night. Either way, if she wound up in trouble it wouldn't be long before someone questioned why Professor Bircham-Fowler's secretary was trawling the underpasses of the South Bank.

'Yes, I know, Mona, I get your point. Mrs Kilsyth can assist us, and I mean assist.' He waggled a finger at her. 'No telling us what to do, no saying we're getting it all wrong; in fact, no whinging of any kind.' He turned the finger back toward himself. 'I am in charge here.'

She looked at Mona, and shrugged. 'Whatever you say – Guv.'

The address for Elijah was annotated with a description of how to get there.

'We're looking for a church hall, Guv, down one of these backstreets. I'll check the map on my phone.'

'Where would we be without the map?'

Mona glared at his back. Greg's A–Z app had proved invaluable, even if Paterson did glare at her every time she consulted it. She wondered how he would prefer to navigate the streets of London. He might know every close, cut-through and rat run of Leith, but here they were on foreign territory.

'According to the *map*, Guv, it's the next road on the right.'

'Mrs Kilsyth,' she touched her arm to stop her walking past the turning. 'We're down here.'

'Theresa, dear, call me Theresa.' She smiled and obediently followed her.

'I'm Mona.'

'Mona.' She nodded. 'A lovely name. And your boss is called?'

'Mr Paterson,' said the Guv, without turning round.

Theresa rolled her eyes. 'Where are we going?'

'We're visiting a community project. The worker here knows everyone, apparently. Number 27, Guv, this is it.'

Paterson knocked on the front door, which opened under the force of his fist. 'Hello?'

They followed him into an old-fashioned church hall. The wooden floor creaked under their weight. The room had seen better days: the elegant cornicing on the ceiling was offset by the peeling paint on the walls. Half a dozen tables had red polka dot plastic covers over them, and a number of homeless men sat at them, drinking tea. Mona looked them over. They were a mixed bunch: old, young, black, white. The one thing they all had in common was an expression of extreme weariness. As homelessness went, these guys were on the front line. No sofa surfers here, this was the hardcore sleeping-under-bridges brigade.

There was a serving hatch in the corner of the room, with a strong smell of soup emanating from it. Paterson wandered over and knocked on the wood. 'Hello?'

Two middle-aged black women appeared, their hands full of crockery and dishtowels. One of them stepped forward, her eyes full of suspicion. 'Yes?'

'Sorry to disturb you. We're looking for Elijah?'

A head popped out of a doorway. 'Someone say my name?' The accent was broad East End. The man was black, as tall and as broad as the Guv, but wearing a grin that suggested an infinitely more cheerful disposition. 'Because if you are looking for Elijah, consider him found. How can I help you?'

'We were given your details by Detective Sergeant Paterson. We're down from Scotland looking for an, ehm, missing person.'

'DS Paterson? A good man. Very understanding when we have our little local difficulties here.' Elijah laughed, a big booming sound, then shook each of their hands in turn. 'You guys cops as well?'

Paterson made a non-committal noise. Fortunately Elijah didn't follow it up.

'So, who's the dude you're looking for? Or is it a lady?' He looked round the café. 'We don't get so many women in here.'

89

'It's a man,' said Mona, and produced the picture of the professor.

Elijah took it from her and studied it closely. 'No, sorry. Can't say I've seen him.'

'Take your time.'

He handed it back. 'No, really. He's a weird-looking dude, and I ain't seen anyone in tweeds like that.'

'Have you seen this woman?' Theresa elbowed them both out of the way, and waved the photograph of the professor's daughter.

Mona wouldn't have thought it possible, but Paterson radiated even more fury than he had earlier. Elijah looked surprised. 'Oh, yeah, what's her name again?'

'You know her?' asked Paterson. 'Is she a rough sleeper?'

'Nah, she ain't no rough sleeper. She works for a charity – the Homeless wotsit UK lot? Know who I mean? This is their annual sleepout.'

'A sleepout?'

'Yeah. They all bed down on the Embankment to draw attention to the lack of resources to tackle homelessness. They always get a few famous people to join them, you know, soap stars, that kind of thing. It gets a lot of publicity for them.'

'Any idea of her name?'

'Oh, now you're asking.' Elijah stood staring into space, his brow furled. 'Lovely girl she is. Sure it was something beginning with M, like Mary or Margaret.' He slapped his forehead. 'Maria! Her name's Maria.'

'Maria Bircham-Fowler?' asked Theresa, again to the Guv's annoyance.

'Don't think so.' He shook his head. 'Nah. Weren't something like that. Something more exotic, I think. I thought she was foreign?'

'Possibly,' said Mona, reluctant to show her ignorance. Theresa might be able to shine some light on this. 'Would you be able to give us the proper name of the charity she works for?'

'You people are taxing my brain today! Homeless something UK. Homeless Hearts, I think? Something like that?'

'Hearthless Hearts UK.' A voice drifted out from the kitchen.

'Antoinette – you are an angel! That woman,' he pointed into the kitchen, 'she never forgets anything, not a name, or a face. She's very popular with our clients. So, if she says Hearthless Hearts UK, then that's what it will be.'

'Any idea where their offices are?'

'I visited them with one of our gentlemen a while back. They were at Pillars Lane then, but that was probably about a year ago, but I didn't hear anything about them moving. Antoinette!' he yelled in the direction of the hatch. 'Hearthless Hearts – they still down at Pillars Lane?'

'As far as I know.'

'We'll start there then. Thanks so much for your help.'

'Always happy to support the police. Though we do take donations for our work ...'

Paterson smiled and dug into his pockets for a tenner, which he laid on the polka dot table. 'It's great that there are immune people like yourself doing this kind of work.'

'Immune?' Elijah's big booming laugh sounded again. 'I ain't immune.'

The three of them stared at him.

'Aren't you scared of catching the Virus?' asked Theresa.

'Nah.' He put his hands together as if praying. 'The Lord will protect me.'

91

4

Alessandra slammed the front door shut behind her, and stomped down the path with Bernard and Carole following in her wake. She tutted impatiently as Bernard struggled to find his car keys. 'Go and hurry up, will you? I want this over with.'

'If you'd turned up for your scheduled appointment it *would* be over with,' said Carole.

'Think you're smart, don't you?'

'Found them,' said Bernard, opening the car. 'Please get in.'

Alessandra tutted again, but climbed in without further protest.

'Well, she's a charmer, isn't she?' said Bernard.

'Yeah, but she's also a woman who is working as a prostitute, and had both her eyes blackened not so long ago. It could all just be front, especially if she thinks that McNiven guy is watching.'

'I suppose. Well, at least we've got her to her Health Check.'

'We're not at the clinic yet. Do you want to ask her questions or shall I?'

'Be my guest.'

'OK.' Carole turned on the intercom. 'So, Alessandra, we are here because you missed your Health Check. Was there a reason for that?'

She shrugged. 'Just had a lot on.' She pulled a long strand of hair out at a right angle from her head, and started wrapping it round her fingers. 'I forgot about it.'

'You know that it's an offence to miss your Health Check? You'll get a letter in the post with a warning if this is the first time that you've missed a Check, but there will be a fine if it's happened before.'

She looked less than terrified at this prospect. 'Right. Whatever.'

'*Have* you missed a Health Check before?'

She appeared to think about this. 'No.'

'And I need to confirm your address. You said you were living at 84 Morningside Crescent?'

'That's right. I was just visiting Stevie.'

'So, you're a friend of Mr McNiven?'

She looked frustrated. 'Stevie said I didn't have to answer any questions, I just need to get the test thing done.'

Carole turned back to Bernard and switched the intercom off. 'She seems pretty on edge. Do you think she's OK?'

Bernard looked at the passenger in his mirror. 'It'd be amazing if she could be described as OK, given her photographic history and the company she keeps. Do you think she's on drugs?'

'Pretty likely. Maybe that's why she's in such a mood – she's in need of a fix?' She turned the intercom back on. 'Alessandra, are you OK? Is there anything we can do to help you?'

'I just want to do the bloody test!'

Bernard winced as the voice came through loud and clear. He pressed the button to give them privacy. A judder went through the car.

'Did she just kick the back of our seats?' asked Carole.

'I think she did.' He looked at the mirror again. 'And I can see her swearing away to herself.' He started the engine. 'Let's get her Health Check over as quickly as possible.'

'OK. But after that I'm going to try again to get her to accept some help.'

Bernard grunted. He didn't fancy Carole's chances.

'Right. We're here.' They pulled up at the Health Check Centre, which was located in a doctor's surgery on Colinton Road.

'I don't know this one,' said Carole.

'It was the nearest. Let's hope they are co-operative.'

'What if they say they can't do it?'

'Well, the law says they are supposed to prioritise the emergency Health Checks, so let's hope they are up to date in their training on the legislation. Anyway, I suppose we better get her out.' He looked at Alessandra in the rear-view mirror. She caught his eye and flicked him the finger. 'OK, Carole, are you ready for this?'

'Not really. Do you think she'll try to do a runner?'

'I hope not. Imagine having to go back and tell Maitland we'd lost her? But she's let us bring her this far, so, come on, let's get this over with.'

He held the door open for Alessandra. 'We're here.'

She grunted and slid across fake leather upholstery. As she got out she pushed the door wide, nearly knocking Bernard off his feet. He cursed his stupidity, and was relieved to realise Alessandra wasn't attempting to make a break for it. In fact, she wasn't trying to go anywhere. She leaned back against the car, her thumbs tucked into the pockets of her jeans.

'I need a fag before I go in there.'

Bernard was torn. He hated smoking but he had an overwhelming desire to get the Health Check over, and if a cigarette was going to make it go more quickly …

'OK, but be quick.'

'Well?' She was looking at him, expectantly.

'What?'

'Give me a fag then.'

'I don't smoke.'

'But I don't have any fags.'

Carole took her arm. 'Then you're not going to be able to have a smoke before you go in, are you?'

'Fuck's sake.' She shook Carole's hand off, and gave the car a kick with the back of her heel.

Bernard hoped she hadn't scraped the paintwork. 'That's enough of that.' He gingerly took her arm, and Carole grabbed the other one.

'Fucking police brutality this.' She tried to shrug both of them off, and the three of them half-fell through the door into the surgery.

The waiting room was full. The entire pensioner population of Colinton appeared to have chosen today to visit their GP, and a sea of grey perms turned toward them and watched as Alessandra successfully shook off first Carole's arm, then his own. She then let rip with a range of profanities that the OAPs were unlikely to have heard before, unless they had spent a considerable part of their youth in the merchant navy. Bernard felt compelled to take control of the situation.

'Enough of that language, Ms Barr,' he shouted.

His raised voice woke the only baby in the room, who immediately started to howl. Bernard did his best to ignore the stares, and pulled Alessandra in the direction of the front desk. The receptionist eyed them nervously.

'We're here from the Health Enforcement Team.' Bernard flashed his card. 'We need an emergency Health Check.'

'An *emergency* Health Check.' The receptionist looked slightly bemused. 'I don't know if we do that.'

'You do,' said Bernard, hoping to God that the HET's database was up to date. He couldn't bear the thought of dragging Alessandra to another clinic.

She looked doubtful. 'I'll speak to the practice nurse.'

The receptionist reappeared with a woman in her thirties, in the blue tunic and trousers uniform of a practice nurse. 'You are the gentleman from the HET, I take it, after an emergency Health Check?'

He nodded, relieved that she seemed to know what he was talking about. She gestured to him to step away from Alessandra, and spoke in a low voice. 'Is she under arrest?'

'No, just late for her Health Check.' Bernard passed over his Defaulter sheet. The nurse looked at the picture and winced.

'Is she suffering from drug withdrawal symptoms?'

'Possibly.'

'Likely to turn violent?'

Bernard thought about the footmarks on the car. 'Possibly. Are you happy to do the Health Check?'

'I'll do it but I want you and your partner on the other side of the door.'

He nodded. 'Just give us a shout if you need us.'

The nurse turned toward Alessandra. 'Ms Barr? Shall we go through?'

''Bout time.'

Alessandra followed the nurse through the waiting

area and into her room. Bernard waved Carole over to him. 'I said we'd stand just outside the door.'

Carole nodded. Bernard thought he saw a hint of relief on her face that they'd made it this far. Alessandra was having her Health Check, and as soon as that was completed they would have no further commitment to her. They didn't even have to offer her a lift home. He wondered if Carole would still be intent on encouraging Alessandra to take up some form of support. Maybe he was getting old and cynical, but he wondered if it was worth it. She wasn't going to accept their help, he was sure of that. In fact, he was pretty sure that getting her next hit was Alessandra's main priority. Perhaps they could phone Social Work or something like that, alert them to a vulnerable individual? Although social services' resources were stretched wafer thin, like everyone else's.

He gave his arms a good stretch. He certainly shared Carole's feelings of relief, but there was also some other emotion at play. Today had been awful, scary, challenging, and most of the time he'd felt completely out of his depth. But they'd got through it. Minor scratches to the car aside, the two of them had triumphed, finding an obviously difficult Defaulter and getting her safely into her Health Check. And they hadn't needed the help of Maitland, Mona or any other ex-cop to do it. Maybe, just maybe, he could do this job. His train of thought was interrupted when the nurse's door opened again.

'Ms Barr wants to visit the Ladies before she leaves, if you could escort her?' She looked at Carole. 'Toilets are just back toward the main entrance, and then the second door on the right.'

Carole nodded. 'OK, Alessandra, shall we ...'

97

'Don't need a fucking escort.' She stormed off along the corridor, with Carole hurrying behind her.

The nurse beckoned him into her room. 'That was a bit of a ruse, to be honest. I wanted a quick word with you before she left the building...'

They were interrupted by the sound of someone yelling.

'Let me go!'

This was followed by a chorus of pensioner outrage, and the lone baby started its wailing again.

With a feeling of impending doom, he wrenched open the door and ran back out to see Carole crouched on the floor. He dropped down beside her, and was horrified to see her face was pouring with blood.

'Kicked 'e.' Carole waved in the direction of the front door. 'Go 'fter...'

He ran back along the corridor and out into the street. There was no one to be seen. A couple of school kids ambled into sight.

'Did you see a woman run past?'

They shook their heads and walked off, laughing and looking over their shoulders at him.

Alessandra had vanished.

He returned to find Carole sitting on a plastic chair in the waiting room, with a white towel held against her face. A group of elderly ladies were standing round her. As he approached, one of them took it upon herself to update him.

'That woman went mad!' She looked at him, pure fury on her face. Bernard wondered if she was holding him in some way responsible.

'She pushed this lassie over then kicked her in the face. She might have broken her jaw.'

'It's OK, Mrs McGregor, I'll see to it.' The nurse gently steered her away, then turned her attentions back to Bernard. 'Your colleague needs to go to Accident and Emergency immediately. I've had a look and I don't think it's broken but she should be properly checked out and X-rayed.'

''Ust get out of 'ere.' Carole stood up, her hand still holding the towel against her face.

'Yes, of course.' He took her arm, and guided her toward the door, the faces of the small crowd watching them go.

'Excuse me.' The nurse stopped them. 'Because of all this nonsense we didn't get a chance to finish our conversation.'

'OK,' said Bernard, his mind already busy planning his route to A&E.

'How much do you know about the woman you brought in?'

'Next to nothing, to be honest. We suspect she might be a prostitute, and possibly takes drugs. But other than that we just picked her up and brought her here.'

'I see.' She nodded. 'Well, I just wanted to tell you that whoever that woman was, her blood group conclusively tells me she's not Alessandra Barr.'

Carole lowered the towel slightly. ''Uck.'

5

'Pillars Lane. It doesn't look far on the map, Guv.' Mona traced a finger from where they were to the offices of the Hearthless Hearts UK charity. 'We can probably walk it.'

'Hmm. Give me another look at their website.'

Mona handed over her phone. 'See, Guv, on their page about the sleepover you can see there's a sentence saying "For more information call Maria …" and if you look really closely at the sleepover photograph you can see that guy from *EastEnders*.'

'Fascinating. Would have been helpful if they'd included a picture of Maria, or a surname.'

Theresa stood on tiptoe trying to look at the screen. 'Oh yes, he's the café owner from Albert Square, isn't he?'

'If you two ladies are quite done discussing the soaps, I wonder if you could give us a minute alone, Theresa?'

She looked surprised. 'OK. I'll wait over there.' She headed over to the edge of the walkway, and stood looking out across the Thames.

'What's up, Guv?'

'Just trying to get my head round how we're going to play this. We can't just bowl up there and start asking questions.'

'Seemed to work OK with Elijah.'

'Yeah, but we had a strong introduction from the local police, and also, he was the happiest, most trusting man in the world. There's nothing to say that we'll get the same reception at this place. Some of these charities can be pretty hostile to people working in Virus policy. You know, all the usual civil liberties bullshit.' He glanced over at Theresa. 'And I'm not sure that having Miss Moneypenny running round with us is exactly going to help.'

Mona followed his gaze. 'We do make a pretty odd-looking trio, Guv. Any suggestions?'

'Yup. I keep herself occupied, and you do a solo trip. Less danger of her mouthing off about something that she shouldn't be.'

'Fine, Guv, totally makes sense. Theresa's not going to like it, though.'

'She can lump it then. This is my investigation, and what I say goes.'

She smiled at her boss's attempt to put his foot down. There was something else that was bothering her, though. 'Guv, do you think that Maria knows about her father? According to Theresa she hasn't seen him in years. We might not get the best response if we barge into her place of work, talking about her dear old estranged dad.'

'Don't see we have much of a choice. You'll just have to play it by ear. Hoi!' He shouted over to Theresa. 'Stop lazing around. We've got things to do.'

She pulled a face and walked over to them. 'Top-level security meeting over?'

'Yes, and we decided that Mona is going to handle the next bit solo.'

Theresa stared at him. 'Over my dead body!'

101

Paterson sighed. 'Come on. We can walk and argue at the same time.'

Pillars Lane was a narrow street, with buildings four storeys high on either side of it. When Mona looked up she had the uneasy feeling that the buildings were leaning inward, as if their upper floors had edged slowly closer in the centuries since they were built, and would one day come to rest against each other. Optical illusion or not, this meant that daylight was in short supply at ground level. The buildings were old redstone, crumbling in patches, and looked like they'd been there since Dickens was a lad. Mr Dickens would probably have noticed a few other changes though: where once these blocks would have thronged with families who called them home, today they housed a range of different offices, perched on top of coffee shops interspersed with the occasional barber.

There was a lack of helpful numbering, so Mona walked slowly, checking the doorplates as she went. She hoped Paterson was going to be OK. Theresa had argued her case for coming with her for the ten minutes it had taken them to walk to Pillars Lane without stopping to draw breath. Paterson had borne this manfully, responding only with the word 'no' at regular intervals. However, outside Katalina's Coffee Stop Theresa had made one too many insinuations that Paterson was incompetent, in over his head, and didn't know what he was doing, and he had responded with a suggestion that Professor Bircham-Fowler had probably run off because he was fed up with her nagging. When Mona had left them to it, Theresa was using her bag to assault a public official going about his business, to the general entertainment of the Coffee Stop's patrons.

Mona located number 89, and pressed the buzzer for Hearthless Hearts UK. The logo against their name showed a fireplace with a tiny heart burning in it, which made her smile.

'Hello?' The intercom sprang into life.

'I'm here to see Maria Bircham-Fowler.'

'Who?'

A van drove past her, and she leaned in closer to make herself heard. 'Maria?'

'There's no one works here with that name.'

'It's about the annual sleepout?'

There was a pause. 'You'd better come up. Fourth floor.'

The door buzzed, and she entered before the girl could change her mind. Inside the building was even darker than the street outside, and it took a second or two for her eyes to adjust. She wandered up and down the narrow passageway on the ground floor, then reluctantly accepted there wasn't a lift and set off up the stairs. As she approached the fourth floor, a door opened slightly and a hand emerged.

'Can I see your Green Card, please?'

Mona held it out, and the hand took it. Through the crack, Mona could see a young woman with long dark hair framing a serious face. She frowned at the card, but eventually opened the door wider, and handed Mona her Green Card back. 'You're interested in the sleepout? It's not for a couple of months but we're always keen to meet people who want to participate or sponsor it.'

Mona nodded enthusiastically. 'It's a great event. But really I was interested in catching up with Maria.' She

103

pulled out the photocopied picture. 'This lady?'

The girl stared blankly at the picture for a moment, then nodded when recognition hit her. 'I do remember her. She was working here when I started, but she moved on a couple of weeks later. Didn't you realise she's not here anymore?'

'No, I haven't seen her for years, and she's still listed as the sleepout contact on your website.'

'Is she?' The girl's face grew even more serious. 'We lost our IT guy a couple of months back.'

'Oh, I'm sorry.' Mona wasn't sure what this meant. Lost to the Virus, or lost to a better paid job? Either seemed entirely possible. 'I've not seen Maria for years. When I knew her she was Maria Bircham-Fowler, but she might have got married since then...'

She tailed off, hopeful that the girl would jump in with a name. She didn't.

'She's still Bircham-Fowler then?'

The woman looked blank. 'That doesn't ring any bells, but like I said our paths only crossed for a few weeks. Sorry.'

'Do you know where she works now?'

'Some other charity, I think.' She was starting to look suspicious. 'Why are you looking for her?'

'Oh, we were at uni together.' Mona tried for an airily casual tone of voice that she wasn't quite sure she pulled off. 'I saw her picture in the paper and made up my mind I'd look her up next time I was in London. Of course, I didn't realise she'd have moved on by then. Anyway, thanks for your help.'

'Do you want to leave a card or anything? I can ask her to contact you if she ever pops back in.'

Mona considered this for a second, and decided that it

wasn't worth it. 'No, it's OK, thanks.' She backed out of the office with the girl still staring doubtfully at her, and trotted back down the stairs.

The café was surprisingly busy; Mona wondered where the people had come from. Afternoon meant that office workers should be in offices, and they were a bit off the beaten track for tourists. It was also so hot that anyone with any sense would be sitting outside in the shade, sipping something cool. But maybe they served the best scones this side of the river. For all she knew they were in the gastronomic heart of the City, Foodie Central. A waitress approached her, and without waiting to be asked Mona pulled her Green Card out of the bag. The waitress glanced at it and looked round the room. 'I'm not sure we've any tables at the moment...'

'It's OK, I'm meeting some people here.' After a second reviewing the room, she spotted Paterson and Theresa tucked away in a corner. From the body language it looked as if the argument that had been raging when she left them had been replaced by mutual sulking. 'They're over there.'

Theresa looked up eagerly as she approached. 'Did you find out anything?'

Paterson tutted. 'Remember that whole "this is my investigation" discussion? Mona answers to me, not you.'

Mona smiled and slowly pulled out a chair.

'So,' said Paterson impatiently, 'did you find out anything?'

'Not a great deal, I'm afraid. The woman I spoke to said Maria's not worked there for a while now, despite what their website says. And she either didn't know where Maria is now, or wouldn't tell me. She did say that she was working for another charity...'

'OK, we can follow that up.'

'I can look online, Guv, but it could take a while. All we've got for sure is a first name, and a vague lead that she works for a charity, of which there must be hundreds in London. And that's assuming that the charity that she's working for actually lists its staff on its website ...'

'I get the picture.' He put a hand up to stop her. 'We're not going to get this done and dusted today, so I better check in with Stuttle to see if he wants us to go home.'

'Home?' Theresa looked outraged. 'You can't just pack up and ship out. One of Scotland's most valuable assets in the war against the Virus is out there on his own. He could be in trouble.'

'I know. You don't have to convince me.' Paterson looked pained. 'And the professor being in trouble is exactly what I'm worried about. We've tried to find him discreetly but the time may have come to contact the Met about this. The longer he wanders around the streets of London on his own the more chance there is of something happening to him.'

'But then ...' Theresa looked suddenly vulnerable.

'What?'

'This episode could end Sandy's career, particularly if we don't get him to his Health Check.'

'I know. I'm sorry.' Paterson pulled out his mobile. 'But it's really not my decision to make. I'll see what my boss says. I'm going out to phone him – Mona, get yourself a drink if you want one.'

Theresa played absentmindedly with the salt cellar, frowning.

'If we go home, you should come too,' said Mona. 'It's dangerous for you to be wandering around on your own.'

'Go home?' Theresa pursed her lips. 'And do what – prepare for retirement?'

'No.' Mona wondered exactly what age Theresa was. She'd guess around sixty, but she'd be hard pressed to say which side. 'You'd still have a job with the university, I'm sure, whatever happens with the professor.'

Theresa shook her head. 'No, if Sandy's career is over, so is mine. I couldn't work for anyone else, not after all these years. And with my reputation, I'm not sure any of the younger academics would rush to snap me up as their PA.'

'I'm sure your reputation isn't bad...'

'You don't get the nickname "Maggie Thatcher" because you are overly approachable and highly loved.'

'Well, you do look a tiny bit like her. And your style of dress...'

'Are you saying I play up to it?' She glared at Mona, then laughed. 'Of course I do! I'll use anything that will persuade the bright young chauvinists that I work with to give me a little respect. Which is all fine and well until I need one of them to employ me.'

Mona tried, and failed, to think of anything comforting to say, and they sat in silence until Paterson reappeared.

'What did Stuttle say, Guv?'

'Well, after five minutes of impugning my detecting abilities, he said to give it another day. He remains very keen for your man to make his Health Check.' He poked Theresa's shoulder.

'He is not my man, Mr Paterson, as you are well aware. And let's stop wasting time.' She stood up. 'Let's get Sandy found.'

'Of course.' Paterson nodded. 'Right after we find us a hotel in Central London that meets the very stringent budget limit set by the HET office. We may need a time machine.'

107

6

Bernard stood with his foot on the bottom step of the stairs up to his office. He was having a great deal of difficulty in getting his other foot to move. Try as he might he couldn't work out a way to frame the day's events that wouldn't result in a torrent of abuse from his temporary boss. Whichever way you looked at it, taking the wrong Defaulter to a Health Check smacked of incompetency. He could argue the mitigating facts that they had a very poor quality photograph to work from, and a woman claiming to be the person they were looking for. He guessed neither of these things would cut much ice.

Carole had gone straight home from A&E, leaving him to single-handedly bear the brunt of any yelling that was going to take place. Not that anyone would have yelled at Carole. The state that her face was in meant that she would get nothing but sympathy. The blame was his, and his alone. He looked at the stone steps ahead of him, and decided that nothing, but nothing, was going to get him mounting them.

'And I just said to him, "Kev, if you ever see her again, that's like you and me finished, right?"'

Marguerite's distinctive voice carried through from reception, and suddenly Bernard found himself half a flight up and climbing. The only thing worse than explaining the situation to Maitland would be explaining it to Marguerite, who would want all the gory details and might even cry as an expression of her empathy. He ran the last few steps.

'Maitland?'

'What?' The voice came from inside Paterson's cave. Bernard did his best to assess the tone, and decided it was resting somewhere between irritation and fury. He decided that he better brave his wrath and walked into the office.

Maitland was surrounded by even more piles of paper than he had been before they left. The paper-work currently covered not only the desk, but most of the floor as well. Perhaps Maitland had some kind of organisational system that wasn't immediately apparent to anyone else, but to Bernard's eye it looked like chaos.

'The Parliamentary Committee papers,' said Maitland, by way of explanation. 'Didn't realise there would be quite so much to get through. How did you get on with the Defaulter?'

'We found her and took her in for a Health Check ...'

'Great. Good work. Make sure you write it up fully.' Maitland returned to leafing through the documents in front of him. After a few seconds he realised that Bernard hadn't actually left and looked up again.

'Except that it wasn't actually Alessandra Barr.'

Maitland stared at him. 'You took the wrong person for a Health Check? How is that even possible?'

'Remember yesterday we went to Alessandra Barr's Green Card address in Morningside, and she wasn't there, but there was a man there called Stephen McNiven? Well, we went to Stephen McNiven's house and—'

'Can you just cut straight to the part where you cocked up without the half-hour preamble?'

'I'm getting there! This woman answered the door and said she was Alessandra Barr and she had Alessandra's Green Card, so we, ehm, believed her.'

'But the photo?'

'The photo on the Green Card is terrible. It could be almost anyone.'

'And you didn't think it was a bit convenient, her answering the door and agreeing to come for a Health Check?'

'No, why would I? There was obviously a connection between McNiven and our Defaulter, and she had the Green Card. Honestly, if the HET can't provide us with good quality photographs ...'

'OK, OK, I take your point. I assume this fake Barr woman is now under arrest for impersonating a Health Defaulter?'

'Actually, no.' He paused, while he tried to figure out the most concise way to describe the second disaster of the day. 'There was a bit of an altercation at the Health Check clinic, and unfortunately she kicked Carole in the face and ran off.'

'Kicked Carole ...' Maitland looked horrified. 'Is she OK?'

'She's black and blue from here to here.' He pointed to the top and bottom of his face. 'I took her to Casualty and they said her jaw wasn't broken, just badly bruised. The doctor suggested that she went home immediately for a couple of days' rest. She was pretty shaken up, as you can imagine.'

'What am I ...? I mean, what should we ...? Ugh.' Maitland plonked his elbows on top of two of the piles of paper and rested his head in his hands. 'I'm not sure how we're supposed to respond to this.' He looked up at Bernard. 'Go on, then. You've memorised the entire procedures manual – what do we need to do?'

'I haven't memorised the whole manual, I only memorised the bit about disciplinary procedure in case Mr Paterson decided to throw the book at me one day. But, for what it's worth, I think all today's activities are now the problem of Police Scotland ...'

'We should call them ...'

'I spoke to them already when we were at A&E. They've had a statement from Carole and me, and they were going to talk to the Health Check clinic staff. We've given them the address that we found her at, and they're going to follow that up. So I think we're OK.'

'OK?' Maitland looked incredulous. 'We're now down to a team of two people and you call that OK?'

'That wasn't what I meant.'

Bernard waited for Maitland to start shouting, but he seemed preoccupied. 'Well, you'd better come with me to this Parliamentary thing tomorrow. You obviously can't be trusted on your own.'

'But ...' A million worries were competing for space in Bernard's brain.

'What?'

'I'm concerned about Alessandra Barr, and by that I meant the *real* Alessandra Barr. She's missing, but somebody else has her Green Card. How much can you do without a Green Card? I mean, you can't buy food, you can't get on a bus, you can't access any kind of services. And yet we still haven't heard of her being picked up by the police or anyone.'

'You think she's dead?'

'It's possible. Equally, if she is working as a prostitute, she could probably survive for a while without linking into the formal economy. But leaving without her Green Card suggests she had a hurried exit, and I didn't much like that McNiven character. I'd really like to be out there looking for her.'

Maitland sighed. 'We get this Committee thing out of the way, then we'll both concentrate on finding her.'

'I've never been to a Parliamentary Virus Committee before.'

'Neither have I.' He looked slightly doubtfully at the papers spread in front of him. 'Bernard?'

He looked up at him, and for a moment Bernard thought he was going to ask for help. 'What?'

The moment passed. Maitland shook himself. 'Nothing. Go home.'

7

Tap, tap, tap.

She stared at the door, trying to work out if someone was knocking, or if it was just another of the hotel room's quirks. In the two hours she'd been searching the Internet, she'd become familiar with the clank-clank of the plumbing system, the excessively loud creaking of floorboards in the room above her, and the general reverberation caused by anyone in the hotel closing their door. It was just as well she was going to be working through the night, because she didn't fancy her chances of sweet dreams.

Paterson hadn't been joking when he'd stressed the 'budget' in 'budget hotel'. As time was of the essence, he'd been keen not to move too far from the city centre. Cross-referencing price, location and the availability of three rooms had left them with just one choice: the Hotel Exceptionnel. The hotel was located in an old mansion block; she suspected every room in the original house had been subdivided several times to create accommodation that housed a double bed with a sliver of space around it. The level of customer service they'd encountered when checking in suggested that it wouldn't be worth complaining. In fact, the level of English spoken at the reception desk made it unlikely any complaints would be understood, far less acted upon.

Tap, tap, tap.

'Mona?'

She shut down the lid of the laptop, and opened the door. 'Guv? What's up?'

'Nothing's up.' There was a certain hunch to Paterson's shoulders that contradicted this. 'I just wanted to tell you I've booked a table for us in half an hour.'

'A table? I was just going to get some room service and carry on with my Internet searching.'

'How's it going?'

'Not so great.' She opened up the laptop again. 'I tried lots of Google search combinations. You know – "Maria" plus "charity" plus "homeless", etc., but didn't turn up anything. So now I'm going through the pages of individual organisations registered with the Charity Commission as having a London base, and looking at their staff teams. But it's going to take a while ...' She waited for Paterson to nod, and tell her to get on with it.

'Yeah, but you need to eat, and a break would do you good.'

She was confused by the sudden interest in her well-being. The Guv wasn't usually supportive of the idea of meal breaks, despite Bernard's many attempts to outline their Health and Safety benefits. And given his current frame of mind toward her his concern was all the more baffling. 'But ...'

'Mona, you're coming with me and so is Theresa.' His hunched shoulders righted themselves into his usual assertive posture. 'We're meeting up with my son again and I'm not sitting in a restaurant for an hour with him either slagging me off or saying nothing.'

She resisted the temptation to point out how annoying it was when someone was sulking and giving you the cold shoulder, and opted for some nosiness instead. 'Why's he so upset with you, Guv?'

'You know, the divorce and everything.'

'I thought Greg was grown up by the time you split up from his mum?'

'Yeah, but he took it hard, and …' Paterson played with the 'Do Not Disturb' sign hanging on the door handle, 'there was a bit of an overlap between the marriage officially ending and me meeting Mrs Paterson Two.' He stared at her as if some kind of response was required.

'Oh.'

'I mean it was over in all but name of course …'

'Of course.' Seeing as Paterson had only just started speaking to her again, she wasn't going to blow it by some sarcastic remark along the lines of, *'And your wife just didn't understand you, did she?'* Unlike the new, and considerably younger, Mrs P. She wondered how much older than Greg his stepmother was. Perhaps it would come up over dinner.

'But he's only heard his mother's side, and there are two sides to every marriage.'

'Of course.' Mona stifled a smile. Two months with barely a word in her direction from Paterson, and suddenly she couldn't shut him up. In fact, her boss was so keen for company that he appeared to have invited Theresa to dinner as well, and she could hardly be described as a fan of his. Mind you, if Greg was anywhere near as good as his father at sulking, Paterson was right to look for all the backup he could muster.

'Foyer in twenty-five, Guv?'

'Where is she?' Paterson looked at his watch, irritated at Theresa's non-arrival.

115

Mona looked round the tiny reception area in case they had missed her. The two chairs and the pot plant didn't appear to be hiding anyone. 'Maybe she fell asleep ... oh, look, here she is now.'

Theresa's heels came clattering down the stairwell. She appeared to have somehow managed to produce an entirely new outfit from the small bag she'd been carrying all day, and also refreshed her make-up. 'Quite some establishment you've booked us into here, Mr Paterson.'

Theresa's voice carried across the whole of the room. Mona glanced over at the reception desk, but the clerk didn't look up from the magazine he was reading.

'The HET's budget doesn't go far in Central London,' muttered Paterson. 'Consider yourself lucky we found anywhere round here that had three rooms available at such short notice.'

'I will "consider myself lucky",' Theresa's voice grew even louder, 'if I get out of this place without acquiring fleas.'

The front desk clerk looked up this time, and slowly lowered his copy of *Cycling Weekly*.

'Shall we go?' asked Mona, hoping that he didn't do something disgusting in Theresa's room while they were out. She had the overwhelming desire to scratch her neck, which she sincerely prayed was down to the power of suggestion, rather than their beds actually containing bugs. She shoved her hands in her jeans and tried to concentrate on her surroundings.

It was still warm, the air dry and baking in a way that it hardly ever was back in Scotland. Mona had forgotten what London felt like, the airless evenings with crowds of people standing outside pubs, glasses in hand. In spite of everything, she found herself quite enjoying the atmosphere. She was definitely going to book a long weekend here when she got home. See the sights. Take in a West End show.

'What kind of food does this restaurant serve, Mr Paterson?' enquired Theresa.

'My son recommended it. It's called The Bamboo Garden, so I'm going to take a guess and say it's not jellied eels.'

She nodded, evidently satisfied with this. 'I do enjoy a nice Chinese meal. Is your son joining us?'

'Yep – and there he is.'

Greg waved from the doorway of the restaurant, but didn't smile. Mona hoped that Theresa was in a really, really talkative mood, because there was no way that she would be keeping the conversation going single-handed. She surreptitiously pulled out her phone to check the time. If she had her way, she'd be out of there in forty minutes, and back surfing the virtual presence of the charities of London.

'Mona.' Greg nodded to her, and stuck a hand out in Theresa's direction. 'You must be Mrs Kilsyth. Lovely to meet you.'

He ushered them through the door, and stepped in after them, leaving Paterson to follow his back into the restaurant.

'Hello to you too, son.'

A Chinese woman in a green button-necked top came over to greet them. 'Welcome to The Bamboo Garden.' The look was Far East but the accent suggested that she'd been born within spitting distance of their current location. 'Table for four?'

They ordered quickly, accepting all the suggestions

made by their waitress. Mona sensed she wasn't the only one who would be glad to have the meal over and done with. The only thing that would persuade her to linger here was the air conditioning. She was still adjusting to the southern temperature. Despite the cooling air from above, she still had to resist the temptation to use one of the menus as a fan.

Greg broke the silence. 'So, Mona, how is the search going?'

'Not so good, I'm afraid. Early days though, and I'm sure we'll have more luck tomorrow, wouldn't you say, Guv?'

'It's gone *terribly* so far.' Theresa paused while their round of drinks arrived, and took a large swig from her glass of chilled white before continuing. 'Terribly. Your father's organisation has put no resources into this search at all.'

Paterson glared at her, over the top of a pint of Diet Coke with ice. 'Apart from dedicating two of the HET's finest to it, you mean.'

Theresa's face reflected her doubts on that matter, and she reached for her wine glass again.

'But I admit our search is going more slowly than I'd like. I was hoping you could help me do some asking around with the rough sleepers on the Embankment.'

'Oh, we're going back?' asked Theresa.

'We,' Paterson pointed from himself to Greg and back, 'are going to the Embankment. Mona is going to keep scouring the Internet for signs of the missing daughter's current employment, and you,' he said, using a digit to good effect in Theresa's direction, 'are going to get your beauty sleep.'

She looked offended. 'I require no such thing. My time

would be much better spent doing something useful to actually find Sandy.'

The arrival of the Chinese Banquet for Four interrupted the argument. Paterson took the opportunity to turn back to Greg. 'So, are you able to help me search? You know the lie of the land far better than I do.'

He shrugged. 'Yeah. I can spare a couple of hours.'

The silence lengthened. Mona looked at her phone again. 20.05. Could she eat up and be out by quarter past?

'So,' Paterson turned to Greg again, 'how are things with you?'

'Fine.' Greg's eyes didn't move from his plate.

'And how's your mother?'

Greg stopped eating, and did a world-class impression of finely controlled rage. It was like watching the Guv listen to Bernard lecture him on some aspect of political correctness, say, gender politics or the socio-demographic division of health inequalities. 'I really don't want to talk about Mum with you.'

Paterson tutted. 'I'm only asking after her health.'

'Her health stopped being your concern once you walked out on her.'

'These spring rolls really are delicious, Mona, aren't they?' Theresa's tone was sprightly, with a slight undercurrent of desperation.

'Yeah, they're great.' She started chewing even faster.

'I visited China once, you know ...' Theresa began a monologue about a university trip to Beijing, stopping only to drink her wine. It was a very long story, for which Mona was eternally grateful, and she told it well. Paterson and Greg wolfed down their remaining food in aggressive silence and by the time Theresa had concluded her story, everyone had cleaned their plates.

119

'I'll get this.' Paterson snatched the bill.

'Let me at least pay half,' said Greg.

'Expenses,' muttered Paterson, slapping a wad of notes on the table. 'Come on then. Let's get the professor found.'

Theresa and Mona watched them walk off in the direction of the Tube station, two very similar silhouettes, walking three feet apart and not speaking to each other.

'Well, that was a fun experience.'

Theresa laughed. 'If I'd wanted an evening of awkward silences I'd have phoned my daughter-in-law.'

'You've got kids?'

'Yes, one son. You sound surprised? He's thirty-seven and has absolutely failed to settle down and give me grandchildren. Far too busy jetting off on holiday every five minutes. So, how do we get back to the hotel from here? I have to admit I wasn't really paying attention, I was just following Mr Paterson.'

'Me too. But we haven't come far.' Mona looked round to orientate herself. She remembered crossing the road to get to the restaurant, but did they turn up the first street or the second to get back? As she stared across the road something caught her eye. A man in sunglasses was leaning against the wall of a café, apparently engrossed in his phone. She stared at him. Something was wrong with his appearance, and it took her a second or two to work out what it was.

'Has the temperature dropped, Theresa?'

'Not so that I've noticed. I'm absolutely melting.'

The man across the street was wearing jeans and a bomber jacket, challenging clothing on a warm summer's evening when everyone else was walking around in shorts and t-shirts. She took Theresa's arm. 'Let's get back.'

She glanced over her shoulder as they left. The man didn't look up or move, but she had the sensation that he knew they were on the move. Maybe she was being paranoid. Tourists came from countries far hotter than the UK, and dressed accordingly. Maybe she was looking for problems that just weren't there. Or maybe ...

'...am I boring you, Mona?'

She realised that Theresa had been talking to her. 'No, I'm sorry, it's just I thought I saw ... No, it's nothing.' She was relieved to see the neon sign for the Exceptionnel appear. 'Look, here we are. See you downstairs at eight for breakfast?'

Theresa nodded. 'Good luck with your surfing.'

'And, Theresa?'

'Yes?'

'Lock your door tonight, OK?'

8

The bus was crowded, hot and heaving with commuters making the journey from city centre to suburb. Bernard was squeezed into a double seat on the upper deck, trapped against the window by a large besuited man with a great many belongings. His laptop bag was wedged into the side of Bernard's thigh, and despite his best attempts at discreet wriggling, he couldn't shift it.

He resigned himself to the pain, and began replaying the events of the day. Whichever way you looked at it, an attempted Health Check fraud and a colleague with a boot in the face wasn't what you'd call a good result. He wondered if Mona or Maitland would have done things differently. Was there some finely honed police intuition that would have alerted them that they'd got the wrong person? Some experience gained the hard way that made them better placed to spot when they were being lied to?

And Maitland was right, there was bound to be a vast amount of paperwork attached to this: incident reporting, witness statements, liaison with Police Scotland. To say nothing of someone having to explain all this to Mr Paterson when he got back ... Bernard realised with a start he was approaching the stop for his new flat.

'Excuse me.'

The man sharing his seat gathered up his bags to let him past, but by the time he'd squeezed out his stop was long gone. He alighted on an unfamiliar street, and set off in what he hoped was the direction of his new home. On a day like today, he'd give anything to be back at his old flat, with his wife. Well, almost anything. He'd give Carrie anything in the world apart from the one thing that she really wanted from him.

He turned the corner and was delighted to find himself back on a street that he knew, Park Road, which was named after the small public green space that ran the length of it. The other side of the street was taken up with shops, all of which were closed for the night. Assuming no further wrong turns he'd be at his new flat in five minutes. Would Megan be in the kitchen, whipping up something delightful for tea? Would she extend her hospitality again, and offer him some food? If so, he'd really have to repay the favour, and cook her something in return. Although his attempts at cooking tended to be functional at best. Maybe he should take her out for a meal; he'd noticed a couple of local restaurants that looked quite passable. Though that might be drifting into dangerous territory, because it might look suspiciously like a date.

Although ...

He shook himself and focused on the present. In case he did get the offer of a home-cooked meal as soon as he got in, he'd better get the evening's phone calls out of the way. He perched on the wall of the park, and leaned back against the metal railings. Who to phone first? Carole, to check if she was OK? Mona, to see how things were going in London? Carrie, to see ... well, for no very good reason at all.

He opted for Carole first. Her number was answered almost immediately by a man, which gave him a moment of anxiety. This was probably Carole's husband, who was, no doubt, furious about the day's events. Bernard couldn't begin to imagine how angry he would have been if anyone had hurt Carrie. Would Carole's husband consider him responsible for not protecting Carole? Because that would make two of them. He took a deep breath. 'Hi, this is Bernard from the HET.'

'Oh.' Rather than angry, he sounded disappointed. Bernard felt relief, as well as a slight confusion at the unexpected response.

'I expect you want to speak to Carole.'

'Yes, if she's ...'

He heard the sound of a conversation in the background, which seemed to consist of Carole being urged to keep the call short.

'Hi, Bernard.' Her voice was thick and unfamiliar, as if she was talking through a mouthful of tar.

'How are you?'

'Sore.' She sighed. 'An 'orried.'

'Worried?'

''ichael didn't go to 'hool today, an' he's 'ot answerin' his 'one.'

Bernard mulled this over. A likely translation was 'Michael didn't go to school today, and he's not answering his phone.' It explained the response he'd had when he rung. 'Oh, that's not good.' Bernard's mind went back to their earlier conversation. 'Probably just him trying to assert his independence?'

'Prob'ly, but we're still 'orried.'

'Are you going to contact the police?'

There was a pause. 'Maybe.'

He understood Carole's dilemma. Better to know what Michael had been doing with his day before drawing the attention of the law to it. 'OK, I better let you go. Call me if I can do anything.'

He scrolled through his address book until he found Mona's number. A wave of doubt hit him as he looked at the screen. She hadn't felt it necessary to phone him, and if they did speak she might ask how the search for Alessandra Barr was going. He wasn't sure he was ready for that particular conversation, especially if Mr Paterson was listening in to the call. He quickly returned to the address book and pressed the number of his former home. The phone rang and rang, until the answering machine kicked in. Bernard felt a sudden sense of loss. There was no reason why Carrie should be sitting at home, waiting for the phone to ring. He tried her mobile, and counted the rings from one to twelve until he got the voicemail.

'It's Bernard. Just wanted to see, you know, how you were. Anyway . . . speak to you soon. Bye.'

Why hadn't she picked up? A range of possibilities crowded into Bernard's head. She could be in the bath. Carrie liked a long, hot soak, and she probably wouldn't leap out of the suds just to answer the phone. She might even have taken the precaution of turning her phone to silent, to make sure she wasn't disturbed. That would be it. Not any kind of illness, or accident, or her not wanting to speak to him ever again. It would just be a bath thing. He stared at the phone for a few seconds, then redialled the number, and counted the rings again.

'Maybe just let me know if you are OK once you get this? Just a quick call. I know you wanted some space, but now I'm worried . . . Anyway, call me. Thanks.'

If she wasn't pissed off with him already, she would be now. He checked the time. He should head back to his digs, and see what Megan was doing. But the streets were

125

quiet and he was enjoying the solitude. The absence of Carrie had unsettled him, and, lovely as his new flatmate was, he wasn't sure he was up to making small talk. He tipped his head back against the railings, and enjoyed the evening sun on his face for a moment, before getting to his feet. He couldn't sit there forever. And maybe Megan would have opened another bottle of wine, although he didn't really approve of drinking two nights running.

He walked slowly, hearing the echo of his footsteps on the deserted street. After a few steps he realised he could hear two sets of footsteps. He speeded up. The other set of steps, though irregular, kept pace with him. He stopped and turned, in time to see a figure disappear into the park. Bernard stared after him, but didn't get a good enough view to make an impression. Jeans, brown leather jacket perhaps? Either way, the person didn't seem intent on doing him harm. Probably wasn't interested in him at all. He shook his head. He was getting paranoid.

He arrived at the new flat and put his key into the lock of the front door.

'Bernard, is that you?' His new flatmate's voice echoed through the flat.

He stuck his head into the kitchen. There was a pot bubbling away on the stove, curry if the smell was to be believed, but no sign of a cook.

'I'm in the living room.'

He pushed open the door. Megan was sitting on the sofa, a glass of wine in her hand. In the two weeks Bernard had lived there he'd only ever seen her in jeans, or the white uniform that she wore to work. Today she had on a green dress, with a pattern of a bird repeated over it. It ended at the knee and he couldn't help but notice a pair of shapely legs tucked underneath her.

Megan picked up the remote control. Her long bright pink fingernails made a clicking sound as she turned the TV off. 'I've made enough curry for two, if you fancy some.'

'That sounds great. And it smells great as well.'

'There's a bottle of Rioja on the go, as well, if you'd like a glass.'

His phone buzzed. 'Sorry, I just need to ...'

Megan nodded, and started pouring him a large glass.

He was delighted to see a text message from Carrie, proving she was alive and still speaking to him. He pressed the screen to open it.

Stop calling me. WE NEED TO MOVE ON.

Bernard realised that despite the health impact of drinking continuously without a rest day, he really, really would like a large amount of wine. And if it meant he went over the recommended weekly units for a man, he really didn't care. He dropped his rucksack on the floor and sat down, rather heavily, on the sofa next to Megan.

She handed him a glass. 'Sláinte!'

WEDNESDAY

DROWSINESS

I

Mona woke with a start as some part of the hotel's plumbing bang, bang, banged its way into life. She checked her watch and groaned. Her brain held a vague memory of lying back on the bed, somewhere around 2am, aiming to close her eyes for a minute while her body summoned the energy to get changed and go to bed. Now, six hours later, she was waking up still in her clothes from the day before.

Stretching, she wandered over to the mirror to see exactly what the damage was. Crumpled trousers. Creased top, with a couple of sweat stains under each armpit for good measure. Stick a couple of twigs in her hair, and she'd have the whole through-a-hedge-backwards chic thing sewn up.

She wished she'd had the nerve to pack a full change of clothes, but she'd worried about incurring Paterson's wrath if she brought a decent-sized bag. She showered, brushed her teeth, and sprayed half a can of Impulse all over. She put a new top on, and cursed her stupidity when she couldn't find her hairbrush. Smoothing her hair with her hands, she returned to the mirror. It wasn't great, but it was going to have to do until she could buy a comb.

Arriving downstairs, she found there was a limited

range of options on the laminated breakfast menu that was pinned to the wall of the dining room. Anything more complicated than a bowl of cornflakes seemed to incur an additional cost, and she wasn't sure if Paterson's limited budget would spring for bacon and eggs. She turned to see an unsmiling woman with a notepad standing behind her.

'Full English, please.' Paterson would just have to lump it. She couldn't walk the streets of the capital without a half-decent breakfast inside her. It was bad enough that she had to spend the day looking like a tramp, without spending it going hungry as well.

'Please take a seat.' The woman gave a wave in the general direction of the tables, and retreated to the kitchen.

'Over here,' Paterson shouted to her from a seat by the window. She was glad to see that he looked as crumpled as she was. 'What did you order?'

'The works.'

'Good choice.' Paterson pointed at his empty plate.

'Can we afford two London breakfasts?'

'Cameron Bloody Stuttle can reach into his personal slush fund and pay for them.'

She smiled, and yawned again.

'Were you up all night on the Internet?'

'Until the early hours.'

'Any joy?' asked Paterson.

Before she could answer, she heard the familiar sound of heels clicking in her direction. She turned to see Theresa bearing down on their table. In contrast to their dishevelment, Theresa looked as fresh as a daisy. Her hair was maintaining its Mrs Thatcher wave, her skirt was completely uncreased, and if Mona wasn't mistaken, she had a fresh blouse on. Her handbag must have Tardis-like properties.

'How is everyone?' Without giving them time to answer, she moved on to her real area of concern. 'Any word of Sandy?'

'Sorry.' The Guv shook his head. 'I was out for a good few hours with Greg last night, seeing if anyone on the Embankment had spotted him. No luck, I'm afraid. I think he might have moved on.'

Theresa's face fell. 'Well, that's really very disappointing.'

'I may have a lead.' At around 1.45 that morning, just as her eyes were beginning to feel like sandpaper every time she blinked, she'd come across the website of the Youth Today charity. Hidden within its fundraising pages she'd found an entreaty to 'contact Maria' if you wanted to get involved in raising money, next to a picture of what was unmistakeably the woman they were looking for. 'I think I've found where Professor Bircham-Fowler's daughter is working.'

'What's her surname?'

'Didn't get a surname, but there's a picture of a Maria and I'm pretty sure it's her. And I'm not too worried about the lack of name because either she'll be at work or we can get it from her colleagues and ... oh.' Mona stopped as a large plate with a greasy selection of sausages and bacon was shoved in front of her. 'Ehm, thanks,' she said, to the retreating back of the waitress.

Paterson's phone started to vibrate, bouncing around the table top.

'Don't recognise the number,' he said, staring at the screen. 'Hello? Yeah, Elijah. Hi.'

Mona and Theresa stared at each other as they tried

to work out if Elijah was bringing good news or bad.

'Is he hurt?'

Theresa let out a small sound, and gripped Mona's arm. Mona could feel Theresa's fingernails digging deeper into her skin, while Paterson uh-ed and yup-ed his way through the rest of the conversation.

'OK, Elijah, many thanks for letting us know.'

He put his phone down on the table.

'What ...?' began Theresa.

'Don't panic,' he said, holding a hand up in her direction, 'but Elijah has some news. He's been asking around for us, and one of his clients thinks he saw the professor in an altercation with some, ehm, "gentlemen" late last night, somewhere near King's Cross station.'

Theresa's hands shot to her lips. 'Oh, poor, poor Sandy. Was he hurt?'

'Don't think so. According to Elijah's source, the professor was asking if anyone had seen a particular woman – Maria, obviously – and was paying for information. He got his wallet out to give cash to a couple of King's Cross charmers, and the inevitable happened.'

'They stole his wallet?'

'Yup. Elijah's contact didn't think he was hurt, but he is now out there without any money.'

'Time to call it in, do you think, Guv?' Mona put down her knife and fork, her appetite suddenly gone.

'What do you mean "call it in"?' Theresa frowned. 'Do you mean give up?'

'No, I'm not thinking about giving up,' said Paterson. 'But I do think that we need to talk to my boss about involving the Met.'

'And have it leaked all over the news by the end of the day?' The waitress who had been heading toward their table heard Theresa's tone, and made a quick retreat. 'We might as well just kiss Sandy's reputation goodbye right now.'

'See sense, Theresa. Up until now we haven't had any information that he's in danger, but now we're pretty sure he's been involved in an altercation, probably been mugged. He's an absent-minded professor, not a streetwise teenager, and now he's wandering the streets of London without any money.'

'No, he's not.'

They both looked at Theresa in surprise. 'Sandy is not as much of an innocent abroad as you two seem to think.'

'Really?'

Theresa fixed a stern eye on Paterson. 'Sandy was a visiting lecturer in New York in the eighties, back at the height of its crime wave. I'm sure you can remember the stories about what it was like. In those days everyone had a tale about the time that they were mugged, or had a knife pulled on them. Sandy himself had several hair-raising encounters in the subway. But it taught him a thing or two about life, and since then he's always carried a mugger's purse, full of cash but nothing else. He'll still have his cards on him.'

Paterson looked sceptical. 'Maybe, if they didn't give him a good kicking and steal those too.'

'And Sandy always has an emergency £20 note hidden where no muggers would ever look.'

The Guv pulled a face. 'I think that counts as too much information.'

She tutted. 'I was referring, Mr Paterson, to his sock.' She stood up. 'Come on, we need to find him.'

Paterson didn't move.

'We could have a quick scout round King's Cross before we phone, Guv?'

He considered this. 'OK, we'll give it until lunch-time before I phone Stuttle. I'll check in with Greg for any incidents at King's Cross. You two follow up the daughter angle.'

2

Maitland was late.

Bernard had been standing next to the pond outside the Scottish Parliament building – their agreed meeting place – for the best part of twenty minutes. As usual, he'd arrived early, and had spent the first ten minutes admiring the post-modern curves of the landscape. The Parliament building had been controversial when it was built, and even now, the best part of twenty years later, it still provoked a wide range of emotions from the inhabitants of Edinburgh.

He, however, was a huge fan of modern architecture, and the appearance of the building brought him nothing but pleasure. He liked the way the structure curved like an upturned boat, particularly on a cloudless day like today, when the outline was silhouetted against a brilliant blue sky. He liked the contrast of the cold grey walls with the brown lattice woodwork. He liked the uplifting messages carved into the building's walls. And that was only his feelings about the *outside* of the Parliament. When he considered the bright and airy interior of the building, he could really wax lyrical.

He checked his phone. *Five to*. Maitland was now officially twenty-five minutes late, despite living less than ten minutes' walk from the building. The sunshine that had been so pleasurable was now beginning to feel oppressive. He watched a group of backpackers laugh and flirt and pretend to push each other into the pond. With every passing minute he was getting increasingly anxious that he'd misunderstood the instructions that Maitland had given him yesterday. He was just about to dial Maitland's number, when his colleague's distinctive silhouette appeared at the side of the Scottish Parliament.

'Where have you been?'

Maitland looked paler than usual. Bernard wondered if Maitland had had a sleepless night; *he* certainly had. He'd spent the small hours alternating between worrying about the Committee, and fretting over the text message he'd received from his wife. When he'd finally fallen asleep, round about 3am, Bernard had then had some rather unsettling dreams about his new flatmate and her long and elegant legs. 'Moving on' obviously all began in the sub-conscious.

'I'm not late.'

'We said half past!'

'No, we didn't. Come on, let's get this over with.' He strode off in the direction of the Parliament's entrance, moving so fast that Bernard had to run to catch him up.

'Is that the Parliamentary Committee documents?' He pointed at the sheaf of papers that Maitland had tucked under his arm.

'Of course it is. What else would I be dragging around with me?'

Bernard tutted silently to himself. His filing would have involved a ring-binder, dividers and several different colours of highlighter pens.

'You are prepared for this, aren't you, Maitland?'

'Of course I am.' Despite the snippiness of his tone, Maitland didn't look entirely convincing.

'It's just that it's really important that we do a good job while Mr Paterson is away.'

'Thanks for the pep talk, Bernard, but I'm on it.' Maitland pushed open the door to the Scottish Parliament.

'It wasn't a pep talk. It was just a continuation of my concern that Mr Paterson left *you* in charge of an administrative task that you are completely unsuited to.'

'Well, save it for later.' Maitland waved at someone.

Bernard turned round to see Cameron Stuttle, who was walking briskly in their direction.

Maitland lowered his voice. 'This is united front time.'

Bernard sighed, and nodded. 'You're probably right.'

They emptied their pockets of keys and coins, took off their belts, and surrendered them all to the security screening machine. Bernard was relieved, as he was every time he visited, to make it through the electronic entry system without setting it off due to a missed 50p hidden deep within a pocket. Throughout the whole rigmarole, Maitland kept up a steady stream of small talk with Stuttle, discussing the weather, the state of Edinburgh's roads, and the inconvenience caused to Stuttle on a daily basis by the number of tourists on the streets outside his office. He then indulged in some gentle banter about football, involving the respective performance of Edinburgh's two main teams. Bernard didn't quite understand the discussion, but he was grudgingly impressed. He would be the first to admit that he wasn't adept at light conversation. Left to his own devices, they would have spent the time in silence, or discussing the influence of Henry Raeburn's picture of *The Skating Minister* on the angles of the trigger panels.

Stuttle motioned them over to a quiet area of the foyer.

'Are you chaps on top of things, in the boss's absence?' His grin seemed a little forced, and lacked its usual spontaneous cheer. 'Be better if this all went smoothly and nobody asked too many questions.'

Bernard wondered why Stuttle was being so circumspect. 'What kind of questions?'

Maitland elbowed him, discreetly but painfully. 'I'll do my best, sir.'

'Good man.' Stuttle gave Bernard an appraising look. He'd seen that look before from his ex-police colleagues, usually after he'd asked one too many questions. And in this particular case, one question appeared to be one too many. But he couldn't help himself. As far as he was concerned, it was always better to know what was going on, so that you could be prepared for it. And right now, what he really wanted to know was where were Mona and Mr Paterson, what were they up to, and why was Stuttle worrying about it?

'Come on then, chaps. Let's get our seats.'

Bernard looked around as they walked out of the foyer and up the wooden stairs to the main chamber. He'd only ever been in the public area of the Parliament before, and felt a small, irrepressible frisson of excitement as they moved into the heart of the building. The chamber itself was smaller than he'd imagined it would be, having seen it only on TV. When his son died, he'd watched hours of footage of the debates on the Virus, as if understanding what was going through politicians' minds might help him to come to terms with his loss. After a few days of watching, he'd grown to understand that nobody actually knew anything. Virus policy was educated guesswork, a series of decisions based loosely on research, and tempered by the level of restrictions on their liberty the electorate would tolerate. It might be a crisis, but everyone in the chamber still wanted to be re-elected.

Bernard followed Stuttle into a row of seats where the politicians usually sat, with Maitland's sheaf of papers digging into his neck as his colleague followed close behind. Two civil servants were scurrying about in front of the room, preparing seats for the arrival of the Committee members. They seemed to be taking a long time to perfect the seating arrangements, but from what Bernard had heard, the Committee Chair, Carlotta Carmichael, tended to expect perfection and nothing less. The public gallery was filling up with members of the press, and hidden in the dark of the rafters were the cameras that would record the entire proceedings for the Parliamentary Channel. Occasionally, edited highlights of the Committee made it onto the teatime news. All in all it wasn't a good place to make a mistake, and judging by the slight tremor in Maitland's hand, he knew it.

Stuttle leaned across to speak to Maitland. 'Before you say anything, you need to press the microphone button.'

Bernard remembered the time that Mr Paterson had accidentally broadcast his views about the Parliamentary Committee Chair to the entire chamber by leaning on the microphone button at exactly the wrong moment. He crossed his fingers that Maitland did something equally inept. He had every confidence that Maitland would manage to equally offend Carlotta; he managed to offend most members of the HET on a daily basis, and Ms Carmichael was renowned for her ability to see offence in statements where none was intended.

'Gotcha,' said Maitland, and gave Stuttle a slightly shaky thumbs-up.

141

A silence fell as the Parliamentary Committee filed in and took their places, Carlotta Carmichael sitting in the middle seat. Bernard watched her with interest. As a keen follower of Scottish politics he was well aware of her career. She'd been a junior minister, leading on a fairly minor enquiry into health inequalities, when the Virus had struck. She'd had either the foresight, or the good luck, to get herself elected onto the Infectious Diseases Short-Term Working Group back in the days when everyone assumed that the Virus would go the way of all the other airborne panics, and die an almost immediate death. But the Virus had rallied, and the Working Group gave way to a fully-fledged Parliamentary Committee. And due to Carlotta's skill at the dark arts of politics, she'd been elected as its first, and to date only, Chair.

Paterson hated Ms Carmichael with a passion, ostensibly because she was 'another of those politicians that makes a name for herself by slagging off hard-working front-line staff'. Word in the office was that his real dislike dated back to his Lothian and Borders police days, when he'd stopped *Mr* Carlotta Carmichael behind the wheel of a BMW doing 52 mph in a 40 mph zone, and attempted to give him a speeding ticket. It hadn't made it to court, a fact that neither Paterson nor the MSP for Upper Lithdale had ever forgotten.

Carlotta hammered on her desk, demanding silence, which she got almost immediately. 'Let's make a start, shall we? NHS Lothian, can you explain these appalling figures ...?'

Bernard's mind drifted as he listened to the beleaguered NHS rep try to defend whatever it was that was currently being regarded by the Committee as indefensible. Carlotta gesticulated as she tried to communicate how annoyed she was with the figures, NHS Lothian, the Virus, and everything else that was getting in the way of her single-handedly restoring order to the land. No one could accuse her of a lack of passion about her work. Bernard thought she was a very attractive woman, in a certain way. He'd never noticed that about her before, but then he had been noticing the way women looked a lot recently, ever since he'd finally accepted his marriage was in its death throes. And Carlotta was a good-looking woman, well-groomed and passionate, although she could do with smiling a bit more.

Like his new flatmate. She never stopped smiling. Last night they'd sat in front of the TV, eating curry and sharing a bottle of red. Megan had had him in stitches, commenting on the trashy programmes they had watched. He couldn't remember the last time he'd laughed like that. Not for ages, certainly not since the death of his son had done for his marriage, his happiness, and his faith in the future. But Megan, lovely long-legged Megan, had got him smiling again. He was so glad he…

'And where is the Health Enforcement Team? I believe John Paterson is the representative?' Bernard snapped back to the present, as Carlotta made a show of looking round the room. There was a degree of artifice in her movements that made Bernard wonder if she already knew that Paterson wasn't here. Had she rumbled whatever it was that his colleagues were up to? For the first time since Mona and Paterson had left, Bernard was glad that he wasn't in charge. He sat back, and prepared to enjoy Maitland arsing it all up.

'I'm here in place of Mr Paterson,' said Maitland, in a less than confident tone.

'And you are?'

'I'm Maitland Stevenson, a HET officer in the North Edinburgh team.'

Carlotta leafed through her paperwork. 'I'm not seeing any apologies for absence from John Paterson listed here.'

'I'm sorry. It was quite short notice.'

'Is he ill?'

Bernard could see Stuttle tense, and edge his finger toward the microphone button.

'Ehm no, he's not ill. He's just taken some annual leave.'

'Annual leave?' Carlotta could not have sounded more disgusted if Maitland had confessed that his boss had just nipped out to murder some puppies. 'Does he not realise the importance of this Parliamentary Committee?'

There was a pause. Maitland's erstwhile pastiness of face was being replaced by a deepening blush. 'He does think this Committee is very—'

Carlotta interrupted him. 'And are any other members of your team on "annual leave"?'

There was a longer pause. 'One other team member is on leave.'

'And is anyone else not at work?'

Again, Bernard had the feeling that Carlotta already knew the answer to that.

'One member of staff is off sick.'

'So, to get this straight, of the five members of your team, only one is currently out in the field?'

The chamber was treated to an even longer pause. 'Actually he's here with me.'

Carlotta clutched a hand to her bosom. 'Oh well, we can all rest safely in our beds knowing that the HET office is being managed so competently that there are

144

no actual HET officers working in the whole of North Edinburgh.'

Stuttle couldn't contain himself any longer and pressed the microphone button. 'We have contingency arrangements in place...'

'We'll get to SHEP in a minute. What I'd like to know, Mr Stevenson, is what prompted two of your colleagues to take annual leave, at limited notice, when it was obviously going to leave you short-staffed?'

'Well, ehm... uh.' Maitland gave up trying to respond and looked over at Stuttle, who kept staring straight ahead.

Carlotta fixed her stare on him for a moment or two longer. 'I think we have heard quite enough from the HET for one session. Let's move on.'

An aide sidled over to her.

'Actually, I'm being told we are out of time, so I'll bring this session to a close.'

Maitland scooped his paperwork up, dropping a few sheets as he did so, and made for the stairs.

'Maitland ...' Bernard hurried after him, eager not to miss the opportunity to rub salt in his wounds, followed by a bit of vinegar. He had a lot of payback for his colleague, and this was definitely time.

'Not a word, Bernard. Not a single word.' He moved off in the direction of the exit, and was swallowed up by the throng of people coming out of the Committee. Bernard allowed himself a moment's full-fat smugness, which was rudely interrupted by the appearance of Stuttle at his side.

'What was your colleague playing at?' he hissed. 'Has he never heard of the concept of discretion?'

Bernard was torn between the desire to give Maitland

145

a kicking, and the need to defend the honour of his team. 'In fairness, Mrs Carmichael did seem to already know about Mr Paterson's and Mona's absence. I don't think he told her anything she didn't already know.'

'No, but he drew a lot of other people's attention to it.' He thought for a moment. 'If she does know about his absence, was it one of your lot that told her?'

'No, I wouldn't have thought so.' He thought back to his suspicions from the previous evening. 'But maybe someone else is keeping an eye on us?'

Stuttle eyed him for a minute. 'You hear from Mrs Carmichael, you let me know. And tell your colleague he's an arse.'

'I will,' said Bernard. *With pleasure.*

3

The woman at the reception desk wore oversized red glasses, and a confused expression.

'I don't understand,' she said, leafing through a large folder which appeared to contain handwritten diaries for everyone in the organisation. Mona was glad to see the HET wasn't the only workplace failing to grasp the organisational opportunities presented by Microsoft Outlook. 'Why would Maria arrange to see you today when she's had this week booked as annual leave for months now?'

Mona's heart sank; if Maria was sunning herself in Lanzarote that would bring their one line of investigation to an abrupt end. 'She's off on holiday?'

'No, just getting some work done on her flat, I think.' She snapped the folder shut. 'I can see if anyone else can help you, but if it was about a grant application we might be struggling, because funding is pretty much Maria's baby, and the boss isn't in today either ...'

Mona manoeuvred herself further into the office. Unlike the previous charity they had visited, this was a modern, open-plan building. A couple of staff were tapping away at computers, and in a glass-fronted meeting space a woman was addressing a small group of young people, a couple of whom appeared to be more interested in their phones than the content of her presentation.

'Gillian, did Maria say anything about coming in off leave today?'

The only other woman in the office looked up from her computer and shook her head. 'No, don't think so.'

Above the woman's head there was a large whiteboard with the location of all the staff written on it. Maria had 'annual leave' written against her name in big red letters. Unfortunately nobody's surname was included.

'Do you have a business card for her? I can give her a ring to reschedule.'

'Of course!' The receptionist looked relieved that there was an acceptable solution to the problem, and began rooting around in her desk drawer. 'Here you go.'

Mona looked at the card. *Maria Sánchez-Lewandowska. Funding Officer.*

'Thanks. You've been very helpful.'

She ran down the steps and looked up and down the street to see where Theresa had got to. Mona had gently suggested that it would be better if she visited the charity by herself, and had been taken by surprise when Theresa had agreed. She'd been prepared for more of a fight. Mona wasn't sure if her sudden compliance was due to the fact that Paterson wasn't here to argue with, or if the stress of their searching was taking its toll on her. But where had she got to? Mona hoped that she hadn't taken off without her. Progress might be slow, but she'd a feeling that might be about to change.

'I'm here.' She turned to see Theresa, who was fanning herself with a magazine. 'Sorry, I went in search of shade. This entire street is a suntrap. Success?'

'I think so.' She showed her the business card. 'Can't

be too many Londoners with a moniker like that. Looks like part Spanish, and what do you think that is, Polish perhaps?'

'Well, Spanish would make sense. Her mother ran off with a Venezuelan PhD student. Sandy was devastated.'

'Might have been helpful to mention that at some point, Theresa.'

'I would have done if I'd thought for one minute that the relationship had lasted all this time. The student was a good few years younger than Sandy's wife, you know. We all assumed it was just a fling.' She lowered her voice. 'Between you and me, that student was a very handsome young man.'

Mona smiled, and looked at the card again. 'And judging by the double-barrel I guess Maria married an Eastern European.'

'Married!' Theresa looked wistful, and Mona stared at her in surprise. 'I knew her as a little girl,' she explained. 'She was a pretty little thing, very talkative; much more her mother's daughter than her father's, to be honest. So I'm allowed to be pleased that she's all grown up and married. Anyway, what will you do now – run her through your Green Card database?'

'No.' Mona pulled up Google and started typing. 'That leaves a pretty big digital footprint – they log everyone who accesses a file. Seeing as we're trying to stay below the radar I'm going to start with the electoral roll.'

'Can you do that on your phone?'

'Hope so.' Mona scrolled through the government website. After a couple of minutes' searching, she found what she was looking for. 'Got her!'

'Really? All this time she was a couple of clicks away on a website?'

'Yup. All it took was the correct name.' She reached into her bag for her phone. 'Let's work out how to get to her house from here.'

Maria's address led them to a row of terraced townhouses in Clapham, on a tree-lined street which once must have been a highly desirable location for Victorian families and their servants. Now, Mona assumed, the sub-divided buildings were highly desirable starter flats for London's army of young professionals. Their particular interest was in number 75, which currently had the door to its communal stair propped open. Builders in blue boilers suits were carrying items out of a van marked m&k plumbing and into the building.

'I don't see why we can't just go in.' Theresa peered round the side of the tree. One of the plumbers caught sight of her and gave a cheery wave.

'Could we be a little bit discreet? The Guv said to wait for him.'

Theresa snorted. 'I'm not sure what exactly he's going to bring to our meeting. He's been singularly unsuccessful in finding out what happened to Sandy at King's Cross.'

'That's not entirely true. We do know that from what Greg could establish, nobody meeting the professor's description was either arrested or found in a distressed state last night.'

'I suppose.' She sighed. 'No news is good news.'

A taxi turned into the street, and Mona caught sight of her boss's unsmiling face on the back seat. 'I think this is the Guv now.'

He climbed out, shoving his wallet back into his coat pocket. 'There's going to be an expenses claim and a half after this trip. So, have you definitely found her?'

'Well, we've found the home residence of Maria Sánchez-Lewandowska. So unless there are two Maria Sánchez-Lewandowskas in the Greater London area, I think we've found her. And fair play, we were due a break.'

'It'll be a break if the professor is sitting in her living room drinking tea. Otherwise, it might be just another dead end.'

'Thanks for the positive frame of mind, Guv. So, what are we going to tell her when we go in there?'

'The truth,' said Theresa.

Paterson glared at her. 'I believe Mona was asking me?'

'I don't care who she was asking. We should tell the poor girl the truth.'

'And what exactly is your interpretation of "the truth"?'

It was a good question. Mona wasn't certain that she could explain the actual reason for their mission, beyond the fact that Cameron Stuttle was up to something, he wasn't going to get his own hands dirty and Paterson hadn't had the balls to tell him to get stuffed.

'The *truth*, Mr Paterson, is that I am a colleague of her father's, and I'm worried about him.' She sighed. 'Desperately worried.'

Paterson thought for a minute. 'Actually, that's probably the best angle we can go for. But perhaps, as a novelty, you could let Mona and me actually do the talking this time?'

Theresa rolled her eyes but she led the way across the street. They waited at the gate as two men navigated an olive-green plastic bath out of the doorway, down the path, and into a skip.

151

'Can see why she's getting rid of that, Guv.'

'Had one like that when we were growing up. It was the height of fashion, I seem to remember; my mother was very proud of it. Anyway, which number do we want?'

'75b. Just follow the dust and plumbing professionals.'

The flat's front door was propped open with a large earthenware vase. Paterson knocked loudly. 'Hello?'

A young woman appeared in the hall, a cardboard box in her hands. She was tall and slender, with long dark hair that fell to just below her shoulders. Mona wasn't sure, but she thought she could spy a bit of a bump in her stomach area. Was the imminent arrival of a baby the reason for all this renovation?

The woman put the box down, and smiled. 'Oh, I thought you were the builders. Are you looking for me?'

'Are you Maria Sánchez-Lewandowska?' Paterson made a brave attempt at the correct pronunciation.

'Yes.' She looked a little cautious.

'I'm sorry to just appear on your doorstep like this, but we need to speak to you about your father.'

Her face immediately scrunched with worry. 'Xavi? Has something happened? Is he OK?'

'Sorry, I should have been clearer. Not your stepfather, Ms Sánchez-Lewandowska, I meant your biological father, Alexander Bircham-Fowler.'

Her face continued to betray her emotions, with a look of surprise being quickly followed by a grimace of annoyance. 'I really don't want to discuss him. I haven't seen him since I was a child.'

Mona worried that Theresa would leap in at this point to defend the professor, with a potted history of his attempts to look for her followed by a list of his many good points, but silence reigned. Theresa had been uncharacteristically quiet throughout all of Paterson's attempts to win Maria's trust. Mona had half-expected her to elbow her way past them and throw her arms round the professor's long-lost child. She turned to look at her, and noticed that she was using a small white handkerchief to dab her eyes.

Maria seemed to be getting increasingly irritated by their presence. She held on to the door and Mona could see her attempt to edge away the vase that was holding it open. Any second now the door was going to be slammed in Paterson's face and he would have to wedge his size twelve brogue into the gap before it closed. She assumed that he was ready to do so; he had a face that brought out people's inner door-slamming instinct.

'Anyway, who are you people?'

'We, ehm, work with Professor Bircham-Fowler in Edinburgh.' Paterson leaned casually but effectively against the door, to hinder any attempts at closing it. 'Unfortunately your father has been missing for two days now. Our last reported sighting of him was here in London.'

Her face was becoming less readable, possibly as she became less certain of how she felt. 'I'm sure it will be something to do with his work. My mother always said he was a workaholic. I'm sorry but I don't see what that has to do with me. If it wasn't for his continual appearance on the news I wouldn't even know what he looked like.'

'We thought he might be trying to find you.'

'I haven't seen him in the best part of two decades.' Irritation was returning to her voice. 'Why would he suddenly be looking for me?'

'Because someone sent him this picture.' Mona pulled the photocopy out of her bag and handed it to her.

She stared at it for a few seconds. 'That was on a sleepout to raise funds to tackle homelessness. I used to work for the charity that organised it.'

'We know that, but we don't think your father does. He's dropped everything to come to London to try to find you because he thinks you're homeless and sleeping on the streets. We know he has been searching for you on the Embankment. No one has heard from him since he left for London and we're worried that he has come to harm.'

Maria leaned her head against the door and her hair fell across her face, obscuring her expression. Mona thought she could sense that her previous irritation was turning into distress. It couldn't be easy, having three strangers appear on your doorstep, dredging up memories of your childhood. And that possible baby bump – should they try and ease off on the stress, get her sitting down, nice cup of tea perhaps?

She felt a rustle at her back as Theresa pushed past her. 'Seven years old!' She reached for Maria's hand, and held it between her own. Maria looked up in confusion, flicking her long hair back over her shoulder.

'You used to be in and out of your dad's office all the time. And here you are, all grown up ...'

Maria pulled away. There was no ambiguity about her distress now, and Mona could see tears starting to streak her face. Maria pushed the photocopy back toward them. 'You need to go. Now.'

A builder appeared at the top of the stairs. He stood there looking them over, obviously trying to figure out what was going on.

154

'But...'

'Please, just leave!' Her voice was getting louder.

The builder took a step forward. 'Everything OK, Mrs S?'

'Yes, fine. Please carry on.'

With a stern glance at the three of them he disappeared into the flat.

Maria bent down and moved the vase away from the door. 'My father hasn't been here and I've no interest in seeing him.'

'I'll leave my card in case you do hear from him.' Mona held the closing door, and pressed the card into Maria's hand. 'I know this is difficult for you but we absolutely do need to hear from him if he makes contact with you.'

The door closed behind them with a thud.

'That went well, Guv.'

Theresa missed the sarcasm in her voice. 'It went dreadfully.' She started scrabbling around in her handbag, and produced her handkerchief again. 'She's never going to speak to us again, or to Sandy. He was obviously trying to make things right with her, and we've just ruined any chance he had of a relationship with her.'

Paterson sighed, and pointed over the bannister. 'And to make matters worse, we're trapped.'

A middle-aged plumber and what looked like his apprentice were manoeuvring a bath up the stairs. It was a narrow space, and judging by the repeated cries of 'easy there' and 'take it slow' the older man was intent on getting it up the stairwell without scraping the wall. They stepped back to allow them space. Mona hoped that Maria wasn't too upset to open the front door, otherwise the bath was going to have to remain precariously balanced on the landing, or even worse, return back to the bottom of the stairs before they could escape.

To her surprise the door opened again, and Maria stood there. 'Excuse me!' She was looking at Theresa. 'Are you Mrs Kilsyth?'

Theresa stopped dabbing her eyes. 'Yes, I am.'

'I remember you.' Maria's voice cracked. 'You were always very kind to me as a child.'

Theresa pushed Paterson out of the way, and reached out to Maria. 'Your father was, and is, a workaholic. I'm sure he made a very bad husband, and possibly not a great dad. But I know that he did love you very much, and it broke his heart when he lost touch with you.'

Maria's face disappeared under her hair again, but her heaving shoulders left no doubt that she was upset. Tears were also streaming freely down Theresa's cheeks. Mona looked over at Paterson, who rolled his eyes. He made a generalised hand movement indicating that she ought to do something, which she returned with a specific shrug of her shoulders, indicating that there was no way she was getting in the middle of that.

A scraping sound followed by a mild oath alerted them that the bath had reached the top of the stairs.

'All right to bring this in, Mrs S?'

Maria fled into the flat without answering.

The plumber looked at them in confusion.

'I'd take that as a yes, chaps.'

'Right you are. Easy there ...'

Their way now clear they walked slowly down the stairs, Theresa sniffing and dabbing as she went. 'Do you think she'll ring us if she does hear from Sandy?'

'I don't know, Theresa.' Paterson held open the front door to let them both pass through. 'But let's hope so, because right now we've not got any other leads.'

A figure on the other side of the road caught Mona's eye. 'I wouldn't say that, Guv.' She pointed at a man standing in the shady spot that they had recently vacated. 'Isn't that...'

'Sandy!'

4

Maitland had been sitting in Paterson's office with the door shut for over half an hour. There were a number of things that he could be doing in there: licking his wounds, e-mailing Stuttle to apologise, crying down the phone to Kate. Bernard's favourite fantasy was that Maitland was busy writing a long and detailed e-mail explaining the reasons for his resignation, starting immediately. Although given the difficulties that the HET had in recruiting staff, it would take more than gross incompetence to get a resignation letter accepted. No, Bernard had to accept that neither he nor Maitland was going anywhere. They were stuck with each other, and had to work together. So if Maitland wasn't going to come out and let Bernard gloat over him, he was going to have to go in.

He knocked and without waiting for an invitation walked in. Maitland was sitting with his head in his hands.

'What?'

'I wondered what you wanted me to do, what with you being *in charge*.' He included an air quotes gesture in case Maitland hadn't grasped his tone of voice.

'How about you finding your Defaulter, what with you being *a HET officer*?' Maitland returned the air quotes. 'Then at least there's one thing Carlotta bloody Carmichael can't get annoyed about.'

'I'd be delighted to, but Carole's off sick, and we're not supposed to wander round solo, which is probably a good precaution given the fact that the fake Defaulter was violent...'

Maitland sighed. 'I get it, Bernard. You're scared of what might happen. After all, Carole was the muscle in your partnership and if she got beaten up, God alone knows what might happen to you.'

Bernard opened his mouth to say something witty, but, annoyingly, nothing came out.

'So,' Maitland folded his arms across his chest, 'what do you know about this fake Defaulter?'

'We're not looking for the fake Defaulter – that's Police Scotland's job now.'

'I get that, loser, but if someone was so keen for us not to pursue Alessandra Barr that they sent a ringer to take her Health Check, then there's some kind of cover-up going on. And our fake Defaulter must know why. So, to repeat my question, what do we know about her?'

Bernard grudgingly admitted to himself that Maitland had a point. 'We know her blood type.'

'Not hugely helpful in narrowing our search.'

'And we found her at Stephen McNiven's house.'

'And you met Stephen McNiven at the house where Alessandra Barr was registered. I wonder who owns those houses?'

'Land Registry search?'

'At last you're making a sensible suggestion. Close the door on your way out.'

Bernard fumed back to his own computer, and logged on to the Registers of Scotland website. He was

159

disappointed when the first house turned out to be owned by a company. He was less disappointed to find the second house also owned by the same company. He picked up the phone to IT and gave some instructions to Marcus.

'Both owned by the same company, Maitland. I've got Marcus looking into it.'

'Great.'

Bernard waited for Maitland to issue some further instructions, but he just sat smiling smugly at him. Eventually Bernard gave in and asked, 'OK. So what do we do?'

'Well, you could go back to the two addresses that you've been to, but I'm guessing that they'll be quiet as the grave just now ...'

Bernard's phone beeped. 'It's Marcus.' He read the screen. 'The company only owns four houses.'

'Any information on who owns the company?'

'The company secretary is Scott Kerr, lives at Falcon Drive, which is also in the very nice bit of town called Morningside, and which just happens to be one of the company's houses.'

'Well, start there.'

'On my own?' His stomach was a lift shaft, hurtling toward his feet. 'Why can't you come?'

'Because Stuttle is coming over to yell at me some more.' Maitland looked distinctly glum at the prospect, which failed to trigger any sympathetic response from Bernard. 'Any minute now he'll be here, breathing fire.'

'Well Stuttle's not going to be best pleased if he knows you are flouting HET regulations and sending officers to follow up Defaulters on their own ...'

'Oh, for ...' He drummed his fingers on the desk, then

sat bolt upright. 'I know. Take Marcus. He's always keen to get out of the office.'

'Marcus?' Bernard shifted from foot to foot. 'But he's …'

'Even more of a nancy boy than you are?' Maitland grinned. 'Man up, Bernard, and do your job.'

'But the regulations say …'

Maitland made a clucking sound.

'I'm not chicken! Fine. I'll go, and if I die in the line of duty we can add that to the list of things you've messed up since Paterson left.' He flounced out.

'What, like taking the wrong person to a Health Check? Believe that was your cock-up, Bernie.'

Bernard grabbed his coat. He wondered if he was ever going to win an argument with Maitland.

5

'Professor, we've been looking for you.'

Bircham-Fowler did not look hurt, or particularly distressed. A little dishevelled perhaps, but then Mona was not about to throw stones on that particular front, not after two days tramping the streets of London in the blazing sun. The professor appeared to be coping with the heat better than she was; how anyone could wear a tweed jacket when it was 28°C in the shade was beyond her. He did appear to have made the concession of removing his tie.

'We're with the HET.' Paterson stuck a hand out for the academic to shake. He ignored him, and focused on Theresa.

'Did you see her?'

She nodded. 'Yes, Sandy, and she's beautiful.'

'Oh, Tess. Do you think she'll talk to me?'

Theresa patted his arm. 'I think she will but not today. You've taken her by surprise. Give her a bit of time to get used to the idea.'

'Mona.' Paterson's voice was low and urgent. 'Ten o'clock.'

She turned in that direction. A bearded man, and a younger clean-shaven guy were sitting in a dark blue Ford Fiesta, both of them engrossed in their newspapers.

162

'Could be nothing, Guv.'

'Could be, or it could definitely be something. Who reads newspapers in this day and age? Anyway, let's not take any chances. You get hold of the prof.'

She nodded. 'Theresa.'

Theresa looked momentarily annoyed that her conversation with the professor had been interrupted, then saw the look on Paterson's face. 'Is something wrong?'

'I need you to do something for me. I need you to go back into Maria's house and stay there.'

'Why?' She frowned.

'Just trust me, please.'

She stared at him, and Mona could see her thinking this request over.

'We will keep the professor safe, I promise.'

'You'd better.' She patted the professor on the arm again, then crossed the road without a backward glance.

'OK, Prof, time to go.' Mona and the Guv took an arm each and started walking.

He looked back over his shoulder in the direction of the house. 'But my daughter ...' He stopped walking. 'I'm not going anywhere.'

'We're being followed, Professor. You may be in danger.'

'But ...'

'Don't bring that to your daughter's house.'

This was the right tactic. The professor started to stride swiftly and purposefully along the street. The Ford Fiesta pulled out and drove slowly along behind them. It was *definitely something*.

'Not exactly discreet, is it, Guv?'

'I'd say worryingly indiscreet. It could be a diversion, you know, keep us so involved in watching them that we

163

run straight into someone on foot. Let's get somewhere busy. We need crowds.'

'The High Street is to our left,' said the professor. 'I've just come from there.'

'Let's try here, Guv.' A path led off from Maria's street, seemingly housing the back doors and recycling bins of a number of local businesses. At the end of the lane, some 200 metres away, they could see shops and a smattering of people. 'We cut up here and they can't follow us in the car.'

'Come on, Professor.' Paterson pulled him into the lane, with Mona gently pushing his back.

'I'm going as fast as I can.' He stumbled, and Mona took a firm grip of his arm. Looking over her shoulder she could see that the Ford Fiesta had parked at the bottom of the lane, cutting off their chance of retreating back in that direction if they needed to. She was beset by a horrible suspicion that they had been deliberately herded this way.

'Can we pick up the pace a little, Professor?' asked Paterson. 'Just in case there's a welcoming party at the end of the lane.'

Crowds were their best hope. They needed to be in amongst a large group of other people who could witness any attempt on the professor's liberty. Get the professor onto the High Street, into a busy café, and they could phone Stuttle for instructions. She assumed this turn of events would take him by surprise; if he'd thought the prof was in danger of anything more than missing a Health Check, she was sure there would have been more than just the two of them dispatched to find him.

The lane was narrowing due to the row of bins and she squeezed closer to the professor in order to fit past, wrinkling her nose at the smell of refuse. The back door of a pub swung open, and they heard a brief blast of rock music. A drunk staggered out, swaying right across their path.

'All right, love.' He bumped into her. 'Fancy a dance, darling?' She pushed him away, and he bounced against a bin before staggering off.

'Ow,' said the professor. 'Something's bitten me.' He pulled his arm free of her grip, and started fiddling with his shirt.

'Keep moving, Professor,' said Paterson. 'We're nearly in a safe place.'

Mona looked round. The drunk had vanished, a remarkable feat for a man who minutes earlier had been staggering all over the place. There was also no sign of the Ford Fiesta.

The professor ground abruptly to a halt, causing Mona to bump into him. 'Look.' He held out a small metal object. 'That man stuck this into me.'

'Fantastic,' said the Guv. 'Someone's poisoned him. OK, sir, let's get you moving while you still can.'

Mona took his arm again, and they stepped out on to the High Street, the professor wobbling as they went.

'I have to say I'm feeling rather woozy.'

'Just try and keep upright, sir. Let's get him in there.' Paterson pointed at a chain store.

Mona pushed the glass entrance open with her back, and they hauled the professor inside. There was a lift facing them with its doors wide open.

'In here?'

'Why not?'

They bundled him into it and pressed the highest number.

'I'm really not ...' The professor slumped against the wall, and his eyes closed. The Guv put an arm round him to stop him sliding to the floor.

'Jesus, Guv, have they killed him?' She held the professor's face with both hands, and was relieved to find he was still breathing.

'Well, this is a fucking shambles and no mistake.' Paterson stared at her. 'What do we do now?'

6

'Sorry to drag you away from your computer.'

'Oh, Bernard.' Marcus laughed. 'I'm delighted, I can assure you.'

Bernard edged through the hordes of cars on Morningside High Street, keeping one eye on the traffic, and the other on his satnav.

'We're still knee deep in files requiring digitisation, and the joys of that particular job wore off some time ago, let me tell you. Bryce was most annoyed that I was skipping out without him. He was very vocal on the subject.'

'Really?' Bernard struggled to imagine Bryce being loud and outraged. 'Anyway, you know what the deal is – I just need to ask the owner of this house a few questions, and you are here as ...' He wasn't quite sure how to describe Marcus's function.

'I've got your back.' Marcus grinned, seemingly clearer in the role he was providing. 'I've always wanted to say that, but life hasn't ever required it of me before. I never had friends at school who got into fights and required their coats held for them, and I can't say that professionally it's ever been part of the job description.'

Bernard suffered a pang of angst. Maitland's terminology might have been repulsive, but Marcus wasn't ideal back-up material in anyone's books. 'Have you ever been in a fight yourself?'

'Can't say that I have.' Marcus shook his head. 'Not a fight, or an altercation, or even a minor scuffle. Unless you count all the zombies I've killed in the virtual world.'

'OK. I shouldn't really need back-up,' said Bernard, mainly to reassure himself, 'but you never really know what response you're going to get.'

Marcus nodded sagely. 'Especially with the drugs war.'

'Drugs war?' He slammed on the brakes as the car in front found a parking space and stopped abruptly.

'You know, as in the memo?'

Bernard pulled out to overtake the parking car, at the same time as the satnav told him to turn left into Falcon Drive. He decided to focus on his driving, and didn't speak again until they were sitting outside the house they were visiting with the engine turned off.

'Marcus, what did you mean about a memo? I didn't get any memo about a drugs ...'

'Oh, look.' Marcus pointed up and out of the car. 'Someone's watching us.' He waved at them.

Bernard looked in the direction he was indicating, and saw that they were indeed being watched. A woman stood at the upper window of the house, holding back a curtain and staring at them. He decided that if they made it through the visit alive he'd have a word with Marcus about discretion, and make it clear that pointing and waving weren't perhaps the best way to maintain their element of surprise. 'Well, they know we're here so we'd better go in.'

He strode off in what he hoped was a relaxed yet confident manner, which lasted right up until he found he was unable to open the garden gate. He slid the bolt back and forth, and tried to work out what he was doing wrong. Marcus didn't seem bothered and kept up a monologue on the history of Morningside.

'Now, Bernard, you may think that this street is named after a bird, but you would, of course, be wrong. Logical, but wrong. The falcon in question here relates to the former Falcon Hall, built in 1780, which became the residence of a string of wealthy local businessmen ...'

'Really?' said Bernard, having worked out that there was a further bolt halfway down the gate on the inside. He leaned over and pulled.

'All demolished now, of course, apart from the gateway pillars. Let's see if you can guess where they were relocated to.'

The bolt finally gave way, and the gate opened.

'Here's a clue.' Marcus made a series of animal noises, accompanied by the arm actions that represented an elephant, a bird and an orangutan.

Bernard stared at him. 'Edinburgh Zoo?'

Marcus looked delighted. 'Yes!'

As they walked up the path, Bernard reflected, firstly, that that had been a very interesting fact, and secondly, if there was a drug dealer living here, he really wouldn't know who to punch first.

There was an ornate wrought-iron circle on the door-frame, surrounding a white button with press written on it in little black capitals. Bernard did as instructed, and within seconds the door was opened by a woman in her twenties. She radiated personal grooming of a level that suggested that she wasn't up at 6.30am every morning for a quick shower before running to catch the five-to-seven bus. No, this was a regime that obviously took time. Her long brown hair was absolutely, perfectly straight. She must have been wearing make-up although it didn't look like she was, a look he had been told took much more time to perfect than banging on a bit of slap. The clothes were both expensive and immaculately laundered. Bernard, who now noticed these things, could see that she was very attractive. Maybe even as attractive as Megan.

'I saw you from the window.' Her long eyelashes flicked up and down as she looked them over.

'I'm very sorry to disturb you. We're from the Health Enforcement Team,' he flashed his ID card, 'and we wondered if we could have a word with Scott Kerr?'

He waited for her to ask who the Health Enforcement Team were, but she seemed well informed. Surprisingly well informed. Had she been expecting them to visit?

'But Scott hasn't missed a Health Check.'

'Yes, we are aware of that. It's actually in connection with a tenant of his. Or at least someone we think is his tenant.'

'You have a name for this person?' The more she spoke, the more Bernard detected a hint of an accent beneath the perfect English. He couldn't quite place it though: Eastern European? Mediterranean? French?

'Alessandra Barr.'

She shrugged in a very Gallic manner. 'I do not know this name. You must speak to Scott directly, but he's not here at this moment.'

'Any idea when's a good time to catch him?' Bernard stared past her, trying to see if there were actually any other signs of life in the house. All that he managed to see was a grandfather clock ticking away at the back of the hall.

'I really am not sure.'

170

'I'll leave you my card. If he could give us a ring once he gets in we'd be very grateful.'

'I will tell him.' She smiled, and Bernard upped his earlier estimation of her. She was surely some kind of supermodel. Or an angel of some description, fallen to earth and landed in Morningside.

She closed the door on them, and he turned to Marcus. 'So, there was a memo?'

'Yes.' Marcus started walking in the direction of the car. 'All about how there is a drugs war kicking off in Edinburgh due to the death of some kingpin or other. The HET liaison officer popped in with copies for us to discuss at our next team meeting. Gave Bryce and me quite a laugh – as if the pair of us have team meetings.' He giggled. 'Didn't you see it?'

'It would go to Mr Paterson in the first instance for him to bring up at a team meeting, and in his absence it would be ... Maitland.'

Marcus laughed. 'Ah, yes, that great processor of paperwork. Bryce is still bearing a grudge against Maitland for the time he ordered six previous address checks, and when we'd done all the work and sent it back he said they were the wrong thing, he wanted previous employment checks, and we said well why did you fill in a previous address request form ...'

'OK,' said Bernard, interrupting what appeared to be turning into a very long anecdote. 'I'll have the whole memo thing out with him when I get back. Are you coming to the HET office?'

'No, sadly, I'd better get back to Fettes.' He paused with his hand on the car door. 'That was a fine-looking woman back there.'

'I did notice – she really was a very attractive lady,

wasn't she? Probably just as well Maitland wasn't here. You know what he's like around good-looking women.'

'Quite.' Marcus did an impersonation of a dog with its tongue hanging out. 'Anyway, talking of fine-looking women, how's Mona?'

Bernard noted the exaggerated casualness to the question. 'She's fine. Her usual self.'

'Would you happen to know if she is, ehm, seeing anyone?'

'How would I know?' He wasn't being evasive. Bernard really had no idea if Mona had a boyfriend. Despite long, and often boring, hours of searching for Defaulters together, their conversation rarely strayed into their private lives. In all his time at the HET Mona had never volunteered any information on the subject, and, in return, had shown a very limited interest in Bernard's current marital situation, to his enduring frustration. It would have been good to talk to someone on the subject, get a woman's point of view.

'But she's not mentioned anyone?'

He shook his head. 'No, I can honestly say she hasn't. But she is, as you said, a fine-looking woman, so I would imagine that she does have someone but just doesn't want to share that information with her colleagues.'

'Oh, OK. You're probably right.' He smiled, slightly mournfully. 'Just say I said hi, and I'll catch up with her sometime.'

The outer office was deserted when he got back. The room was unbearably stuffy; the absence of his colleagues meant that none of the windows had been opened all day. He opened one on each side of the room, and succeeded in creating a cross-draught that blew a pile of papers off

Mona's desk and onto the floor. He scooped them all back up and weighted them down with an unwashed mug.

The door to Paterson's office was shut. He attempted a discreet peek through the window, and saw Stuttle and Maitland deep in conversation. He felt a little bit disappointed at the absence of shouting and bawling being deployed in Maitland's direction. At the very least he'd hoped to witness some admonitory gesticulation. The door to Paterson's office opened, and he just had time to install himself behind his computer and look busy before Stuttle appeared with Maitland hovering at his shoulder. He was glad to see the look of anxiety on Maitland's face.

'So, hot on the trail of this Defaulter then, Bernard?' Stuttle shot him his usual insincere smile which always made Bernard feel nervous.

'Yes, kind of.' He wasn't sure that 'hot on the trail' really described their current leads. 'Not so easy with Carole being off but ...'

'She called in,' said Maitland, hastily. 'She'll be back tomorrow.'

'Good woman. She's a battler that one.'

Bernard tried to remember if Stuttle had ever actually met Carole.

'Anyway, chaps, glad things are under control here. I'll leave you to it.' He gave them a wave and left. Maitland pulled out a chair and crumpled into it.

'He's in a surprisingly good mood,' said Bernard. 'What did you do?'

'What do you think? I crawled for all I was worth. I think he's thought it over and decided that it's all Carlotta Carmichael's fault. The main thrust of the conversation was him trying to work out how Carlotta knows so much about the ins and outs of the HET. I got the third degree about whether we had a spy in our ranks.'

'And what did you say?'

'I said I'd always thought Bernard's loyalties were a bit questionable.'

'*What?*'

Maitland laughed, long and heartily. 'Ah, the look on your face. Well, you can keep your remaining hair on. I said I couldn't imagine any of my colleagues doing that. Said we were all loyal to the HET's aims, saluted the flag at the start of every day, etc., etc. And he went away fairly happy with us. So, as long as you find your Defaulter without messing up, I think we're in the clear.'

'Maitland, did you receive a memo about drug dealing in Edinburgh?'

The sound of the phone ringing came from his room.

'Hold on, I'll just get that.'

Bernard sighed, and turned back to his computer. He was scrolling through e-mails when Maitland reappeared and threw himself into the chair he had recently vacated.

'This is bad. Oh God, this is so, so bad.'

'What is?' Bernard started to panic. 'Has our Defaulter been found dead? Are Mona and Mr Paterson in trouble?'

'Worse, much worse.' Maitland's head was back in his hands again. 'That was Carlotta Carmichael's office. They said she was so concerned about the running of the North Edinburgh HET that she's coming to visit us tomorrow.'

'Can she do that?'

'I don't know. Probably – she is our ultimate boss, I suppose. I'm waiting for Stuttle to phone me back. This is a nightmare.'

Bernard looked round the office. There were piles of files everywhere. The wind tunnel he had inadvertently created had rearranged some more of Mona's papers on to the floor. Each and every desk held a collection of mugs with varying degrees of mould. 'We'd better tidy up.'

7

'We can't stay here, Guv. Sooner or later someone is going to want to use the facilities.'

They were closeted in a disabled toilet on the top floor of the store, a cramped and airless space that was not designed to accommodate three people.

Paterson contemplated their dilemma. 'Have you got any paper in that bag?'

Mona dug in and pulled out a notebook.

'That'll have to do.' He wrote 'Out of Order' on it, and stuck his head out of the door to attach it.

'Do you think he'll be OK, Guv?'

The professor was propped up on the toilet, leaning against the wall and snoring softly. He looked relaxed and at peace, the polar opposite of how she currently felt.

'He looks OK to me, based on the fact that he's breathing normally and not throwing up or fitting or anything. My guess is that bloke has pumped him full of sleepy-juice, but I don't particularly want to risk his health, whatever else is at stake. I'm thinking we need to call an ambulance.'

'And say what? How do we explain what's happened?'

Paterson opened his mouth to speak, but stood there without saying anything. 'I don't know,' he admitted.

'Guv, what *is* going on? Whoever is tailing us had ample time to drug the professor, kill him even, if they wanted to, while we were inside Maria's flat. Why wait for us to appear?'

'I don't think they want him dead; a suspicious death risks turning him into some kind of martyr, sets off all kinds of conspiracy theories. My guess is that they want to discredit him.'

'How does pumping him full of sedative discredit him?'

'My guess, and it is just a guess, is that they want some shots of him apparently drunk, dishevelled and sleeping it off in a doorway. On top of him taking off, and missing a Health Check, they've got a great story to rubbish him if they've got a tame newspaper to do it for them.' He ran his hand in the air as if spelling out a headline. 'Top Boffin Cracks Under Pressure. Professor Ga Ga. Bircham-Fowler Fowls Up ...'

'I get the picture, Guv. But why wait for us to appear on the scene?'

There was a silence. In the mirror, Mona watched her boss think. 'I can only assume that they, whoever they are, want us discredited as well. The professor's been a big supporter of the HETs. His research is the main academic underpinning of our work. If the press decides he's a fruitcake, it'll be guilt by association. And a picture of us aiding and abetting an apparently incapacitated prof would implicate us nicely in all this.'

'They've already got a story just by us being in London.'

'I'm sure Stuttle can concoct something to explain that away.'

Mona caught his reflection's eye. 'Unless he's planning

to hang us out to dry. Two HET officers gone rogue. After all, we're officially on leave.'

His reflection quickly looked away. 'I'm sure it's not that.'

Mona took the professor's pulse. 'For what it's worth, Guv, I don't think they've poisoned him either. His pulse is normal and he doesn't have a temperature. Would your son have a friendly medical contact that could have a look at him?'

Paterson looked at her, and at the door, obviously torn between the different courses of action. Eventually he nodded and pulled out his phone. 'No signal. Damn. OK, I'm going out to call him.' He paused by the door and after listening for noise for a second or two, decided that the coast was clear and headed out.

The heat was becoming unbearable, and her lack of sleep was beginning to catch up with her. Mona inspected the floor and wondered if it was clean enough to sit on. She decided she was already so sticky and disgusting that ten minutes sat on the floor of a toilet couldn't make her much worse. Crouching down, she leaned back against the wall and watched the professor breathing deeply in and out. He looked entirely peaceful, and there was something very restful about watching him, like the sensation of watching goldfish swim round and round. Her eyes were just beginning to close when there was the sound of feet outside the door.

'Oh, it's out of order. That's ridiculous. We should complain to the manager.'

Mona held her breath, and hoped that the professor didn't choose this particular moment to start snoring loudly. She didn't fancy explaining the situation to an outraged store manager if he opened up to find a noted academic and his friend had just popped into their disabled loo to have a nap.

'No, Mum, just leave it. There's one on the ground floor, we'll go there.'

Mona breathed out, wishing Paterson would hurry up. Eventually someone was going to discover them, or possibly their bodies if they didn't get some additional oxygen soon.

There was a knock on the door, which made her jump. 'Mona.' Paterson's voice, low and urgent.

She unlocked the door and Paterson's hand appeared, clutching a bag. 'Get him into these.'

It contained a large sun hat, and a pair of sunglasses. '*Really?*'

'We can stop them getting a decent photo of him at least.'

'Do you think there's still someone hanging around?'

'Well, there were a pretty limited number of places that we could have disappeared to with the prof in this state. If you were in their position what would you be doing?'

'I'd be methodically checking the shops.'

'Yup. And if our optimistic thinking is right, all they're after is a photograph, but let's not push our luck. Come on, give me a hand getting him upright.'

'We're leaving?'

'Yup. Greg's bringing a car and meeting us at the back door. I've had a recce of the shop, and I didn't see any familiar faces, so it looks like now's our chance to make a, well, I was going to say run for it, but the prof's not looking too athletic.'

'He's over six foot tall, Guv, and he weighs a ton. There's no way we're getting him out of here discreetly.'

'Well, we can't stay here much longer, not without suffocating.' He handed Mona her bag. 'Oh, and turn your mobile phone off. I don't want anyone tracing where we are going.'

'Phone hacking? Who exactly do you think is looking for us?'

'That, Mona,' said Paterson, as he hooked his hands under the unconscious professor's arms, 'I really don't know.'

8

'When did we last tidy up in here?' Maitland lifted a pile of files from Carole's desk and looked round for somewhere to put them. 'This place is a disaster area.'

'I don't know what you mean by "last tidied up",' Bernard said. I don't think we've ever tidied up. We've just accumulated more and more files with every case we've undertaken, and we've left them lying about in the hope that someone is going to eventually establish a filing system.'

'Do you think that there is any chance the admin department could establish that filing system before tomorrow morning?'

'No. I think we would still be arguing with them tomorrow morning about whether it was their responsibility or not to do our filing. Anyway, Marguerite has been helpful. She's lent us this from the admin department.'

'A room divider?'

'Yeah, I thought we could place it strategically in a corner, and pile all this junk behind it.'

Maitland nodded appreciatively. 'One of your better ideas, Bernie. Although productivity in the admin department has probably slowed to zero now nothing can get in the way of their gossiping.'

'The admin assistant that was sitting on the other side of it from Marguerite didn't look too pleased.'

'Yeah, it probably had certain sound-absorbing qualities that you'd appreciate if you were sat next to Marg. Anyway, her loss is our gain. Stick it over there.'

Maitland dumped the files behind it, and looked in disgust at the layer of black dust covering his hands. 'This place is never going to be tidy by tomorrow.'

'And we don't know what time she's popping in?'

'No, for the third time I don't know what time her broomstick will be landing. Maybe we'll be forewarned by the swarm of bats.'

Bernard considered whether to respond to this, and decided that he must. 'Likening a woman in authority to a witch-like figure is a little bit on the sexist side.'

'Oh, for ...'

Bernard's phone rang. 'Hold that thought.'

Maitland looked exasperated, but headed back into his office, stopping only to wipe his dusty hands down Bernard's sleeve.

It was an unfamiliar number. There was a moment or two of what sounded like sobbing. 'Bernard?'

A woman's voice. It didn't sound like Carrie, even allowing for the fact the woman was obviously in distress, and it definitely wasn't Mona. He couldn't think of any other women who would phone him *in extremis*, unless ... 'Megan?'

There was another choking sob. 'You need to come home. There's been a man here ...'

'A man? What man?'

There was a loud sniff on the other end of the phone, followed by some gulping for air. 'I've called the police. Please, Bernard, can you come here immediately?'

182

'Of course.' He was about to ask her for more information about what was going on when he realised she had hung up. He turned round to find Maitland, only to see that he was standing behind him.

'What was all that about?'

'I need to go.'

'Now?' Maitland's jaw dropped. 'You're kidding me. Look at this place – there's a good few hours' work left.'

'I know, I'm sorry. But that was my flatmate on the phone in floods of tears – I think she's been attacked or burgled or something.'

'Attacked?'

'Yeah, I don't know quite what's happened; she was saying something about a man being in the house. Anyway, she's just called the police and wants me to go home.'

Maitland looked at his watch. 'Jeez, it's after seven. I need to go as well.'

'Are you seeing Kate tonight?'

'Probably not as much of her as I'd like to see, but yes. Can we both get in for seven tomorrow, give this place another going over?'

'Good plan. See you then.'

Bernard hailed the first taxi he saw, and sat back trying to work out what had happened. It was possible that Megan had been attacked by a stranger in her own home, but statistically, of course, this was unlikely. Women were always far more likely to be attacked by someone they already knew: boyfriends, husbands and family members were all first in the frame when violence had occurred. But Megan hadn't given him any indication that she'd felt threatened. And Megan didn't seem the type to let a man … What was he saying? There was no such thing as a type – abuse could happen to any woman, he knew that.

So, was there some ex-boyfriend she hadn't mentioned? He felt an unaccustomed pang of jealousy; he'd been with Carrie so long that the last time he'd had to deal with love rivals was when he was a teenager. Though, of course, a sensitive soul like himself would look great in comparison to some loutish brute who was free with his fists. Unless, that is, Megan was anticipating that he was going to avenge her wrong, in which case he'd have to admit he probably wouldn't come out of it well.

He got the taxi to drop him off at the end of the street, so he could scope out whether there was anyone still hanging around. It proved to be an unnecessary precaution, as there was already a Police Scotland car sat opposite the flat's gate. As he approached the front door he spotted broken glass on the path, and saw that the small window at the side of the door had been shattered. He supposed this would allow someone to reach in and open the door. Poor Megan. Had she been burgled?

'Hello, I'm back.' He pushed open the door to the living room. At one end of the couch sat a large middle-aged policeman; he seemed strangely familiar. He'd taken off his high-vis jacket and draped it across his knee, and his notebook was resting on top of this. The notebook seemed to have a great deal of writing in it. Megan was curled up at the other end of the sofa, red of eye and nose, with a large hanky in her hand. She leapt up when she saw him, and for a moment he thought that she was rushing toward him for a comforting hug.

She wasn't.

'He was looking for you, you know.' Both her tone and her pointing finger were accusatory.

'Who?'

'The man.' She started to cry.

Bernard reached out to her but she batted his hand away.

'Might be better if you sat down, sir.' The policeman gave him a smile that was twice as polite as it was warm. 'I'm PC McGovern.'

'OK.' He lowered himself a little distractedly into an armchair. 'Megan, what happened?'

She gave a loud sniff. 'He asked was I Bernard's tart, and said if so I'd better watch myself. He said you were in trouble with some pretty bad people.'

'What people?' He wasn't aware he knew any bad people, far less was in trouble with them.

'He said you should mind your own business. Then ...' She stopped for a cry. 'Then he grabbed me by the throat.'

'Oh, Megan ...' He went to stand up again, caught the policeman's eye, and lowered himself slowly back down.

'So, Mr ...' PC McGovern stopped to check his notes, 'McDonald. Have you been keeping some bad company?'

'No, I—'

'Are you a user of illegal drugs, Mr McDonald?'

'No, of course not. I'm a—'

'Any debts? Gambling perhaps?'

'Oh, for heaven's sake! None of the above. I'm a HET officer.'

PC McGovern sat back in his seat and stared at him for longer than felt comfortable. 'Oh, you're one of that mob.' He turned back to Megan, and patted her arm. 'Now in light of the shock you've had I'm going to suggest that we all have a cup of tea. Mr McDonald can help me.'

'I can do it.' She half stood up.

'No, no, miss, you relax.' He caught Bernard's eye and jerked his head in the direction of the door.

'What's going on?' PC McGovern closed the kitchen door firmly on the two of them. 'What have your lot been up to?'

'Nothing.' Bernard realised why the policeman looked familiar. He had an undoubted similarity to Mr Paterson, particularly the expression on his face as he interrogated him. 'Well, nothing out of the ordinary anyway. Just chasing up Defaulters, talking to potential witnesses. The usual.'

'Really?' The PC looked sceptical. 'Because one of my colleagues was called out yesterday to deal with a HET officer who'd had a boot in the mouth, and here I am today talking to a HET officer who's had a visitation.' He pointed at the kettle. 'Stick that on, we're supposed to be making tea.'

'Oh, right.'

'So you lot are treading carefully aren't you? It's pretty grim out there at the moment.'

'I know. There was a memo.' Which he still hadn't actually set eyes on.

'I'll need to report this to our HET liaison officer. Is John Paterson still in charge at your end?'

'Yes, but ...'

'Him and I go way back. Maybe I'll give him a ring about this.'

'He's on annual leave,' said Bernard, quickly. He couldn't bear the thought of Paterson and his looka-like discussing his situation. He imagined they would be very much in agreement about his shortcomings.

'Well, see that you report all this back to him. And chop chop, get the lassie her tea.'

'What do I say to Megan about all this?'

'As little as possible, until we work out what's going on. Be a bit evasive, but reassuring, and make sure you keep an eye on her.'

Bernard nodded, but wondered who was going to be keeping an eye on *him*. After all, he was the person this mysterious man was looking for. He couldn't quite bring himself to ask PC McGovern this though; he had a mental image of the policeman and Paterson catching up with each other in the pub. *And then, Paterson, get this, the wee chap says, 'Who's going to look after me?'* Cue the pair of them laughing their heads off.

Megan seemed a little calmer when they returned. 'So, is this to do with your work?'

'Possibly.' *Be evasive.*

'Am I in danger?'

'I don't know, Megan. I've really got no idea what is going on.' He caught PC McGovern's eye and realised this probably didn't qualify as reassuring. 'But I'm sure it'll be OK.'

'We'll keep an eye out on the place, Ms Parker. And you'll have Mr McDonald here for company.'

'No.'

Bernard and PC McGovern looked at each other. 'No?'

'If Bernard is responsible for bringing this trouble to my door, then I don't want him here.'

'But if I move out you'll be here on your own.'

'No, I won't. There's an, ehm, friend I can call.'

Bernard focused on the pause before 'friend'. So there

was an ex. And not the thuggish sort, not the kind that pushed girls around, kicked kittens, laughed at old ladies. No, she had to have the kind of ex that you phone up in a crisis. The kind that was sensitive enough to listen to her distress, but manly enough to offer protection against a violent world. He hated this 'ehm, friend', whoever he was. 'Fine. I'll get out of here first thing in the morning.'

'No, I want you out of here tonight.'

He looked at PC McGovern, who raised his eyebrows sympathetically. 'Best do what the lady says, son. I can drop you off somewhere.'

'Fine.' Bernard turned on his heel, and marched into his room. He threw a bag onto the bed, and started grabbing handfuls of his clothing and shoving it in. Was Megan's insistence that he move out immediately because of the shock she'd just had or was it due to her desire to have her 'ehm, friend' all to herself? Fine. *Fine. Fine. Fine*. If she wanted him out, he'd go. But the question was, where to?

Not to his mother's. He really didn't want to bring any trouble in her direction. And he'd have to sleep on the sofa. He could go to a hotel, but that could be expensive. And, cowardly as it might be, he didn't want to sit alone in a hotel room, waiting for a thug to find him.

Then he remembered. There was a perfect solution to his problem. A smile played across his face as he zipped up the bag.

He was owed a favour.

9

Paterson slowly opened the door and looked out. Mona watched as the back of his head swivelled left, then right.

'I think we're OK. Ready for some heavy lifting?'

They grabbed an arm each and put it round their neck.

'He's a deadweight, Guv, and both you and the professor are a foot taller than I am. Is this going to work?'

'We don't have a lot of choice.' He pushed the door open with his foot, and narrowly missed hitting a passing member of staff.

'Oh.' She looked at them in surprise. She was a small woman, in a smart, dark trouser suit which had a shiny badge pinned to its lapel, pronouncing her to be 'Robina'.

'Sorry,' said Paterson, 'but my dad here has had a funny turn.'

Robina looked concerned. 'Do you need an ambulance?'

'No, no. He has these turns quite regularly. My son's picking us up in the car from the back door, we're just struggling to get him there.'

'Oh I see.' She frowned. 'Would you like to borrow a wheelchair?'

'You have a wheelchair?'

'Of course!' She looked delighted at the chance to help.

189

'Just give me two minutes.' She disappeared through a door marked staff only.

Paterson winked at Mona. 'Sorted.'

'Can we put him down, Guv, or at least lean him against the wall? My back is killing me.'

'Let's prop him up.'

A metallic voice came over the store's intercom. *'Can we have a wheelchair to the disabled toilet on the fourth floor, please?'*

They looked at each other. 'If I was methodically checking out the shops on the High Street, that announcement would pique my interest,' said Mona.

'Crap. I'll hold him. You summon the lift for a quick getaway.'

The staff only door opened again, and Robina reappeared. 'They usually only take a minute or two.'

'Great. Really, can't thank you enough.' Paterson's eyes were scanning the shop as he spoke.

The lift doors opened, revealing an elderly black security guard and a sturdy leather wheelchair. Mona thought she'd never seen a more welcome sight. She stuck her foot into the lift to stop it from closing. The security guard raised his eyebrows. 'That's not good for the lift.'

'Sorry, just keen to get him out of here and into the fresh air.'

Robina took control of the wheelchair. 'I'll pop the brakes on while you manoeuvre him in.'

'Thank you so, so much.'

The professor was lowered into the seat with more speed than grace. His head lolled forward, and his arms fell limply over the sides of the seat. Mona was trying to make him more comfortable, when a prolonged burst of coughing came from Paterson. Amongst the expectoration she thought she heard the word 'beard'. She looked out across the store, and sure enough, the bearded man she had seen in the car outside Maria's house was watching them from behind a row of kid's t-shirts. To make matters worse, he was on his phone.

'So, it was the back door that you wanted?' asked Robina, rather more loudly than either of them would have liked.

'Yes,' said Paterson. 'Maybe you could show us out.'

'Of course!'

The three of them, and the security guard, all got into the lift. Mona would have killed for two minutes alone with her boss in order to plan what they needed to do. As it was, all they could do was exchange glances, while Robina chatted.

'And are those Scottish accents I hear? Do you live down here?'

'No, just visiting for a few days.'

'Oh dear, I hope your dad taking ill doesn't spoil your break.'

'We'd all be much happier if he was fighting fit. We really would.'

The lift pinged open. They stood for a moment, half-expecting the other man from the car to be standing there. Paterson pushed the professor slowly out into the shop, then stopped abruptly. 'Mona, why don't you steer?'

She saw the familiar figure of the other man from the car, and took control of the wheelchair. 'Which way to the back door?'

'Left,' said Robina. 'Follow me.'

She wheeled the professor toward the exit, aware that

191

Paterson was no longer at her side. Glancing back, she saw him deep in conversation with the security guard, gesturing discreetly in the direction of the man they were trying to avoid. She suppressed a smile. Paterson would be drawing his attention to some shoplifting that was taking place. Any minute now the man from the car was going to be marched off to the manager's office to explain himself.

Her good humour evaporated as she spotted the man with the beard loitering by the back door. He was holding something black in his hand at hip height. She stopped in shock, then realised. *Not gun, phone.* The Guv was right, they didn't want the professor dead, they wanted footage.

'Robina, could you take him for a second?'

'Of course.'

Mona made as if to push open the door, as a pretext for putting her body in between the professor and the lens.

'It's an automatic door, you don't need to do that.'

'Oh, OK.' She stepped backwards, so far into the man's personal space that anyone else would have complained. He neither moved nor spoke. As soon as Robina's back disappeared through the door she turned to face him. He didn't catch her eye but turned and walked away, as slowly and calmly as if he'd just popped in for a quick shop.

'What's going on?' Paterson.

'That was Mr Beard – with a camera. Did you get rid of the other one?'

'Emptying out his pockets in the manager's office.'

'Is this your car?' Robina called to them.

'You take charge of him,' said Paterson. 'I'm on paparazzi duty.'

She went outside and was relieved to see Greg standing by a large, dark car.

'Can you get Grandad into the car?'

He glanced at Robina, and nodded. 'You take one arm, I'll get the other.'

'Is there anything I can do to help?' asked Robina.

'No, we've got this.'

After a lengthy period of pushing and pulling, the professor was finally sat upright in the middle of the back seat, Mona and a seat belt keeping him vertical. She leaned back out of the car. 'Robina, thank you so much for your help.'

'No problem. I do hope your grandad's OK.'

Paterson appeared and dived into the car. 'Time to go.' Greg started the car moving before he even had the door shut. 'Thanks again, Robina,' he shouted through the remaining crack in the door.

She gave a slightly confused wave after them. As they pulled away there was a flash from across the street.

'Did someone take a picture?' Greg asked.

'I think it was a traffic camera,' said Mona, twisting round to look. 'You were parked in a loading bay. I hope you don't get a ticket.'

'He'll be paying if I do.' He jerked a thumb in the direction of his dad. 'Anyway, what happened in there?'

'As I said on the phone, someone got to the prof here, and we encountered a couple of less than friendly sorts in the children's department.'

'Who's behind all this?'

'We don't know.'

Greg's expression in the mirror was pure scepticism. 'Really, Dad? Not a clue?'

'No! We've been sent down here without any of the information we actually need to keep him safe.'

There was a moment or two's tense silence.

'Do you think they got any useable footage, Guv?'

'Hard to tell,' he said. 'They'll have some hilarious footage of an old man being manhandled into a car, but they're going to have a job confirming that it's him.'

They both looked at the professor in his sunglasses and hat. He looked ridiculous, but also unrecognisable.

Greg indicated right and turned onto a multi-lane dual carriageway.

'Where are we going, son?'

'Call me Greg. I don't need a constant reminder of our relationship.'

Paterson looked both hurt and irritated. 'Where are we going, *Greg*?'

There was a pause before Greg grudgingly shared the information. 'We're visiting a friend of mine who's a nurse. She'll give him the once-over and tell you if he should go to hospital, or if you just need to find somewhere for him to sleep it off.'

Paterson looked out the back window of the car. 'You'll make sure we're not followed?'

'I do know how these things work, Dad. This is my job, after all. And it's a job that I'd like to keep, so can you make this the last favour that you ask for?'

'Yes, of course.' There was a wounded tone to Paterson's voice that Mona recognised only too well. 'Wouldn't want to impose.'

Greg tutted but said nothing, and the silence stretched on uncomfortably. It reminded Mona of being in the car with Bernard. Until she'd been partnered with Bernard she'd been unaware of the many different shades of silence that existed. There was companionable silence, the best sort, and to be fair, much of the silence she shared with her partner was harmonious. But there was also wounded silence, when she'd said something that offended his core beliefs, like saying that the *Daily Mail* might have a point from time to time. Then there was needy silence, when Bernard thought he had offended her, but couldn't think of anything to say. And she'd take any of those over Bernard's attempts to get her views on his current marital problems.

But right now, an in-depth dissection of the ins and outs of Bernard's relationship would seem like light relief compared to the toxic silence in the car. She looked out the window and yawned. Her late night was catching up with her, and between the heat and the motion of the car she could feel her eyes closing. She dug her cardigan out of her bag, rolled it into a ball, and propped it up against the car door, using it as a makeshift pillow. Within minutes she slipped into a restless sleep. She was half in a dream, vaguely aware still of the sounds of the traffic, but also with a sense of being pursued by something nameless but bad. She woke up as the car ground to a halt.

'We're here.' Greg twisted round in his seat. 'Time to liven up.'

Mona stretched and stared out the window at her surroundings. They were in the middle of a housing estate. On both sides of the road, grass sloped down to a series of red sandstone multi-storey blocks. Bookending the blocks there were stairwells, and each block had outside balconies that ran the length of the building.

'Does your friend by any chance live on the ground floor?' she asked.

He smiled. 'Liz lives on the third. Sorry.' He looked suddenly serious. 'And it goes without saying that if this goes wrong we keep Liz's name out of this, OK? She's going out on a limb for us.'

'Totally.' Mona nodded. 'We were never here.'

'Or,' said Paterson, 'if we were here, your friend had no idea why.'

'I preferred the "you were never here". In fact, I really wish you weren't here, but we are where we are.' Greg started the car again. 'Right. I'll get you as close as I can to the stairwell, then you two get him out while I go and park.'

Five minutes later the four of them stood at the foot of the multiple floors of concrete stairs, three of them contemplating the difficulties of their task.

'If we drag him up there, Guv, he'll have broken ankles by the time we reach the first floor.'

The sound of approaching footsteps stopped him from responding. Two black women in full African dress appeared, one holding a baby and the other dragging a toddler by the hand. The two women nodded as they went past, and the toddler eyed them with suspicion, twisting round to stare at them as his mother pulled him out of the building.

'Sod it. It's not going to be discreet, but we'll have to carry him up like a big sack of spuds. You get his head, son – I mean Greg – and I'll take his feet.'

The two of them manoeuvred the professor into a portable position, and started up the steps.

'Easy now,' said Paterson.

Mona had to clasp a hand to her mouth to catch her laughter, as a memory of Maria's builders and the bath came into her mind. She doubted Paterson was equally concerned about not scraping his cargo on the paintwork.

'Can you knock on that one, please?' Greg pointed to a blue door with a pot plant at its side. Mona obliged, and after a second or two it was answered by a young woman in jeans, who yawned then apologised.

'Sorry, I was on a late shift. I've not been up long.'

'Please don't apologise,' said Paterson, setting down the professor's feet. 'We're really grateful you can help.'

She opened the door wide. 'Come through to the living room and I'll have a look at him.' There was an accent of some sort – from Australia or perhaps New Zealand.

They placed the professor as gently as possible into an armchair, and Liz knelt at his side. She pushed up the professor's jacket sleeve and held his bony wrist between her thumb and forefinger. She listened for a minute, her eyes on her watch. 'His pulse is normal.'

She picked up what Mona thought was a pen from her bag, and twisted it until a weak light shone out. She lifted each of the professor's eyelids in turn and shone the torch into them. 'Pupils are dilating normally.'

Dipping into the bag again she produced a thermometer. After holding it in the professor's ear for a couple of seconds, she pronounced that his temperature was also well within the acceptable range.

She dropped the thermometer back into her bag, zipped it up and sat back on her heels. 'I'm not seeing anything that indicates that he is in distress, so my guess is that he's been given a sedative, nothing stronger...'

'So, he's OK then?'

'I'm not saying that.' She held up a hand. 'As a health professional, I would have to advise you to get him into a hospital for a blood test, and find out conclusively what's in his system, and at what dose.'

Paterson stared at the professor, his face betraying an agony of indecision. His gaze moved to Mona. 'I need to speak to Stuttle.' He pulled his phone out of his pocket.

'Mobile, Guv? Is that a good idea?'

He stopped, his finger hovering over the phone. 'No, probably not. Liz, could we impose even further and borrow your phone?'

She nodded. 'Sure. It's in the hall. I'll show you.'

Greg looked less than pleased. 'You shouldn't be involving Liz in this.'

'It's just a phone call, Greg. It's fine.'

'It's not fine.' He went to follow them, then paused at the door and pointed at the sofa. 'You might as well sit down while you wait. I'll get you a tea or coffee in a minute.'

Mona wondered about his relationship with Liz. A friend, or girlfriend? He certainly seemed at home in her flat, right down to the offer of hospitality. She looked around the room again. It was small, crammed full of furniture, books and plants. Could anyone make a room this welcoming, or did Liz have a special gift? The sunlight streaming in helped, undoubtedly. Maybe she'd try a few pot plants in her place when she got home, or a brightly coloured rug.

Today's paper was lying on the coffee table. She glanced at the lead story – the Mayor of London had promised again to improve the Green Card entry system that was apparently causing havoc at rush hour on the Tube – and picked it up to flick through. As she did so, she noticed a small pile of leaflets lying underneath it. She peeled one off the top and started to read.

Why Everything You Know About Virus Policy is Wrong

An interesting title. She read on.

Current Virus restrictions are not sufficient to control its spread. Front-line health workers are constantly put at risk by the monthly Health Check regime...

The leaflet developed its argument using fairly scientific language before concluding that it was 'time to think the unthinkable', without specifying what this unthinkable thought might be. She wondered who the leaflet was aimed at; it was too technical to be aimed at the general public. She turned it over, and at the bottom of the page found a box saying the leaflet was published by the Health Workers' Collective.

Paterson reappeared, closing the door behind him. He lowered his voice. 'That wasn't very reassuring.'

'What do you mean?'

'Well, I stupidly thought that when I told Stuttle about today's events he would have some contingency arrangements for getting us out of here. I thought maybe he'd been a bit economical with the truth when he dispatched us down here, and hadn't bothered to mention that we weren't the only ones who might be looking for the prof. But I got the impression I had taken him completely by surprise. In fact,' he rapped on the table to emphasise his point, 'I got the impression he was shitting himself.'

'Really? So what do we do now?'

'Stuttle says that we're to stay here and await further instructions.'

'So, no hospital? Guv, what if he does take ill?'

'Then it will be Stuttle's problem.'

'Based on one phone call, which he can conveniently forget happened if we get into trouble?' Both their voices were getting quieter, but more forceful.

'Yes, but the problem is if I do the opposite of what

199

he's instructed, he's going to have a hundred per cent recall of what he said.'

'Except, of course, we're technically on holiday.'

'I'm taking responsibility for this one, Mona.'

Greg and Liz reappeared. From the flushed complexions on both of them she guessed they had been having their own quiet but forceful argument in the hall.

'We've been asked to stay put until we hear from my boss. Would it be OK to hang on here for a while?'

'Absolutely not.' Greg's already colourful cheeks were turning purple. 'We agreed that Liz would give him a quick once-over and then he'd be out of here.' He turned to her. 'I should never have involved you.'

Liz looked considerably calmer. 'It's OK, Greg. He can stay.'

'That's very kind of—'

'Shut up, Dad!' Greg looked apoplectic. Mona was again struck by the family resemblance. They seemed to look most alike when they were furious, right down to the same throbbing vein in each of their temples. 'Liz, this is not your problem. You don't have to let some random stranger stay here just because you want to be helpful.'

'Except he's not a random stranger, is he? He's Professor Alexander Bircham-Fowler.'

'You know him?' asked Mona, surprised. She knew the professor was never off the news in Scotland, but was unaware that he was particularly well known in England.

'Oh, yeah. He's a world authority on the Virus. My friends and I have a lot of time for his views.'

'Friends?' Greg spat the word out. 'Those bloody communists from work, you mean? The lefties with the banners, and the websites full of nonsense?'

200

'The words you are looking for are "trade unionists".'

'Same difference.'

The two of them glared at each other. Greg looked away first.

'Fine. Do what you like. But I want it on record that I think this is a bad idea.'

Liz turned to them. 'Do you want to make him comfortable on my bed?'

Paterson walked over to the professor's chair. Greg didn't move, and the other three stared at him. Eventually he snapped. 'Oh for God's sake. Come on then, Dad.'

The professor moved, Paterson reappeared and closed the door firmly behind him.

'Bit of a discussion going on in the hall.'

'I can imagine.'

'Stroke of luck her being a fan of the professor.'

'I think she's quite politically engaged. See this.' Mona handed him one of the leaflets. 'Shame it provoked a lover's tiff, though.'

Paterson ignored the leaflet. 'Lover's tiff? You think they're an item?' A grin spread across his face.

'I just assumed so. Don't you know?'

Paterson shrugged.

'Before we came down here, when did you last speak to Greg?'

He mumbled something that could have been 'Christmas'.

'What was that?'

'December.'

'Oh. As in last Christmas?'

'As in Christmas two years ago. Anyway, if she is his girlfriend, he's done well. The face he's got on him it's a wonder any woman would look twice.'

'And there was me noticing a strong family resemblance.'

The front door slammed so hard that the whole flat rattled.

'Anyway, Guv, back to the matter of the prof. We're running out of time. We need him at that Health Check by noon tomorrow. We can't get an unconscious man onto a plane, even if we had his ID and Green Card. Without the Green Card we can't even get him on a train.'

'I made all these points on the phone to Stuttle.'

'And even aside from his immediate health issues, I'm not sure we can keep him safe. We don't know who these people are who are looking for him, or what they want with him, or with us. Shouldn't we be involving the Met?'

'Again, I made that point to Stuttle, and he was adamant that we were not to involve the police. So, not a whisper of Greg's involvement once we get back.'

'Guv, I really don't like this.'

'I said as much to Stuttle ...' There was a sound of ringing from the hall. 'And I bet that's him. We must have mentioned his name once too often. Beelzebub, Beelzebub, Beelzebub, and here he is in a puff of sulphur.'

'I think a puff of Hugo Boss aftershave is more Mr Stuttle's style.'

Liz appeared in the doorway, phone in hand. 'It's for you.'

'Sorry. Thanks.' Paterson took the phone, and disappeared back into the hallway, pulling the door closed behind him.

'I'll stick the kettle on,' said Liz.

Mona followed her into the kitchen. 'Where's your accent from?'

'Same place as the rest of me: Auckland, New Zealand. Are you from the same part of Scotland as Greg?'

She nodded. 'Edinburgh.'

Paterson appeared. 'That was Stuttle.'

'He pulled in those favours in extra quick time.'

'He's got a vault's worth of favours to draw on, as we know to our cost. Anyway, he's sending a guy with a car.'

A thought occurred to Mona. 'What do we do about Theresa, Guv? We can't just leave her down here.'

Paterson snorted. 'A delicate flower like Mrs Kilsyth? How on earth would she cope? It would be good to check she's OK, but I really don't want to use our mobile or hers.'

'She might still be at Maria's, if we could find a landline?'

'Can I borrow your phone one last time?'

'Of course. You know where it is.'

Mona sipped her tea. 'I still can't get over you knowing the professor.'

'Is he in danger?'

'We hope not,' said Mona, slightly evasively. Much as she liked Liz, she wasn't clear enough where her loyalties lay to confide any of their concerns in her. 'We're trying to keep his visit to London quiet…'

'And you'd like me not to mention he was here?'

She nodded. 'Is that OK?'

'Sure, if it helps Professor Bircham-Fowler.'

'Success!' Paterson came in smiling. 'Directory enquiries came up trumps. She's still at Bircham-Fowler's daughter's place. I think she's been telling Maria everything that's happened over the past twenty years; she sounded high as a kite. Anyway Maria is going to drive

203

her to the airport and try to get her on the next flight back to Edinburgh.'

'Do you think she'll be OK, Guv?'

'Let's hope so.'

'Did you tell her about the professor?'

'Are you kidding?' Paterson grinned. 'I'll tell her all about our adventures once his nibs is safely delivered to his Health Check and standing up to give his speech in Parliament.'

Mona couldn't help but think they were some way off that.

10

'Just here is fine.'

Bernard pointed at the end of Milton Street, a narrow street with tenements on either side, appalling parking, and a fine view of Arthur's Seat if your window was facing the right way. If he remembered correctly, this was where Maitland had his bachelor pad.

PC McGovern double parked the car, and put the hazard lights on. Grateful as he was for the lift, Bernard was very glad to be saying goodbye. The car journey had been fifteen minutes of interrogation about how they were responding to the memo (which he hadn't read), what their future plans would be for responding to these attacks on HET officers (which he didn't know), and what a fine cop like John Paterson was doing wasting his time with the HET nonsense (upon which he really couldn't speculate).

'Before you go.' PC McGovern reached past him into the glove compartment, and pulled out a folder. He leafed through it, then picked out three sheets of pink A4 paper. 'John, or whoever is currently in charge, needs to complete these and fire them over to Ian Jacobsen, our HET liaison person. He'll want to give you some guidance on this situation.'

'Thanks.'

'And can I give you some unsolicited advice?'

Bernard assumed this was a rhetorical flourish rather than an actual question. He nodded.

'Ease off on the search until you've spoken to Ian Jacobsen, or at least until John is back at work. No offence, but you lot are amateurs when it comes to dealing with some of the nasty bastards out there.'

He nodded, but the advice was moot. He had no intention of doing any further chasing after his Defaulter until someone could guarantee his safety. Someone who had a degree of concern for his well-being. Someone who would take his concerns seriously. Someone who wasn't Maitland.

'Thanks for the lift.' He opened the rear door, and picked up his worldly goods from the back seat.

'Take care.' PC McGovern drove off with a cheery wave over his shoulder.

Bernard set off down Milton Street, trying to remember exactly which of the grey stone tenements was home to Maitland's flat. He'd only been there once before, when an early start had involved him picking up Maitland directly from home. He did not remember his colleague being overly grateful for his lift.

The obvious thing to do would be to phone ahead, but he suspected that any pre-announcement of his arrival would result in him being redirected to a hotel, hostel, YMCA, park bench or any other venue that didn't interfere with Maitland's date night. Better to arrive and be shouted at than risk the door not being answered.

He walked up to the first of the tenements and ran an eye over the names on the entryphone. The shifting population of renters meant that most of the names were written on bits of paper, full of scoring-out and Tippexing. Even allowing for the quality of the copperplate, there wasn't anything resembling a Stevenson. The second tenement had a sun-faded entry that looked like it started with an S and ended -son. He filed it away as a possible, and moved on to a third door. There he found a doorbell with Stevenson typed onto a bit of paper and sellotaped over the previous nameplate. In a stroke of luck, the stair door was propped open. The first Maitland would know of his arrival would be the joyous moment when he opened the door and they were stood face to face. He ran happily up the stairs until he found another sellotaped 'Stevenson' and hammered loudly.

After a minute's delay, Maitland opened up holding a £20 note in his hand. 'You're not the Chinese takeaway.'

'No, I'm not.'

'Then why are you here, at my home, outside of working hours?' He pointed the banknote at him, in what Bernard felt was a rather aggressive manner.

'You know how my flatmate, Megan, phoned up earlier, in distress?'

'Yes, sorry to hear that, but—'

'She was attacked at her flat. A guy broke in and threatened her, had her by the throat and everything.'

'Sounds awful, but really a police matter ...'

'The guy who assaulted her was looking for me.'

'You?' He looked sceptical. 'Why would anyone be looking for you?'

Bernard felt his good humour slipping away, being replaced by the usual Maitland-induced irritation. 'I think it's to do with our search for Alessandra Barr.'

Maitland's face clouded over. 'I just cannot get a break on this case, can I?'

Bernard stared at him. 'You? *You* can't get a break? My flatmate is hurt, I get threatened and *you* ...'

Rage overcame any articulacy he may previously have possessed. 'Fuck you!'

'Bernard, language.' Maitland grinned. 'Have you spoken to the police?'

'Yes, and they've given me these forms for you to fill in.' He handed over the pink sheets.

'Do I have to do it now? Kate's here. This can wait until morning, surely?' He looked down and caught sight of Bernard's bag. 'Oh no, no way.'

'But Megan's kicked me out!'

'Go to a hotel!'

'I don't want to stay in a hotel on my own. What if someone is looking for me?'

Maitland looked less than concerned about this prospect.

'Anyway, it's not like you and Kate are going to be, you know, what with her Christian beliefs.'

Maitland stepped out into the hall, and pulled the door shut behind him. 'I know! But I was looking forward to seeing exactly how far the boundaries laid out in the Good Book could be stretched, which I can't do with you here.'

Bernard folded his arms. 'You owe me a favour.'

Maitland grunted.

'Shall I explain the nature of the favour to Kate?'

'Don't you dare!' For the first time in the entire conversation, Maitland looked animated. 'She doesn't know anything about Emma's bunny-boiling tendencies. Oh, God, I can't believe I'm saying this. You can stay for one night, and one night only.'

There were footsteps on the stairs, and a Chinese man appeared carrying an insulated bag.

'Do I get a share of the prawn crackers?'

11

Mona sat back on the sofa, her eyes closing again. Liz had left them in the house while she'd gone out to do some shopping. It was quiet, and she'd have been asleep by now if it wasn't for Paterson flicking through channels on the TV. He seemed unable to settle on watching anything. They'd had thirty seconds of the BBC, thirty seconds of Channel 4, a loud and derisive snort at some American cop show full of beautiful people, then flick, flick, flick up into the high numbers, then back down. She was relieved when he eventually settled on the BBC News Channel.

'Are you looking for something in particular, Guv?' she asked, yawning.

'Nope, just channel-hopping. I suppose I vaguely thought there might be some mention of the professor, but until he misses that Health Check he's not actually newsworthy.'

'He's not going to miss his Health Check, Guv. We'll get him there.'

'Of course, now that we've got the magnificent Cameron Stuttle pulling out all the stops to help us...'

There was a loud knock at the door.

'And that'll be the guy.'

'I'll get it,' said Mona.

She caught sight of herself in the hall mirror. The

reflection showed someone who had undeniably slept in her clothes, woken up, then slept in them some more. There wasn't much she could do about that, but she wished she'd taken the time to brush her hair, and show some semblance of professionalism to whichever colleague Stuttle had dispatched to get them. Oh well, too late now. She took off the chain, and cautiously opened up.

Greg was standing there, and judging by the look on his face he was not any better disposed toward them than he had been when he left. In fact, had it not seemed impossible, he looked even more annoyed.

'Where is he?' He pushed past her.

'Guv, Greg is here,' she shouted, by way of warning.

He flung open the door to the living room. 'I said, no more favours.'

Paterson looked up, his expression a mixture of surprise and annoyance. 'And I heard you loud and clear. Exactly what additional burden have I placed on you since you left here less than one hour ago?'

Greg's fury appeared to be reaching eruption point. She tactfully inserted herself into the flight path between Greg's fist and Paterson's face. 'What's going on?'

'I get into work only to get immediately summoned into the boss's office. He tells me I'm driving my dad and an unnamed VIP all the way to Scotland, which he is not happy about, by the way, but he's had orders from above.'

'That sounds like Stuttle, right enough.' Paterson sighed. 'This wasn't my idea, Greg. Honest. But it's obviously occurred to my boss that he could make use of the son he knows I have in the MET. Would have been nice of him to mention that on the phone.'

Greg stared at him. 'And he's got the clout to do that?'

'Clout implies that he commands respect and obedience. I'm sure there's a better word to describe a self-serving toe-rag whose main skill is an ability to accumulate favours. But either way, he gets things done.' He tapped the remote control distractedly on the side of the table while he thought things over. 'Did you say that you had already been working with me?'

'No. I thought it best not to.'

Paterson looked relieved. 'Good man. One thing for Stuttle to involve you in this, quite another for me to do it off my own back.'

Greg shook his head. 'Jesus. I have a life here, you know, Dad? One that was going just fine without any input from you. Now Liz isn't speaking to me, my boss has got the hump, and best of all, I've got to drive all the way to Edinburgh.'

'I can see why you are annoyed, son ...'

'Greg!'

'Greg. I am sorry about getting you and your,' he paused, 'friend involved in all this.'

Greg dismissed this with a wave of his hand. 'Well, I'm here now. We may as well get him moved. And if he takes ill en route it's your responsibility, not mine.' With a final glare in the direction of his father, Greg headed toward the bedroom.

Paterson swept an arm in the direction of the door. 'After you. Our carriage awaits.'

Mona smiled, and followed Greg.

12

'Bernard, take a proper helping, there's plenty for all of us!'

He smiled at Kate, and tipped a sizeable portion of beef in black bean sauce onto his plate, then ladled a couple of spoonfuls of rice and a handful of prawn crackers on top for good measure.

'Maitland always orders a mountain of food.'

'Which he generally enjoys eating,' muttered Maitland.

Bernard watched the happy couple on the sofa from his vantage point cross-legged on the floor. Not for the first time, he marvelled at Maitland's ability to secure himself extremely attractive girlfriends. He'd moved seamlessly from the blonde and willowy Emma to Kate, who was curly-haired, curvy and possessed of a smile so warm it was a miracle that any man could restrain himself from hugging her.

Maitland, on the other hand, had features that stopped several feet short of handsome. Perhaps his countenance was attractive when the muscles were pulled into something other than a sneer, but Bernard saw other facial expressions so rarely he'd be hard pressed to comment. Maitland's love life confirmed Bernard's long-held view that there was no woman who could not be successfully wooed if you had enough height and enough confidence.

Kate picked up the bottle of red and tipped the

remaining contents into Bernard's glass. He murmured his thanks, and took a large mouthful. It tasted both smooth and expensive. Good food, great wine, and best of all a look of glowering hatred on Maitland's face as he watched Bernard tuck in to the dinner he had paid for. It was almost pleasurable enough to make him forget that someone out there was looking for him, for reasons that he didn't understand.

'I'll put these in the bin.' Kate started to pick up takeaway cartons and plates.

'No, let me.' Bernard made to stand up.

'Don't be silly!' She motioned to him to sit back down. 'You've had a terrible shock. You take it easy.'

As soon as Kate was out of the room the look on Maitland's face morphed from miserable to murderous. He unwrapped his long legs and aimed a kick in Bernard's direction. 'You could have stayed in a hotel you know,' he hissed.

Bernard was hit with a redoubled willingness to help Kate, and get out of reach of her boyfriend's foot. He picked up the remaining plates. 'Not with some unidentified hard man looking for me.' He backed out of the living room, with Maitland still glaring at him, and shouted back. 'For all I know Alessandra Barr's boyfriend wants to kill me. I mean we've both seen the photo of what he did to her.'

The living room held its silence.

'Alessandra,' said Kate. 'Is that Spanish or Italian?'

Maitland pushed past Bernard and helped himself to a beer from the fridge. 'We shouldn't be talking shop.'

'It is Italian, I think,' said Bernard, ignoring him. 'Which is interesting, now that I come to think about it. We haven't really explored that angle. Maitland, do we

213

have any contacts in the Scottish-Italian community that might know her? And it's OK, I didn't want a beer.'

'It's OK, you weren't being offered one.' He took a long drink. 'Hmm, tasty.'

'Maitland!'

He shot a sulky look at Kate, but opened the fridge. Bernard quickly retrieved a bottle of Bud before Maitland 'accidentally' shut his head in the door.

'Italian-Scottish.' Maitland's expression changed to one of grudging acceptance. 'Well for once, Bernie, I think you've come up with something that's not totally a bad idea. There's a guy I worked with when I was a cop who was Italian. Well, of Italian descent anyway. Jimmy Rossi. Give me two minutes.'

Bernard and Kate installed themselves in front of the TV. She flicked through the channels, but kept the sound muted, which Bernard took as a signal that she was really after conversation. 'Sorry for ruining your date night.'

She patted his knee. 'There will be plenty other date nights. Maitland would never have forgiven himself if anything had happened to you tonight.'

Bernard wondered, not for the first time, if Kate had an entirely accurate picture of her boyfriend. He also wondered how someone as intelligent as Kate – who was, according to Maitland, on course for a First in her degree – could possibly be gullible enough to swallow Maitland's nice guy persona. Maybe the fact she was studying Divinity was something to do with it. She was probably pre-programmed to see the good in everyone, even Maitland. He forced his lips into a smile. 'Well, he is very considerate.'

Kate settled on the TV news, and current affairs took up all of Bernard's attention. The Virus was not the first item, which was good because there were obviously no heightened threats. It was also bad, because it meant that the Virus had slipped from being the lead item to being routine news to be fitted in between cabinet rebellions, trade talks and the *And Finally* heart-warming closer. Virus news coverage had passed from acute to chronic.

The ad break came on and he realised that Maitland hadn't reappeared. From the way she was staring at the door, Kate seemed to have the same thought. 'Is Maitland still on the phone?' she asked.

'I'll go and see.'

He knocked gently on the bedroom door. 'Maitland?'

His colleague was sitting on the end of the bed, his phone in hand. 'I think we're in trouble.'

Bernard felt a sudden weakness in his legs. He sat down heavily beside Maitland. 'Oh, God. Why?'

'I've just had a very detailed family history of the Barrs. Apparently they're a big Glaswegian drug family ...'

'How could you not know that? You were in the police!'

'Yeah, for a whole eighteen months before I got seconded to the dead-end street of the HET. And I was based in Edinburgh. I could have told you who was dealing in Leith or Craigmillar but expecting me to know the ins and outs of the West Coast suppliers is a bit much.'

'OK, sorry. I'm just feeling a bit nervous. I don't like the thought of a major bunch of drug dealers visiting me at home.'

'You're fine. Stop worrying.' His brusque reassurance was slightly undermined by him walking through to the hall and locking and bolting his front door. Bernard followed him but was shooed back into the room, and

Maitland pulled the door shut behind them. 'Kate doesn't need to hear all this. Anyway, the Barrs. Or as they were originally, the Baresi family. Arrived here from the backwoods of Italy, and set themselves up in Glasgow back in the 1920s. The first thing Papa Baresi did was anglicise the family name, hence the Barrs.'

'But Alessandra is a totally Italian name.'

'I know. Old Man Baresi thought changing his name would make it easier to fit in, but from the sound of things their name was the only thing they changed. They kept all the Italian traditions, and later generations went overboard on the Italian first names.'

'Why didn't they change their name back to Baresi?'

'I don't know! This is all third-hand via my colleague; I'm not an expert on the history of the Glaswegian Italian community. But if I had to speculate, I'd say that because they did such a bang-up job of creating the Barr brand as being a bunch of nutters who would stab you as soon as look at you, they probably thought it was too good to waste.' He stood up. 'I'm just going to check that lock again.'

'Oh dear.' Bernard sat down again on the edge of Maitland's bed, and tried to breathe. 'I'm not sure that this is making a lot of sense. I'm getting the impression from our investigations that Alessandra Barr is a prostitute, working in Edinburgh. Doesn't really fit in with her being from a big Glasgow family. Or with her being a prostitute.'

'But the Glaswegians were looking to move into the East Coast drugs market – there was a memo or something?'

Bernard glared at him. 'Yes, Maitland, apparently there is a memo.'

'I'm going to have a look at that paperwork Police Scotland gave you as soon as I get back.'

Bernard realised to his extreme dismay that Maitland had just picked up his coat. 'Back?'

'Yeah, don't wet yourself, but I'm going to have to escort Kate back to her halls.'

'Oh.'

'I'm not having her travelling back alone with these nutters out there. You'll be fine here. Just be sure to lock the door behind us.'

'Maitland, am I in danger?'

Maitland paused for rather longer than Bernard would have liked. 'Short answer, Bernie, is that I don't know. We need to get rid of that mad bat Carlotta tomorrow, then as soon as she's out the door we're talking to Police Scotland. We've got a contact for them, haven't we, on those sheets you gave me?'

Bernard nodded.

'We're going to have to put your case on hold until they tell us it's safe to proceed. Maybe they can get us some back-up, or something. Anyway, Paterson will be back soon and all this will be his problem.' He stood up and shouted, 'Kate, come on, I'll see you home.'

Bernard hovered in the hallway as Kate pulled on her coat. She looked anxiously at the two of them. 'Is everything OK? You two were closeted away in there for ages.'

'Fine, yes, no problem.' He attempted a smile. 'Just work stuff. Sorry again about ruining your night.'

'And again – don't be silly. Goodnight, Bernard.' She threw her arms round him in a bear hug, provoking a look of outrage from Maitland which under any other circumstances would have delighted him.

'Lock the door behind us, and stay out of my room.'

Bernard nodded. 'Be quick.'

THURSDAY

BREATHING DIFFICULTIES

I

Mona was losing grasp of time. Once they'd left London and turned onto the motorway, the drive had grown increasingly monotonous, without buildings or landmarks to relieve the tedium. She felt like she'd been staring at the same dark nothingness for ever, but her watch showed 2am, which meant they'd only been driving for two hours. She wasn't sure she could bear another five hours of this.

Greg seemed to sense her boredom. 'Feel free to fall asleep. I won't be offended.'

'Thanks, but I'm too wound up.' Her bones were weary and aching, but her mind was racing, struggling to process the events of the last two days. Some shut-eye would be good. At the moment the obstacles in their way seemed huge, and her mind was already worrying about the fallout of their trip once they were safely back in Edinburgh. Sleep, in her experience, tended to bring perspective; a couple of hours' solid snoozing and she'd be ready to deal with whatever else this journey would throw at her.

'I could turn the radio on if you like?'

'Nah. Don't want to disturb either of our sleeping beauties.' The professor and Paterson were sound asleep on the back seat, their heads lolling from side to side as the car purred along the empty roads.

'It's been an eventful few days...'

Mona sensed this was the start of a conversation, and felt grateful to Greg for making the effort. From his point of view, it must be bad enough having to drive them through the night, without having to keep her entertained as well. 'Yeah. Thanks so much for your help. We'd definitely not have got this far without you, and I know you didn't want to get dragged into all this.'

'No, it's all right. Doing things you don't really want to do comes with the territory of being a cop. I'm more worried about Liz getting caught up in all this.'

'Sorry. I really liked Liz. I take it she's your girlfriend?'

'Sort of. We're very different, as I'm sure you saw. So we get along for a bit, then I'll say something about the difficulties for the police of responding to the Virus and we have a huge argument, and it's all off again.'

Mona wondered if Greg was any less difficult to live with than his father. 'Well, I'm glad you're friends at the moment, because she did us a pretty massive favour.'

'Yep. And she was happy to do so. As she said, she's a huge fan of the prof.'

'You didn't know that before you took us there?'

'No. I should listen more carefully to what Liz is ranting about.' He laughed. 'Don't take this the wrong way, but I'd have given it a miss if I'd known. Liz can be a bit of a nightmare when she's on her soapbox. She'd get herself into all kinds of trouble just to prove a point of principle.'

'What do you know about the Health Collective that she's involved with? Is it all legal?'

'Oh yeah, despite our words back there it is all legitimate trade union stuff. Are they not active in Scotland?'

'Not that I'm aware of.'

222

'Well, according to Liz, the Health Collective thinks the sun shines out of the prof's nether regions. She gave me a pretty thorough run-down of his good points when she was shouting at me in the hall earlier.'

'Oh yeah?' said Mona, intrigued. 'And what are they?'

'Well, her agitator mates think he's the only person who is actually admitting there is a problem. The politicians have agreed their consensus approach to the Virus, which is great in terms of letting the scientists and everyone get on with trying to tackle the problem, but it does mean that they all stick to the line that everything is under control. And the State of Emergency means there's a limit to how much the unions and voluntary sector can do without getting into trouble. Liz is always complaining about the ban on demonstrations, for example, not even allowing immune people to gather in big groups. But she says Bircham-Fowler stands up and tells it like it is.'

'Like it is? And what exactly *is* it like?'

'Well, I'll give you one example. Liz is always banging on about the monthly Health Checks being too far apart to do any good. And that's one of Bircham-Fowler's hobby horses. He'd have them weekly if it was up to him.'

'He's not wrong on that one. By the time someone ends up on our desk, assuming the referral doesn't get lost in the system which it frequently does, it's five weeks since they had a Health Check, then it can take us a couple of weeks to find them. That's a long time for someone to be out there, possibly infectious. Add into that the fact that they're sharing needles or sleeping rough ...'

'Yup, a health disaster waiting to happen. But where would the resources come from to increase the HET team four-fold to enforce a weekly regime?'

'Is that the kind of thing you say to Liz that gets you into trouble?'

He threw his head back and laughed. 'Yes, that's exactly the kind of thing that gets me into trouble.'

Mona smiled. Despite the situation, Greg's laughter was infectious.

'I do love Liz, but sometimes I think she is so naïve. The government didn't make up the State of Emergency with the sole mission of stopping dissent. There really is a Code Black emergency going on. But then I remember that she and her colleagues are right at the sharp end of all this. They're the ones with people coughing and spluttering all over them, and people dying in their arms. And with the unions muzzled, no one's speaking for them.'

She nodded. Like Greg, she could see both points of view. 'So this thing with Liz, is it on or off at the moment?'

'It was all off, and to be honest I thought she might tell me to sling my hook when I phoned up to ask a favour.'

'Lucky for us she's a forgiving sort.'

'She's great. And I think she was quite impressed to have the professor to stay, so maybe I'm back in the good books. Was my dad asking if Liz and I were together?'

'I think he did wonder. I take it you haven't mentioned her to him?'

'Nope. None of his business.' He looked over at her. 'Do you think I'm being harsh with him?'

'Don't ask me. I'm still struggling to picture the Guv as somebody's dad. What was he like when you were growing up?'

'Absent a lot of the time, but you know what police work is like. Pretty strict when he was there. So, in classic bitter child of first family style, it irks me a bit when I hear about him playing football with his younger kids, and going to school concerts and stuff. My brother and I would have liked a bit more of that.'

'He must have done something right. After all, you followed him into the force.'

'I suppose. So, have you got it all sussed with your folks?'

She laughed, softly. 'Hardly. I'm the world's worst when it comes to dealing with parents. I've only very recently got round to telling my mum that I'm gay.'

There was the sound of spluttering from the back seat. Mona turned round and stared at her boss. Paterson's eyes were still closed, and he was sitting perfectly still, not even apparently breathing. His impersonation of a sleeping man was fooling no one.

Professor Bircham-Fowler's head lolled to one side, and bumped against the side of the car. Mona thought she saw his eyes flutter, his eyelashes lifting for a second before returning to rest. A moment later a lengthy fart emanated from his direction. Paterson used this as a pretext to waken up, continuing to ham it up with some look-I've-just-woken-up stretches.

'Think he's starting to come to.' Paterson gave him a gentle prod. 'Professor?'

There was no response. Bircham-Fowler's head flopped back against the leather, and he started to snore again.

'Try him again in half an hour, Guv. I'm sure I saw his eyes nearly open.' She turned round, smiling, wondering if Greg had caught the charade on the backseat. To her surprise, he was staring at the road, his face creased with concern.

'Trouble?'

'I think we've got company.' He nodded toward the back of the car. She turned, and saw another set of head-lights about twenty feet behind them. It was the only other car in sight.

'That car's been keeping pace with us. It's a pretty quiet road and I've been speeding up and slowing down, but it's not shown any interest in overtaking us.'

'Have they been following us ever since we left Liz's?' asked Paterson.

'I don't think so. It's only about twenty minutes since I started noticing them.'

'But we're in an unmarked police car. If they haven't been tailing us since Liz's how would they have found us?'

'I don't know.' His tone was defensive. 'I deliberately didn't use my own car in case they'd clocked it earlier.'

'Someone could have told them.' Paterson peered over his shoulder. 'An inside leak?'

'I don't think anyone other than my boss knows about this little jaunt at my end. He was making noises about this being a discreet operation so I'm pretty sure he'll have been warned not to discuss it.'

'So, what do we do now?' asked Mona. 'Try and shake them off?'

'Pretty much impossible if they already know where we are going.'

'You could try putting some distance in between us and them.'

Greg clicked his teeth as he thought about the options. 'I don't want to speed. If they are police it gives them a perfect excuse to pull us over.' He looked again in his rear-view mirror. 'In fact, I'm pretty keen not to find out what happens if we stop.'

'You think they'd try to arrest us?'

226

'Possibly, if "they" are the police. After all, all they need to do is keep the Prof detained long enough to miss his check, which is less than ten hours away now. Any copper worth his salt could come up with enough excuses to detain him for three or four hours at least.'

'They wouldn't have grounds to arrest him.'

'No, not legitimate ones, and it wouldn't be easy for them to arrest on some made-up charge, what with me being a serving MET officer, on official business … but like I say, all they need to do is hold us up for a good long while.'

'And what if they're not police?'

'I think we have to assume that it wouldn't end well.'

They drove in silence for a few seconds, each thinking about the possibilities. Mona's mind was coming up with scenario after scenario. They could be driven off the road. They could be forced to a halt, and the professor kidnapped. They could all be detained, by persons unknown. She wished again that she'd had some sleep, to help her sort out the likely from the fantasy.

'Dad?'

'Yeah?' Paterson was fully engaged in staring at the headlights of the car behind them.

'We don't know what we're dealing with here. Maybe you should phone your boss and ask for instructions. I know you don't want to use your phone in case it's being hacked, so why don't you use mine.' He handed it to him. 'Less chance that anyone has messed around with that.'

Paterson sighed. 'Fair enough. After all, Stuttle got us into this, so he can tell us what to do next. If we're really lucky he might even tell us what's actually going on here.'

Mona and Greg listened to the one-sided phone conversation. The monosyllables used by Paterson gave little away about the content of the conversation. When he hung up, Mona was surprised to see a broad grin on his face.

'These cars are incredibly easy to hack, according to Stuttle. They've all got a chip in them to allow them to be traced if they're stolen, and apparently if you are a technology geek who knows what you are doing you can hack into that. And Stuttle said, and I quote, he knew the MET idiots would be stupid enough to use a pool car, so he's prepared for this eventuality.'

'Has he prepared for the eventuality of this MET idiot dumping you all on the hard shoulder and leaving you to it?'

Mona leapt in. 'How exactly has he prepared?'

'He's got a couple of guys driving south, even as we speak.'

'Where are we meeting them?'

'Locksbridge Services. Says it does a great full English.'

'So we ditch the car and drive on with them?'

'Even better, we deliver the professor into their tender care and they do the rest.' He grinned. 'Sorted.'

'And did Mr Stuttle deign to tell us who is pursuing us up the M1, or give any indication why?'

'You heard me ask those very questions, but all I got in return was an "all in good time, John". But, as I said, our part in all this is coming to an end, thank Christ.'

'We're not there yet, Guv. These clowns following us could try something. And how are we even going to know who Stuttle's people are? There's lots that could—'

Her concerns were interrupted by a burst of flatulence from the back seat. She turned to see the professor staring at her wide-eyed.

'It's OK, Professor Bircham-Fowler, you are quite safe.'

Recognition came into his eyes, followed immediately by panic. He looked round the car. 'Tess? Where is she?'

'On her way back to Edinburgh, Professor,' said Paterson. 'Travelling in considerably more style than we are.'

'And my daughter, please tell me she hasn't come to any harm?'

'She's fine, Professor,' said Greg. 'Some of my MET colleagues are keeping an eye on her house.'

The professor sighed, and rubbed his temples with the palm of his hand.

'How are you feeling?'

'My head hurts. What happened to me?'

'We think you were injected with a sedative.'

'Poisoned? Oh, dear Lord. Dear, dear Lord.' He shook his head. 'I've made a terrible mess of everything, haven't I? I should never have taken off like this.'

'I think you've been rather manipulated, Professor,' said Paterson. 'Anyone would have reacted the same way when they got that photograph. Your family has to come first.'

Greg snorted.

Mona jumped in before Patersons senior and junior started fighting again. 'The events of the last few days indicate that you've upset someone. Any idea who that might be?'

'I've absolutely no idea,' said the professor, and sighed. 'But I do agree that my reputation is under attack. O tempora! O mores!'

She looked at Greg, who shrugged. For the first time in their journey she wished Bernard was there. He would have got on with the prof like a house on fire, and his translation skills would have been useful.

'O what, Professor?'

'It means, what times we live in.'

Mona thought for a moment. 'I'm still not quite sure what you mean.'

'I mean, the world has gone mad. Since the Virus hit, all our values have been turned upside down. In the good old days you discredited academics by finding them with a rent boy. My entire career would have been over with a *Daily Mail* exclusive entitled "Top Boffin in Kinky Gay Sex Scandal".'

Paterson tutted. 'Yup, read a few of those articles in my time.'

'But nowadays, nobody would be either surprised or particularly bothered if I was homosexual. In fact, I would probably go up in the estimation of some of my students. No, in today's Virus frenzy if you really want to ruin the career of a virologist the one thing that would guarantee it would be missing a Health Check.'

'Well, that's not going to happen, Professor,' said Paterson, cheerfully. 'We're going to get you to that Health Check, and into the Parliament.'

Mona looked over at Greg, who was staring into his mirror again.

'They're speeding up,' he said quietly.

2

Someone was trying to get in. Bernard, who had not moved from his position in the hallway since Maitland left, listened to the sound of a key scraping round in the lock.

'Maitland,' he said quietly, 'is that you?'

'Who's Maitland?' asked a low, gruff voice that he did not recognise. His heart leapt somewhere in the direction of his tonsils, and he looked round the hallway in a frantic attempt to locate a weapon. Should he run through to the kitchen and find something, or would his time be better spent phoning the police? Did he still have PC McGovern's number somewhere?

There was a burst of laughter from the other side of the door, laughter that was childish, mocking, and annoyingly familiar. He peered through the spyhole and saw Maitland doubled over in hysterics.

'Of course it's me. Now take the bolt off the door, you tool.'

Bernard closed his eyes. If he made it through the next week alive, he was going to dedicate the rest of his life to torturing Maitland. His starting point would be giving Kate a good talking-to about what she had got herself into, and how she could do so, so much better.

'Hurry up, Bernie!'

Bernard undid the bolts as quickly as he could, which

wasn't very quickly at all as his hands were still shaking. He pulled the lower bolt back too quickly and caught his finger in it, causing a little row of bloody dots to appear on his skin. Maitland ambled in, grinning.

'That wasn't funny.'

'Yeah, sorry.' His grin turned into a yawn, giving Bernard a view of his fillings and tonsils. He pulled open a door. 'This is the spare room. And remember, you are here for one night, and one night only, so don't get comfy.'

Bernard peered in. Comfy was a danger he didn't think he would be encountering. Given the dimensions of the 'room' he was looking at, claustrophobia or lack of oxygen might be a bigger threat.

'Is this really your spare room? It barely meets the definition of the word room. It's more like a closet.'

'That'll suit you perfectly then, won't it?' he smirked. 'Being closeted?'

'I'm not … oh never mind.' There were more important issues to address than engaging with Maitland's ever-present homophobia. 'Maitland, I don't see a bed.'

'It's in there. It's just got a few things on top of it.' He picked up a brown cardboard box marked 'Uni Stuff' in black marker pen, and dropped it in the hallway. 'See.'

A square foot of red and grey duvet cover was revealed.

'Anyway, I'm having first shot at the bathroom. I'll give you a knock about half-six, OK?'

'Yeah. I'll just carry on excavating my bed, shall I?' He turned round but Maitland had already disappeared into the bathroom. Bernard could hear him noisily relieving himself and singing at the same time. He manoeuvred another three boxes of 'Uni Stuff' out into the hallway, followed by two well-stuffed plastic bags of football

232

memorabilia. Underneath this was a layer of shoe boxes and several bags of what looked like designer clothing. Once all of this was removed he was in a position to confirm Maitland's theory that there was actually a bed in the room, albeit one with an extremely flat duvet. He pulled the cover off, and found a very large, very dead spider lying on the sheet. He picked it up by one of its legs and flung it after the other junk.

'All settled in then?'

'Do you have a lot of guests, Maitland?'

'What were you expecting? Fluffy towels and a chocolate on the pillow?'

'What is all this stuff anyway? Why do you need so many pairs of trainers?'

Maitland shrugged.

'And do you actually wear any of this stuff?'

'What are you – my mother?' Maitland pulled a tracksuit top out of a bag, examined it for a moment and shoved it back in. 'Anyway, I can't wear this stuff *now*.'

'Why not?'

He sighed. 'Bernard, let me explain how men's fashion works, seeing as your dress sense suggests it's not a concept you've ever come across. It all begins with some old lady brand that a hot-shot PR person decides is going to be the next big thing. Early adopters of fashion, such as myself, buy into this and spend a small fortune on the stuff. Then you start seeing the brand appearing on the football terraces, and suddenly every ned in Scotland is wearing the same overpriced gear as you.' He dug into a bag and produced a distinctive fawn checked scarf. 'A case in point. And you know it's time to move on.'

'But why not throw all this stuff out, or give it to charity?'

'Well, I spent a lot of money on it, and it might come back into fashion.'

'You are crazy, Maitland.'

'Yup, but women love me, and you are supposedly back on the market looking for some lady-loving so watch and learn. Now shut up and go to sleep.' He threw the bag he was holding into the far reaches of the closet, where it hit the wall and spread its contents across the floor.

'Maitland, what do we do if someone does turn up here tonight?'

'They won't. And if they do, the door is securely locked and we'll have plenty of notice. Go to sleep, Bernard.'

Go to sleep, Bernard. As if it was just that easy. He stared at the ceiling of Maitland's spare room, then sat bolt upright. He could hear footsteps on the stairs. It was probably nothing; after all, there were five other flats in the building, and they could be returning home to any one of them. The footsteps stopped, and so did Bernard's breathing. Should he waken Maitland? Probably a false alarm but better to be prepared. He crept out into the hall. He was nearly at Maitland's room when he heard the unmistakeable sound of girlish giggling. He slid over to the front door and looked through the spyhole at two young women opening the door opposite. *Neighbours.*

He slunk back to his own room, immensely grateful that he hadn't woken Maitland; he would never have heard the end of it. He climbed back into the dirty sheets of his temporary refuge, and wondered if tomorrow could get any worse than today had been. What could top the day that had started with him being shouted at by a politician and ended with him being threatened by people who sounded more than capable of carrying out their warning? And just to add to the joy of the day, this threat, as well as putting the fear of God into him, and limiting his ability to do his job, also seemed to have stomped all over his first chance at romance since his marriage broke up. Megan, lovely Megan, with the ex-boyfriend who was apparently so much handier than him in a crisis. He probably had better fashion sense too.

And now he was here, stuck in the junk room of a man who spent every working day needling him about his lack of machismo. He really didn't have to bother; over the past few months the universe had made plenty of assaults on his masculinity – he'd already got the message. He'd been beaten up so badly on the Weber case he'd ended up in hospital. *Wouldn't have happened to a real man.* His wife had left him because he refused to get her pregnant. *Real men impregnate anything with a pulse without a second thought.* His female colleague had nearly had her jaw broken. *Real men keep their team mates safe.* And the worst bit, the part that really did make him feel like he had the testosterone levels of a teenage girl, was that he did feel safer with Maitland around.

He sighed. Wallowing in self-pity was making him feel marginally better, but it certainly wasn't making him feel any sleepier. Maybe counting his blessings would relax him enough to drop off. And there were plenty of people out there much worse off than him. Carole, for instance, with her sore jaw and her teenager troubles. Anyone that wasn't yet immune was also much worse off than him. And poor Alessandra Barr, the woman with two black eyes. Or at least two black eyes six months ago when she'd got her Green Card.

235

Six months ago. Six months. That had to be unusual, right? The whole Green Card regime had been established over eighteen months ago, and even a year ago it would have been odd to come across someone without a card. The regime made it impossible to even get a cup of coffee without showing them your credentials. How had Alessandra survived without a Green Card? And why hadn't anyone asked any questions about why she was only requesting one now? Unless ...

He dug his bag out from under the shower of designer clothes, and found his laptop. He logged in and opened up Alessandra's file. He went over the facts again.

Alessandra Valentina Barr
Born: 23 April 1995
Place of birth: Glasgow

It didn't make sense. If Alessandra was part of the Barr clan, why was she working in Edinburgh? Surely it wouldn't be safe? And he didn't know much about gangster families, beyond what he'd seen in films, but he was pretty sure that their womenfolk didn't usually walk the streets touting for business.

Six months. *Six months* with a Green Card. A thought occurred to him. He looked at the time, and decided that it was too late to phone Marcus. He stared at his laptop for a moment or two, then decided to phone anyway.

To his relief the phone was answered on the first ring. 'Bernard! What can I do you for?'

'Sorry to ring so late.' He heard a voice in the background. 'Am I disturbing you?'

'No, that's just Bryce. You caught us, I'm afraid.'

'Really?' He found himself wondering about his colleagues' relationship – what exactly had he caught them doing? Oh God – one night in Maitland's box room and he was turning into him.

'Yes, we were in the middle of a guilty pleasure. We've spent the whole evening rewatching season two of *Buffy the Vampire Slayer*. Call me an old romantic but I do like the early episodes with Angel. Never quite took to her other boyfriends ...'

'Anyway,' Bernard said, eager to head Marcus off from an episode by episode discussion, 'sorry to intrude so late, but I was wondering if you could look something up for me?'

'Sure,' he sounded surprised. 'Something that just couldn't wait, eh? Must be important. Hang on a mo while I get my laptop on to my knee. OK, fire away.'

'Can you search for Alessandra Barr's death being registered?'

'Her death?' He laughed. 'Do you now have so little faith in the HET's admin system that you're worried they've got you chasing after dead people?'

'Something like that.'

He listened to the sound of Marcus typing.

'Only finding one dead Alessandra Valentina, and I'm afraid that was a six-year-old girl back in 2001.'

'Can you check the birth date of that Alessandra?'

Marcus read the date to him. 'Ooh, that's a little bit interesting, isn't it?'

'Certainly is. Thanks, and sorry again for disturbing you. Enjoy your remaining vampires.'

Bernard returned to the hall, double-checked the view from the peep-hole, then dithered outside Maitland's room. He would probably be furious at being disturbed, but right now he didn't care. 'Maitland.'

He was answered by a snore. Apparently his colleague

237

was not having the same difficulties falling asleep that he was. He pushed open the door and crept in. In a slightly louder voice he said, 'Maitland.'

This still failed to rouse him, so he knelt by the bed, and gave his colleague's shoulder a shake. He woke up with a start, his arms flailing.

'What?' He switched on the bedside lamp. 'Bernard, what the fuck? Is somebody here?'

'No.'

Maitland sat up, the duvet falling off him to reveal a lack of nightwear. 'Then you better have a very good reason for waking me up.'

'I need to tell you something.'

Maitland smirked, and pulled his duvet back up to his neck. 'Is it that you've been madly in love with me since the moment we met, and made this whole story up just to get access to my bedroom? Because, no offence, but I'm really not interested.'

'Oh for God's sake, Maitland. I'm not gay, and even if I was and you were the last man on earth, it'd still be no.'

'It'd be easier to believe you if you weren't kneeling semi-naked at the side of my bed.'

Bernard glared at him.

'OK, I'm done. What do you want to tell me?'

'Alessandra Barr.'

'Yep.'

'She's only had a Green Card for six months.'

'Uh-huh. So?'

'So how was she surviving without one?'

He shrugged. 'Cash-in-hand economy.'

'But you need a Green Card for everything – shopping even.'

238

'Maybe she got busted, and that's what made her get a card.'

'Or maybe she's only been in the country six months.'

Maitland finally looked interested in the discussion. 'You're thinking trafficking?'

'I think it's a possibility. I just got Marcus to check to see if the death of an Alessandra Barr had been registered. There was the death of a six-year-old girl registered in 2001, with exactly the same birth date as our Alessandra. They could have used her birth certificate to get the Green Card.'

'And you think the Barrs did this?' Maitland yawned and scratched his chest while he thought. 'A bit callous recycling their dead child's name for one of their tarts.'

'And it still doesn't explain why she's working in Edinburgh, and not on their home turf. But I think there's definitely something in it.'

'Right. Tomorrow, we deal with the old bag Carmichael, get in touch with that Police Scotland liaison bloke, then you get hold of Marcus again. See if he can find anything else out about her on the system.'

'OK.'

'Now get out, close the door behind you, and no sneaking back in for another look at my perfect physique.' He turned off the light and plunged them both into darkness.

3

Mona was developing a crick in her neck from twisting round to watch the headlights of the car behind them. The car had been keeping pace with them for nearly an hour, speeding up as they accelerated, slowing down when required, and always keeping an even couple of car lengths behind them.

'It'll be hilarious if it turns out to be a couple of tourists in the car behind us,' said Paterson, 'just tailing us for a bit of company.'

'Well, let's hope that's the case, but either way we'll know soon enough,' said Greg. 'It's the next exit. Locksbridge Services.'

'Oh,' said the professor. 'Are we stopping?'

'Yes,' said Paterson, but before he could update the professor on their plans, Greg's mobile rang. 'It's Stuttle. Two seconds while I get this.'

'Am I still pulling off at this exit?'

Paterson ignored him and listened intently to the phone.

'Dad?!'

'Yes, yes, go for it!'

Greg swerved sharply off the motorway, hitting the accelerator hard as he did so. The car behind them, as they anticipated, continued to follow them, speeding up a little to maintain its usual distance.

240

'I can't tell if they are tailing us, or if they already know where we are going,' said Mona. 'They didn't seem particularly panicked when you swerved off the motorway like that.'

'If they're locked on to our tracker chip they might not be too worried about losing us. They know they can find us again.'

'Right, troops.' Paterson's head appeared between the two front seats. 'Stuttle's guys are about twenty minutes to half an hour away. They suggest that we get the prof into the service station, in the hope that there are other people around that will force everyone to be a bit civilised. Nice of them to phone up to tell us that because obviously we wouldn't have thought of it ourselves. Anyway, I suggest that Mona and the prof nip inside and have a nice bacon roll or two...'

'Actually I'd very much like to go to the toilet...'

'Mona can supervise that arrangement, sir. Greg and I will wait outside to see exactly what clowns emerge from that car once it finally stops. Is that OK with you, son – I mean, Greg?'

'Fine by me, Dad.'

'I'm a little bit unclear who you all are,' said the professor. 'I thought you all worked for the HET, yet you two appear to be related?'

'I'll explain when we get inside, Professor. Are you ready to move quite swiftly once we get out?'

'I'll do my best, but I'm not that fast at the best of times, I'm afraid.'

Greg turned into the forecourt of the service station. 'Best of luck, guys.'

Mona had her door open before the car even stopped. She yanked open the back door, and pulled the professor

241

upright, with, she suspected, some help from Paterson pushing him. Holding him firmly by the arm, she navigated the professor toward the building. Her pace was obviously faster than he would have liked and he stumbled several times.

'I'm sorry,' he said. 'Not too steady on my pins yet.'

'Understandable, sir, after what's happened to you.' They made it into the brightly lit foyer, just as the car that had been tailing them pulled into the car park. 'Toilets, Professor. I'll be right here – shout if you need me.'

The professor nodded, and she hoped he intended to be quick. With all due sympathy to recent events and the professor's age, this would not be a good time for any prostate difficulties. The bright lights of the services behind her made it difficult to see what was going on in the car park. It was like looking from a brightly lit stage down into the stalls. From what she could make out, the car that had been following them had parked up and turned its lights off. As yet no one had emerged, and she was too far away to see how many of them there were inside it. What were they waiting for? Further orders? Reinforcements? Greg and Paterson loitered by the side of their car, poised for action.

'That's better.' The professor emerged from the Gents. 'Much better.'

'Let's go order some food.'

Mona pushed open the door to the café and surveyed the room to identify the most populous section. It didn't take long – the food hall was completely empty, without a single table of customers.

'Damn.'

'Is something the matter?'

'No, no, Professor, everything is fine. Let's get you some food.'

She peered over the counter. There didn't appear to be any staff either. *Welcome to the Mary Celeste Service Station.*

'Hello?'

A tired-looking teenager appeared from the kitchen, bringing a waft of marijuana with him. 'Yeah?'

'Can we have a couple of bacon rolls and two coffees, please?'

He yawned and nodded. 'It'll be about five minutes for the rolls, is that OK? And the coffee machine is over there.'

He handed them two mugs and disappeared into the kitchen. So much for the safety of other people. It wouldn't take long for the men in the car park to suss all they had to worry about in the way of witnesses was one teenage stoner with a frying pan. She gave the room the once-over. There were no obvious exits other than the way they had come in. If they needed to leave, it was either retrace their steps, or head for the kitchen.

'Take a seat, Professor.' She filled up the coffee cups, all the time trying to see out into the darkness of the car park. There didn't appear to be any sign of movement.

'I really am most terribly sorry about all this.'

'Hardly your fault, Professor. You were manipulated into going to London.'

'And I let myself be manipulated. I'm long enough in the tooth to know how all this works. I've been in academia for over forty years, for goodness' sake! It's not like it's the first time my research has upset people. But whoever sent me that photograph hit on the one area of my life where I can't be entirely rational, though

I should have stopped and thought it through. With a little bit of reflection I might have seen it for what it was. I should have told Tess; she'd have known what to do. And you know, she's going to kill me when we get back.'

'Quite probably, sir,' said Mona, smiling. 'Out of interest, how many people knew you had a daughter?'

'Very few. I made no great secret of the fact, but it wasn't really something that came up in conversation. It's ancient history, really. Most of the people that I worked with then have moved on or retired. Except for Tess, of course. We've worked together for most of my academic life.'

'Apart from your stint in New York.'

The professor looked blank.

'You know, your time at university there in the 1980s?'

'I've never been to New York in my life. The whole place seems terrifying ... Why are you laughing?'

'I'm sorry, I was just thinking about how vigorously Mrs Kilsyth protects your reputation.'

He looked confused.

'Anyway ... back to today. I don't know what you're planning to say to Parliament, Professor, but some people seem very keen to stop you saying it.'

'I'll be saying publicly what I've been saying privately for quite some time. I'm planning to recommend a two-week nationwide quarantine. People confined to their own homes. I want everything shut: workplaces, schools, shops. Everything except emergency services.'

'Quarantines have been discussed before.'

'Not by me. And I have a certain,' he paused, as if uncertain how to phrase something. 'I have a certain credibility which means that I will be listened to by the press and the public. Voters, if you want to call them that.'

'Why haven't you raised the issue of quarantine before?'

'I've been under a lot of pressure not to. It's an incredibly unpopular policy. The government is worried about the loss of productivity. The retailers hate it, because we are already in recession, without taking away a whole two weeks of buying opportunities. Women's charities hate it because they predict, probably correctly, a rise in domestic violence. The police are ambivalent about it. They'd have a quiet couple of weeks but they're concerned about child protection and policing the lockdown. And the usual suspects are going mad about the civil liberties issues. In fact, the only people who like the idea are the health services.'

'So why suggest it now?'

'Because the Virus isn't behaving as it should. By now we should see the numbers of new infections tailing off. The rate of infection has been falling, but in recent weeks we've seen it beginning to rise again. I'm worried that this indicates ...'

'A third wave?'

They were interrupted by the sound of shouting from the car park.

'I think that's our cue to run, Professor.'

'Oh dear. Not again.'

Mona lifted the counter hatch and bundled the professor through. Holding him firmly by the arm, she booted open the kitchen door. The sole kitchen operative appeared to have fallen asleep next to a frying pan with rapidly cremating bacon, but woke up with a guilty start as the door opened.

'You can't be back here!'

'We're not staying.' She found the emergency exit and

hit the bar to open it with her bottom. 'Through you go, Prof.'

The burning bacon finally hit the smoke detector, which began to emit a shrill beeping, and distracted the cook from any further discussions with them.

'Where are we going?' asked the professor.

'We're just going to get ourselves out of the way while my colleagues deal with the situation.' She pulled the door shut behind her and peered into the darkness. After a second or two her eyes adapted to the gloom and she saw what she needed. 'Can we head in the direction of those trees?'

'It's very dark.'

'To our advantage in hiding.'

With a firm grip of the professor's arm, she pushed her way into the foliage. It was hard to tell how far back the trees went, but she could hear the sound of animals in the next field. If she could get them as far into the darkness as possible, they might be able to hide. She wished they could move faster, but she could hear the professor's breathing becoming increasingly laboured.

'Mona,' he panted. 'I'm afraid I need to stop.'

'A little further, sir.'

'I'm sorry, I can't.'

This would have to do. She propped him up against a tree. 'Are you OK?'

'Just need to,' he took a deep gulp of air, 'catch my breath.'

She peered back toward the service station. Even now that her eyes had adjusted to the lack of light it was difficult to discern anything in the darkness.

'Mona,' the professor whispered, 'who are these people?'

'I don't know, sir. As you yourself said your speech tomorrow upsets just about everyone. For all we know it's the militant wing of the small shop owners' association who don't fancy closing their doors for a couple of weeks.'

Personally, right at this moment she was less worried about who was pursuing them than what they were planning to do if they caught them.

There was a sudden burst of light. Someone had followed their route, opening the emergency exit. A lone figure was briefly silhouetted against the fluorescent glow from the kitchen. He stood there, and she could see the outline of his head looking one way then the other. To her horror, she saw him lift his arm.

'Professor, he's got a gun,' she whispered.

The professor grabbed both her arms, and pushed her violently against a tree. Wrong-footed, she tried to work out what he was doing. She was sure that she could fight him off, but she wasn't sure if she was being attacked. If she pushed him away, she risked creating a lot of noise, and drawing attention to where they were hiding.

She heard the muffled sound of gunfire. Was someone shooting at the Guv and Greg? The sound came again, and this time she heard the bullet explode into a branch near them. Not the stifled sound of distance gunfire, then, more the up-close sound of a gun with a suppressor. A gun which was currently being fired into the trees, probably at random, possibly in the hope that it would flush them out into the open. Whichever way you looked at it, though, the gunman was demonstrating a limited concern for their getting accidentally executed by a bullet.

The professor had the full weight of his body pressed

against hers, and she realised what he was doing. He was trying to protect her from being shot. It was a well-meaning gesture, and confirmed her suspicion that the professor was possibly the last decent human being on earth. Unfortunately, his chivalry was likely to get them both killed as there was nothing she could do to protect them with her arms pinned down. She lifted her hands up and pulled at the professor's arms.

'Come out, please. We don't want to hurt you.'

The voice was English. Neutral; it had no particular regional accent, but neither was it Eton-style posh.

'Come out, please, Ms Whyte—'

The voice broke off suddenly. After a brief second of unnerving silence, there was the sound of a thud.

'What's happening?' whispered the professor.

A bead of torchlight was making its way toward the trees. If the gunman got any closer they'd be cornered. The professor's grip on her arms was weakening, and she took the opportunity to push him away. He fell to the ground with a loud thump, twigs and leaves snapping as he landed. Mona winced at the noise. 'Stay there,' she whispered. 'I'll be right back, Professor.'

He didn't answer. Mona moved in the direction of the torch light. Her only hope was to surprise the searcher, knock him off his feet before he found them. Unfortunately, every move she made crunched or crackled. The light stopped moving – had he heard her? After a second's pause it moved on again, coming closer and closer to where she was. She waited until it was an arm's length away and lashed out.

There was a yelp and she pushed forward, kicking and shoving as she went. The flashlight fell to the ground, briefly illuminating her face.

'Mona Whyte?'

She grabbed the flashlight and shone it into the darkness. It lit up a familiar face, although she couldn't quite put a name to it.

'Ian Jacobsen, Police Scotland HET liaison.' He laughed, softly. 'I thought you would be more pleased to see me than this.'

4

'What do you think? Does it look tidy?'

Bernard looked up from the pile of papers he was trying to cram into a lever arch file. It was 8.45am, and they'd been there since seven shifting bits of paper around. There was no definition of tidy that the room could reasonably be deemed to have met. It didn't look tidy. It wasn't going to look tidy. In fact, he wasn't entirely sure they weren't making it look worse.

'I'd say it...'

'Morning, chaps.'

They both turned round, surprised at the intrusion into their office before opening hours, and saw Stuttle standing in the office doorway. He looked exhausted, distinctly grey around the gills, with huge dark circles under his eyes. The tiredness was offset by a surprisingly jolly grin. Bernard wondered what events were causing Stuttle to be both weary and cheery at the same time. Had he been up all night worrying about Mrs Carmichael's visit? He couldn't imagine much that would keep Stuttle awake. And short of Mrs Carmichael's immediate retiral from politics, he couldn't imagine much that would currently make him happy.

'Having a bit of a tidy up?' He looked round the room. 'Good work. Never hurts to polish the surroundings. After all, government ministers think the world smells of fresh paint and Mr Sheen. Anyway, did the minister give you an ETA for her visit?'

'No, sir,' said Maitland. 'I'd imagine it could be anytime today?'

'Ha! That's typical of Mrs Carmichael.' Stuttle smiled. 'Keep everyone hanging around, awaiting her arrival. I took the precaution of checking her movements with her diary secretary. She's got a breakfast meeting at the Royal College of Surgeons, then she's caught up in meetings with the Scottish government from 11am onwards, so if she's visiting it's going to be ...'

The office door opened, causing all three of their heads to swivel sharply in that direction, in the expectation of seeing the head of the Parliamentary Virus Committee enter the room. Instead, the decidedly bruised and battered face of Carole appeared.

Stuttle looked horrified, then recovered enough to speak. 'You must be Carole.' He leapt up to shake her hand. 'I'm Cameron Stuttle. That's one heck of a beating your face has taken.'

"Es. 'Allo.'

Stuttle pulled out a seat and shepherded her into it. 'Though it might be no bad thing for Mrs Carmichael to see the realities that you folk are facing in the field.'

'Won't she just think the HET's at fault for not protecting its staff though, sir?' asked Maitland.

Stuttle sighed. 'A fair point. Mrs Carmichael does have a remarkable ability to make everything the fault of the HETs.'

Marguerite appeared in the office doorway. 'Morning, everyone.' She stopped in surprise when she realised there was an additional person in the office. 'There are two people in to see the HET. They say they've got an

251

appointment, but I didn't want to disturb you before nine o'clock. Shall I send them up?'

'Oh, well,' said Stuttle, 'unless we're going to pop Carole into a cupboard for the duration of the visit, I guess she's going to meet the minister too.'

''reat.' Carole gave a thumbs-up and moved her damaged mouth into a shape that could have been a smile, but probably wasn't.

Stuttle advanced on Marguerite, his hand outstretched. 'I'm Cameron Stuttle, chief executive of the Scottish Health Enforcement Partnership. I'm sorry, I don't know your name.'

Marguerite looked over at them nervously, while she shook his hand. 'I'm Marguerite, one of the admin assistants here, Mr Stuttle.'

'And, Marguerite, were the visitors a curvaceous lady with rather uncontrollable auburn hair, and a tall pale, gentleman with dark hair?'

She nodded.

'Sounds like Carlotta Carmichael MSP and her assistant Paul Shore.'

'Oh my God.' Marguerite slapped a hand to her mouth. 'That woman's an MSP and I never even offered her a cup of tea or anything. She's been here about twenty minutes while I waited for you to be officially open.'

'Twenty minutes?' Stuttle looked pained. 'That will have put her in a good mood. Oh, well, let's get this over with. I'll come down and get them.'

As Stuttle followed her out of the office, the sound of Marguerite's voice drifted back. 'I'm pure mortified, I really am. I should have recognised her off the telly...'

'Carlotta's not going to seem so bad after a trip down the stairs with Marguerite.' Maitland grinned.

Bernard grunted in response.

'Come on, Bernard. Lighten up.'

'I'm just thinking we should have warned Stuttle about what happened to me last night.'

''ot 'appened?'

'I'll tell you later.' Maitland looked dismissive. 'Carlotta's not going to know anything about that.'

'I don't know. She seems to know a lot of stuff that she really shouldn't.'

'And you didn't believe me when I said she was a witch. Well, it's too late now. We'll just have to wing it, and ...'

He broke off at the sound of voices in the corridor. 'There is absolutely no need for you to be here, Cameron. I'm perfectly capable of meeting one of your teams, without you putting your usual sugar-coated spin on everything.'

'I'm just here, Minister, in case you have any questions or queries about strategy that I can usefully answer.'

Carlotta appeared in the doorway, framed by Stuttle and her tall, pale assistant.

'But seeing as you are here, maybe you could start being useful by introducing me to the HET team?'

'This is Maitland Stevenson, who as you know is in charge while John Paterson is on leave ...'

There was a brief snort. 'Yes, there is a conversation to be had about the lax attitude to annual leave in this office, but we'll get to that issue later.'

'And Bernard McDonald.' Bernard stuck his hand out toward Carlotta, and was ignored. Feeling foolish he folded his arms.

'And this brave woman is Carole ...' He stopped, clearly with no idea what her surname actually was.

'Brooks,' Bernard helped him out.

Carlotta glanced in Carole's direction, then her eyes widened as she caught sight of the bruises.

'And what happened to you?'

'An accident in the field, Minister. An operational hazard ...'

'And did the accident leave Carole unable to speak, Cameron?'

He looked annoyed but stepped away. Carole was doing a good impression of a bruised rabbit in a headlight.

'Vas an 'cident.'

Carlotta exchanged a look with her assistant, then let her eyes continue wandering round the room. She turned around as she did so, her heels clicking as she pirouetted through a full 360-degree view of the office. 'There is a distinct lack of organisation in this premises.'

Bernard kept his fingers crossed that she didn't notice the random pile of boxes they had pushed behind a partition screen. He held his breath as she stepped toward the screen. The only thing that could make her even more annoyed with them was if a box of files fell on her. Fortunately her twirling ended with her back to the partition.

'I had expected something a little less chaotic.'

'Well, you know how it is, Minister, with cuts to the budget that we have for administrative support ...'

'Administrative support! I'd say you are overstaffed with admin, judging by the fifteen minutes I spent downstairs listening to the young lady who showed us in conversing with her colleagues about every television programme that she watched last night, while singularly failing to do anything resembling work.'

She paused as if waiting for someone to leap to

Marguerite's defence. Bernard could think of nothing to say. On this issue, if no other, Mrs Carmichael was spot on. Marguerite's ability to avoid work was second to none.

Stuttle reluctantly stepped up to the plate. 'I don't think you can extrapolate from one instance…'

'But I'm not surprised about the lack of management oversight. I've long had concerns about the way the HETs are managed.' She paused again, as if waiting for Stuttle to defend them. He seemed to sense the possibility of another kicking, and kept quiet. She looked annoyed, and continued. 'For example, yesterday's fiasco at the Committee.' It was Maitland's turn to feel the full weight of her glare, but he looked unperturbed. 'That performance indicated that junior members of staff should not be attempting to deal with the complexities of a Parliamentary Committee. Why was the situation allowed to arise that John Paterson was on annual leave with no senior HET officer mandated to substitute for him?'

Stuttle looked over at the minister's assistant. Some unspoken message passed between them, and he leaned over toward his boss.

'These are operational matters, Minister,' he murmured.

She smiled up at him, with all the warmth of a polar bear hovering over a hole in the ice. 'I'm aware of that, Paul. Thank you for your assistance in keeping me right. But what I'm seeing here is the continuous mismanagement of operational issues, which may prompt us to have a review of the strategic direction of the HETs.'

Bernard had no idea what this meant, but judging by the colour Stuttle's face turned, he fully caught her drift.

'With all due respect, Minister, this mismanagement talk is nonsense.'

'Is it?' She arched an eyebrow. 'You can defend the health and safety management of the HET with *two* major incidents involving HET staff in one week?'

Oh God, she did know. He looked up at Maitland, who gave a tiny shrug in return. Bernard kicked himself. He should have told Stuttle the second he saw him; his omission had left his boss at a distinct disadvantage. Everyone stared at Stuttle and waited for his response.

'And how exactly are you defining "major", Minister?'

Their eyes all moved to Carlotta. It was like watching a tennis match, with bluffs and barbs being used as balls.

'Well, I think this lady's face says everything you need to know about the first incident. Perhaps you would care to clarify why the second incident is just a minor, everyday, run-of-the-mill occurrence?'

Stuttle remained silent, and Carlotta smiled, her point well made.

'Time, Minister,' her assistant tapped his watch.

Carlotta stopped smiling. 'Everything that I've seen here today confirms my suspicions. I don't think I have any alternative other than to recommend to my Committee colleagues that we need to immediately move to establish an inspectorate for the HET teams. We need some quality control.'

Stuttle stared back at her, poker-faced, and she turned her attention to Carole. 'Perhaps you could show me to the Ladies, before I leave?'

Stuttle followed them both to the door, which he closed firmly behind them. 'Toilet trip, indeed. She'll be logging every missing bit of paintwork en route to support her theories. And God help us all if there aren't any paper towels in the dispenser! I suppose that would indicate inadequate mechanisms at the HET for the stock control of sanitary supplies and necessitate an immediate parliamentary review? I mean, Paul, really, what the fuck was all that about?'

'Don't blame me, Cam, this is the minister's own idea.' He looked round the room. 'Though you lot didn't exactly help yourselves – look at the state of this place.'

'And what was the "second incident" she was banging on about?' asked Stuttle.

Maitland opened his mouth.

'On second thoughts, put it all in an e-mail to me. I need to be somewhere right now.' He looked round at them all. 'Not the best result we could hope for. Still, must be a world record between an agency being set up to do something and an inspectorate being established to tell them they're doing it wrong.'

'The minister has still got to get the idea through Parliament, so it's not exactly imminent, if it happens at all. Resources implications, and all that,' said Paul. 'Anyway, shall we?' He nodded toward the door.

'Tell your boss I want him in my office the minute he's back at work.' Stuttle pointed a finger at Maitland. 'The minute.'

The door slammed behind them, and suddenly the office seemed very quiet.

'You can tell Paterson about all this,' said Bernard.

Maitland grunted, and looked up as Carole came back in. 'Did she interrogate you all the way to the Ladies?'

''Es but I'm gunfitleble so not a pwoblem.'

'You're what?'

She sighed. Picking up a pen she scrawled a word on a bit of paper.

'Oh, you're *unintelligible*.'

'I need a cup of tea,' said Bernard.

'There's no milk.'

'I'll borrow some from the admin team.'

When he walked into the admin office, five pairs of eyes turned toward him. The one set that didn't was Marguerite's, who had her head in her hands. Her shoulders were going up and down.

'You won't believe what that visitor of yours said to her,' said one of the older administrators, accusingly.

'Was it something to do with working hard and not chatting about TV?'

Marguerite let out a cry of misery, not unlike the sound of a cat losing a territorial dispute. Five pairs of administrative professionals' eyes glared at him, daring him to continue.

'Can I borrow ... actually never mind, I'll go to the shop.'

He hurried out of the building before anyone shot him with a staple gun. He was surprised to find the sun was shining. After the frostiness of the morning's meeting it felt good to bask in the warmth of its rays. While the encounter couldn't have been said to go well, at least it was over. They'd have a cup of tea, and he'd make sure Maitland filled in the forms for Ian Jacobsen properly. With any luck Paterson would be back by tomorrow and no matter how annoyed he was with him, he would have to be more annoyed with Maitland as he was in charge. Bernard would be sure to tell Paterson 'I told you so', though he might do it in sufficiently academic language that Paterson wouldn't be clear enough on the point that he was making to yell at him. He turned the corner, heading toward the small newsagents that kept the HET team supplied with milk, newspapers and unhealthy snacks. Yes, things could be worse. He might even splash out on some Jaffa Cakes.

He became aware of the low grumble of a car's engine, which seemed to be driving along slowly just behind him. Suddenly, the sense of danger that Bernard had been nursing since the events at Megan's returned with a vengeance. Maybe the driver was just stopping to ask directions, but he didn't want to risk it. He turned sharply on his heel, aiming to return in the direction of the HET offices, and bumped straight into a solidly built bald man. He attempted to dive past him, but found his arm being grabbed. Within seconds his other arm was being forced up his back, and he was pushed toward what he could now see was a black BMW.

Without quite registering his feet leaving the ground, he found he was sitting on the back seat, sandwiched between the bald man and a guy in a brown leather jacket. 'Where are we going?'

'The boss wants a word.'

Bernard wondered if he had his mobile with him. Could he dial 999 without anyone seeing him do it? His hand edged toward his pocket.

'Touch your phone and I'll break your arms. Put your hands where I can see them.'

Bernard put his hands on his thighs and watched them tremble.

This made the bald man laugh. 'Relax, pal, if the boss wanted you dead you'd be travelling in the boot. Just sit back and enjoy the ride.'

5

'Mona.'

Somewhere, in a far-off distance from her dream, a man's voice was calling her name. She ignored him. The pull of sleep was strong and she kept her eyes firmly shut.

'Mona.' A hand shaking her shoulder finally jolted her back into the world of wakefulness, and she reluctantly came to. She felt chilled, and every bone ached.

'Sorry to interrupt your slumbers but we're nearly there.'

She smiled at Ian. Despite his comments of the night before, she'd been extremely glad to see him. Their paths had crossed, briefly, a few months earlier when one of their cases had strayed into Police Scotland territory. With his help, and that of his colleague (whom she'd been introduced to while speeding away from the service station and whose name now escaped her), they'd managed to get the professor back on the road and had raced through the night in the direction of the Scottish border.

'I thought I was too wired to sleep, but I pretty much went out like a light.' She turned to the constable on the back seat – Bob, she was pretty sure it was Bob – 'How is he?'

'Good, I think.'

'Has he been snoring the whole way?'

Probably-Bob pulled a face. 'If only it was just snoring.'

'Any word on my guv'nor?'

'Your boss phoned my boss to tell him he was still alive.'

'Oh thank God.' She closed her eyes and allowed a feeling of relief to wash over her. 'Is either of them hurt?'

'Neither has more than bumps and bruises, but they've headed off to Casualty just to be on the safe side.'

'So, what exactly happened back there? Who were those people?'

Ian laughed. 'Some nutters who dislike the tone of the professor's views tried to kill him. And I hit a man who was aiming a gun in your general direction with a very heavy piece of kitchen equipment.'

His tone was dismissive, almost light-hearted. The forced jollity was completely at odds with the gravity of the night's events. She'd expected Stuttle's guys to be businesslike, serious, concerned with the urgent matter of keeping them safe. She wouldn't have been surprised to be bawled out by them, to have her competence questioned about the way things had turned out. She would have found that unfair, and would have told them so loudly and clearly, but she would have understood it. But flippancy? What was this all about?

'What do you mean, "some nutters"?'

'Well, you know what it's like with public figures, especially in this day and age. Every nutjob with a Twitter account is issuing death threats against people like the professor, after they get some bee in their bonnet. You know, they start thinking that he's trying to kill everyone rather than cure them.'

'True, but nutjobs on Twitter don't generally have the wherewithal to lure someone to London, poison him, have him followed, then try to shoot him. That smacks of organisational involvement.'

'Mona,' Bob leaned forward, his hand on the side of her seat. 'Relax! You've done your bit, take it easy now.'

She shifted in her seat so that his hand was no longer touching her. 'He knew my name.'

'What?'

'The guy with the gun, he knew my name. He said, "Come out, Ms Whyte."'

There was a long silence. 'I'm sure he didn't,' said Ian.

'Yeah, Mona, it's been a really stressful few days for you, and I bet you haven't had a lot of sleep. Like I said,' Bob's hand found her shoulder, and patted it, 'you've done your bit. Relax.'

Mona stared out the window, and thought about all the things that were wrong with the conversation. She was tired, weary to her core, but she knew what she had heard last night. She knew also that Stuttle's guys were making a cack-handed attempt to get her so confused about the past few hours' events that she would shut up. What she didn't know – yet – was why. The unmistakeable bulge under Ian and Bob's jackets meant that somebody, somewhere, had authorised this being an armed excursion. Did Stuttle suspect when he sent them down here that things could turn out like this? Or had things gone wrong very quickly?

'You're very quiet.' Ian glanced over at her. 'Are you annoyed with us?'

'No, of course not,' she lied, and forced herself to smile. 'I know none of this is your fault. I'm pretty furious with Mr Stuttle for nearly getting me killed though.'

'Believe me, no one is more freaked out at the turn of

262

events than Stuttle. He's going to want to keep this all very quiet.'

'This would be a very good time to be asking Stuttle for a pay rise,' said Bob, laughing.

'Yeah, totally.' Ian joined in the laughter, which became increasingly strained as Mona didn't respond.

'Anyway,' said Ian. 'Time to wake the professor, do you think?'

'Just before you do, can I ask you something?'

There was another slightly loaded pause. 'Sure. We'll answer if we can.'

'Is the professor in danger?'

'No immediate danger.' Ian took his eyes off the road so that he could make eye contact with her. 'Seriously. We'll give him protection until his speech tomorrow, then there will be a full review of his security arrangements, and those of his family.'

'Including the daughter in London?'

'Definitely. Now that people seem to know where she lives she could be a target.'

'For the nutters on Twitter?'

'Exactly.'

Fuck you, she thought. Her life had been put at risk by people who thought so little of her that they thought she'd buy some cock and bull story about Internet weirdos. And poor, poor Maria. No sooner does her long-lost dad find her than she ends up needing personal protection. Not the best of starts to the prof rekindling their relationship.

Ian pulled off the motorway. Mona watched the little blue dot on the car's satnav twist and turn as they moved closer to the big red arrow that indicated their destination.

Bob gave the professor a gentle shake. 'Sir, we're here.'

He woke with a start, and stared blankly around for a second before recognition set in.

'Good, good. But where exactly is "here"?'

They appeared to be parking in a car park containing nothing except three recycling vats and a Portakabin.

Ian pointed at the building in question. 'That, folks, is the Gretna Green Health Check Centre.'

'And they are expecting us?' Mona looked at her watch. It was only just after 7am.

'Yup, special arrangements have been made.'

The professor opened his door.

'Hang on a minute there, sir. Just need to check in case it's not just the health centre staff who are expecting us.'

Mona saw his hand move to his hip.

'I'm going to do a quick recce. Bob, can you and Mona keep an eye out, and, Professor, if you can get ready to move quickly if necessary?'

'I'm not sure I can do any more running. I'm not twenty-five anymore, you know.'

Ian disappeared round the back of the Portakabin, appearing a second later at the other side. He knocked on the door, had a moment or two's conversation with someone they couldn't see, then went into the building. All the time he was gone, Bob kept up a watchful eye on the surrounding area.

Ian reappeared. 'All clear. Bob – do you want to do the honours of getting him into the building?'

Mona and Ian followed them, then took up position on either side of the door. Inside she could hear the sounds of the professor being greeted by a female voice.

'So this will get the professor off the hook?' She kept her voice low.

'People can arrange to have an early Health Check if there's a compelling reason why they can't make it. You don't get into trouble for having an early Health Check, only a late one.'

'It's still going to look odd, him having a Health Check here.'

'I think you'll find it was prearranged for him by his personal assistant, who knew he would struggle to make it back to Edinburgh in time after he had to attend to some urgent family business in London. There's a paper trail to show that, or at least there should be by now. And from what I've heard about his PA, she'll play along.'

'We met her in London. I think she'd do anything to protect him.'

'She was down there too? Explains why we couldn't find her. Anyway, as soon as he's logged on the system, we're home free.'

'Well, almost. We still have to get him safely to the Parliament building.'

'Believe me, we'll have plenty of reinforcements for that.'

The door opened and the professor emerged, waving a cheery goodbye to the staff.

'OK, sir, ready for the last leg?'

6

'Where are we going?'

He looked at the man who had bundled him into the car. He was very large in a way that suggested that once upon a time he'd been fit and toned, but in the intervening years had developed a solid layer of flab covering whatever muscle definition remained. In a nod to the stereotypes about fat men, he seemed inordinately cheerful.

'We're off to Disneyland, son. The boss wants to buy you some candyfloss.'

'I don't know who your boss is.'

The fat man didn't answer, so he turned to his other captor. He was younger and thinner, and although he hadn't yet spoken, his tanned skin made Bernard think that he was foreign. He wore a battered brown leather jacket, a jacket that Bernard suspected he'd seen before. The jacket that had disappeared into the park when he had twigged that someone was following him. The thought that he'd been watched for days before this made him even more panicked.

'I think there's been some kind of mistake. I'm just a health enforcement officer. All I'm interested in is getting people into their monthly Health Check. I don't care what they do with the rest of their life. It's none of my business.'

266

The man ignored him and continued staring out of the window. Bernard turned back toward his other travelling companion, who grinned at him, then winked.

Bernard could feel his heart racing, and forced himself to take some long deep breaths to stop panic overwhelming him. Should he be doing something to free himself? He could attempt to wave to a passer-by, but this might result in a swift retaliation from one of the other members of the car. Besides, he hadn't seen too many other people on the empty backstreets that they had driven through.

Kidnapping hadn't been one of the eventualities they had prepared for at his HET induction. Being kidnapped had obviously been such a ridiculous proposition that it hadn't even been touched on in the syllabus. Being spat at, being hit, having a knife pulled on you – all of these were dealt with in a single morning of training. The trainer – another cop in the Mr Paterson mould – had finished by concluding 'and of course none of those things are going to actually happen to you lot. Worst you're going to see is a bit of bad language.'

Wrong.

He'd been spat at.

He'd been hit.

And if he hadn't yet had a knife pulled on him, the day was still young.

He couldn't blame the instructor. His training had been over a year ago now, and in that time things had changed. Much had been made at induction about the temporary nature of the post, how they would probably only be needed for a few months. But the Virus was still here and so were they, along with every shyster who thought he could make a quick buck out of the misery caused by the situation, by selling placebos of hope to the hopeless. Or for those who had given up on medicine, conventional or otherwise, there were the purveyors of mind-altering drugs to assist people to forget that there was ever a Virus to worry about. The HET were wandering around in the middle of it, under-resourced, unarmed, and if the last couple of days were anything to go by, totally out of their depth.

The car turned into Bruntsfield, heart of Edinburgh's student land, and suddenly there were shops and people. If he was going to cry for help this was his chance. The fat man sensed his sudden alertness.

'Keep your hands on your knees, son. I wouldn't want to have to break your fingers.'

Bernard felt his stomach heave at the mention of violence. He did as he was told. The car turned off the main thoroughfare and negotiated the empty residential streets of Morningside, where large detached houses were set back from the road behind high stone walls. Bernard recognised where he was. He'd been here before, recently, he was sure of it. They turned a corner and he found himself back at the second house he had visited. The house that had contained a beautiful woman, but no actual sign of Kerr. But he couldn't be the boss in question, could he? He was barely twenty-five.

The car turned into the driveway, the gravel crunching under the tyres.

'Time to get out, son, if your legs will carry you.'

A large hand reached into the car and pulled him out. For all that the thug was joking, Bernard's legs did feel decidedly wobbly at the thought of walking into the house. Was he about to receive a beating? His legs gave way slightly at the thought and he stumbled.

268

The man in the leather jacket pushed open the door, and a blast of music hit them. It was sixties stuff, with high female voices singing in harmony.

'We're back!' yelled the man in the leather jacket. As Bernard had suspected, his English was heavily accented.

The volume was lowered slightly in response to their arrival.

'I'm in here.'

The fat thug nudged him. 'Just follow the sound of the music, pal.'

Bernard looked at him in confusion. The man pointed at one of the doors. 'In there.'

He pushed open the sturdy wooden door, and saw a young man sitting cross-legged on the floor, in front of an old-fashioned record player.

'Grab yourself a seat.'

Bernard lowered himself into a leather armchair, and looked around the room. The furniture didn't match the occupant. It was an older style, expensive, solid, but slightly dated. The kind of furniture his grandparents would have invested in, seeing in it a lifetime of use. But the man on the floor was distinctly of the IKEA generation.

One wall of the room was given over entirely to records, shelf after shelf of thin album spines. The young man lined up another couple of 45s. Bernard watched fascinated as he fitted the records onto the narrow metal pole in the centre of the turntable, and held it in place with the plastic arm. For the second time he was reminded of his grandparents.

Satisfied with his choice of music, the man swivelled round toward him. It took a certain kind of confidence, the kind that Bernard would never have, to be totally in command of the room even when you were lolling on the floor at someone's feet.

'So, you guys were looking for me. I'm Scott Kerr.' He reached out a hand, which Bernard shook, nervously. 'What do you think of my record collection?'

Bernard considered how best to answer the question. He felt as if he'd woken up on *Mastermind* with a specialist category he hadn't chosen. Except the worst that could happen on *Mastermind* would be a humiliatingly low score. He didn't want to think about what could happen here if he inadvertently insulted the man's choice of music. He opted for a safe answer. 'I don't really know anything about music.'

'Allow me to educate you. That music you heard when you came in was The Supremes.'

'Oh, I've heard of them.' He felt a rush of relief. 'Diana Ross, wasn't it?'

Kerr shot him a withering look. 'Of course you've heard of them. Everybody's heard of them. But I bet you don't recognise this band.'

Bernard made a show of listening to the record, but short of the band being The Beatles or ABBA it was unlikely he was going to recognise them. 'It sounds quite similar but I couldn't tell you who they are.'

Kerr roared with laughter. 'It does sound similar, doesn't it? That was the point. But this band, the Tronettes, were Edinburgh's finest girl band, back in the early sixties. And you know who that was on lead vocals?'

With a feeling of panic, he searched his mind for 'sixties' and 'Scottish'. 'Lulu?'

'Naw! That's my granny you're listening to.'

'Wow,' said Bernard, in what he hoped was a sufficiently impressed tone.

270

'My grandad was their manager, and he fell in love with her.'

'That's a really lovely story.'

'Not for her. He made her give up singing when they got married, and she hated him until the day she died. But you probably knew my grandad, Angus McNiven?'

'I'm sorry, I don't recognise the name.'

Kerr sat back on his heels, and regarded him with a look of disbelief. 'Really? I thought you were police?'

'No, I work for the Health Enforcement Team.'

'But they're all ex-coppers, aren't they?'

'No, only about half of us are. I used to work in health promotion.'

He smiled. 'That explains a lot. Anyway, enough of all my family history. I got you here for a reason today. You had a visitor to your home yesterday, didn't you?'

'I wasn't in, but I believe so.' His heart started beating faster. Did Kerr know that he'd already spoken to the police about the incident? Did that make him some kind of grass in Kerr's eyes? Because if he knew one thing from TV cop shows, it was that it never ended well for informants.

'Must have given your wife quite a scare.'

Bernard opened his mouth to contradict him, but thought better of it. If Kerr thought that Megan was his wife, let him. It would stop him ever getting the idea of visiting Carrie. He felt bad, but if it helped to keep his wife safe ...

'So ...' Kerr stretched the word out, 'I wanted to apologise for that.'

Bernard's jaw dropped; he literally felt the bottom of his face make involuntary contact with the collar of his coat. There were many people in this world who he felt

271

owed him an apology, most of them currently working for the North Edinburgh HET, but never would he have suspected receiving an apology in this setting. 'OK. Thank you very much for that.'

'Allow me to explain what happened. It was the work of my idiot cousin, Stevie. He lives at 3 Colinton Gardens, although you already know that. He lives with a lady, and I use the term loosely, called Danielle Campbell, who I think you are also looking for in relation to one of your colleagues getting a boot in the face. Of course, we also apologise for that. You have a job to do, a very important one in these difficult times.'

'Thank you.' This was the most gratitude that Bernard had received since he started in the job. However, he felt that there was a very important issue here that he was not quite grasping.

'So, now you know exactly who has committed these two outrages.' He paused, and Bernard felt that some kind of response was required from him, although for the life of him he couldn't quite work out what it was. He started with the obvious option.

'You want me to have them arrested?'

'No.' The music ended, and there was a silence while Kerr changed the record. Bernard had a brief pang of nostalgia for watching his grandfather doing a similar task when he was a child. Not that his grandfather had been anything as glamorous as a manager of girl bands. His grandad had spent thirty years working in a paper mill just south of Edinburgh, and once retired had never missed one of Bernard's badminton matches. 'I can see why that would be your first instinct, and that's very commendable. And I'm sure your investigations would have led you there over the next few days. But I'd rather you didn't. In fact, I'd like you to do everything in your power to stop them being arrested.'

Bernard was unclear whether to reach for a 'what' or a 'why' first. Kerr sensed his dilemma and laughed.

'I can see I've confused you. And I know that you've got a lot of better things to be doing than sitting here and listening to me moan, but if I can impose on you for a minute or two I'll explain. Can I get one of the lads to bring you a tea or coffee? Or something stronger?'

Bernard declined the offer. He was sure the men from the car would be less than delighted to rush round addressing his hospitality needs. He still wasn't sure where this discussion was going and he definitely didn't want to antagonise them.

'OK. Well, if we can dive back into the McNiven family history for a minute. My grandad took me in after my dad scarpered, and my ma – his daughter – started drinking. And I'll tell you this for nothing, Grandad was an evil old fucker, didn't take any crap off anyone. He fell out big time with my uncle, Stevie's dad, who three months later gets pulled out of the Water of Leith after an impromptu swimming session.'

'He killed his own son?'

'Naw, the Italian-Glaswegians took care of that. Big Og, as everyone called my grandad, just stood by and let it happen. So between my ma's drinking, and Uncle Gus's inability to float, old Og is short of an heir apparent. Now, Stevie is the only son of Og's only son, so by rights he should be stepping up to the mark. And under other circumstances I'd agree with him; I'm all for maintaining dynastic traditions, you know?'

Bernard nodded enthusiastically.

'But Idiot Boy was never going to be able to hold things

together, not while him and his skanky girlfriend are too busy shooting all kinds of junk into themselves. Never touch the produce, that's the motto of any successful drug dealer. Which I assume you know I am?'

'I sort of got it from the context.'

Kerr nodded, approvingly. 'So, Big Og decides that muggins here, his eighteen-year-old grandson, is going to be trained up to run the family firm. And I have to give credit to the man, he's taught me plenty over the past seven years.'

Kerr stretched his arms out and cracked his knuckles. Bernard wondered exactly what skills he'd picked up.

'So I'm loyal to Og, well to his memory anyway. The Virus took him, three months back. I would have liked to give the old fella more of a send-off than he had. If it was up to me I'd have liked the funeral to have brought the traffic to a halt across the whole of Edinburgh, you know? Have the MSPs and lawyers and that all at a standstill while Og's horse-drawn hearse trots past the Parliament. But you know what it's like with undertakers these days. Stack 'em high and plant 'em cheap.'

Bernard nodded in what he hoped was an empathetic manner.

'Now he's gone, every Glaswegian fucker thinks they can move onto the territory that my grandad worked so hard on. And just to add to my troubles, my big cousin thinks that the time has come for him to be having a say in the way things are done. Obviously I'd welcome a bit of input from a family member, but as you've noticed the boy lacks a bit of finesse. I mean, him throwing his weight around like that with your wife? What was that going to prove?'

Bernard gave a wan smile, and hoped the conversation

274

moved away from his 'wife' as quickly as possible.

'And that stunt with his skanky girlfriend – it was never going to pull the wool over the eyes of a HET officer, was it?'

'Of course not,' he lied.

'So, in a lot of ways it would be helpful to have the pair of them out of the way, but I'm a sentimental fool when it comes to family, and unfortunately, he's the only family I've got. And I also know that five minutes in a police cell and he'd start telling you all kinds of stories that I really don't want you to hear.'

'I'm not sure that I can do what you want. The assaults are already being investigated by the police.'

Kerr nodded. 'I was afraid of that. So, Plan B. Here's what we're going to do. When the police come to take your statements, you're going to have a very bad case of memory loss. You're not going to remember clearly what happened, and you are going to raise some questions about whether, on reflection, the HET's response was appropriate, given the intense vulnerability of the skanky little drug-addled ho you were dealing with.'

If he did that Stuttle would kill him before Kerr could. 'But there were lots of witnesses.'

'You leave them to me.'

Bernard's stomach turned over at the thought of the old ladies of Colinton being threatened by the men he'd met today.

'Anyway, you mull that over, because there's a second little issue I need help with. Now my grandad, God rest his soul, did like to wind people up. And, unfortunately, some of his little pranks are causing me difficulties now that he's gone. You've probably sussed from your investigations that we're also in the business of helping

275

gentlemen in need of loving to meet ladies who are eager to help?'

'Prostitution?'

'Yes. And some of our ladies come from overseas, and need a bit of assistance to get Green Cards. You know what the Green Card people are like, with the difficult questions about passports and visas, and that kind of shit.'

Alessandra Barr.

'So Big Og thinks it would be funny to get one of these girls a Green Card in the name of the dead daughter of one of our friends and rivals in the west ... you know where I'm going with this, don't you, Bernard?'

'I'm not sure.'

'Alessandra Barr, Bernard, that's who I'm talking about, the wee lassie I know you've been nosing about after? Now our Glaswegian chums hear about this tart that's wandering around Leith calling herself by the name of their dead bairn, and not surprisingly, they think the McNiven clan is taking the piss. Alessandra gets a good going over, as a wee message to me.'

'So it wasn't you that gave her the two black eyes in her Green Card photo?'

'Oh no, that was me.' Kerr stared up at him, unblinking. 'She was a bit of a mouthy cow when she first arrived. I'd beat seven shades of shit out of any one of my girls if I needed to teach them a bit of respect. I had it in mind to beat the crap out of you, except we're getting along so well here I changed my mind.'

Bernard tried to swallow but found it very difficult.

'Now, apologies again for all the moaning, but I've got a lot on my plate. I've got my idiot cousin to deal with, I've got the questionable loyalties of my men out there ...'

'They seem very loyal.'

'As soon as Og died I doubled their wages to keep them sweet. I've paid up every month so far, but it's not easy with the Glaswegians all over my territory. So I can do without winding up the Barrs any further. If I don't take heed of their warning, the next time they see the lassie called Alessandra Barr she'll end up dead. And I can do without that on my patch. So you get her found, and you deliver her to me. I'll sort out the rest of it.'

'I can't do what you are asking of me.' Bernard closed his eyes and waited for Kerr to hit him. To his surprise, he heard laughter.

'You are very ethical, I like that. When you were round here the other day, you met my wife, didn't you?'

Bernard nodded.

'She's a fine-looking woman, wouldn't you say?'

Bernard had a feeling they were wandering into dangerous territory here. 'She's very pretty.'

Kerr lowered his voice. 'Just between you and me, her younger sister is even hotter. Don't ever tell her I said that.' He leapt up to his feet, and picked an envelope up off the sideboard. 'There's nothing that Maddison couldn't get a fifteen-year-old boy to do. Buy her a drink, steal things for her, deal drugs ... Do you know any fifteen-year-olds?'

Bernard thought for a minute. He wasn't sure that he did. After a second the penny dropped. *Carole's boy.*

Kerr held up a picture for him to look at. 'Pretty poor quality, I'm afraid.'

It was dark and grainy, but still good enough to clearly show Michael and another man in a doorway exchanging money and a package.

'The recording that we've got of him is a lot better.

It's amazing how much a fifteen-year-old will boast about the drug deals he's been involved in when there's a woman of Maddison's quality to impress. Making half of it up, I know, but still plenty in there to embarrass his mum, and her colleagues if it came to light.'

Bernard closed his eyes. *Blackmail.* Another one to add to the list of things that they'd failed to cover in his induction training. What was he supposed to say? He needed to talk to Carole, and Mona and Paterson, or anyone else who could tell him what to do. He played for time. 'Alessandra's registered at your cousin's house. Don't *you* know where she is?'

'She'll have gone crying to someone, they always do. Anyway, you think about what I said. Have a little chat to your colleague about not pursuing these recent unfortunate events too vigorously.' He stood up, and Bernard followed suit.

'You can find your own way home, I'm sure. I'd offer you a lift, but I dare say you'd prefer your own company.'

Bernard, sensing he was free to go, hurried toward the door. Behind him he heard the sound of another record being stacked onto the record player.

'I'll be back in touch.' The music started, the female voices swooping in harmony. 'Oh, Bernard, by the way you're not quite as ethical as I'd originally thought, are you? I know that wasn't your wife, that wasn't Carrie, I think her name is? Didn't see you rushing to correct me though.'

He stopped dead. 'Leave my wife alone.'

'You're compromised, Bernard.' The music filled the room, the female voices swooping mournfully over the guitars. 'Now I know you will tell lies, when it suits you. And as I said, I'll be in touch.'

7

'Eight miles to Edinburgh, everyone, according to that last road sign.'

'Great.' Mona gave Ian a curt nod. Conversation in the car had been limited since they'd climbed back in at Gretna. Ian and Bob had made a few attempts at chit-chat, which Mona had immediately shut down. She was in no mood to play along with their fictions about what she had or hadn't witnessed at the services.

She contented herself with staring out of the window. It would be lovely to be home again. She was going to soak in a long bath, get clean clothes, plan how she could improve the ambience of her living room using pot plants and throws, and work out the best approach to bully Stuttle into authorising a pay rise for her. That was the one sensible thing that Bob had said on this journey; after all, she could have died in that wood. And sure, it was a bit pushy to imply the channels that she might have to pursue, but then Stuttle knew all about bullying.

The professor leaned forward. 'I live in Newington, but I was wondering if you might be able to drop me at my offices at the university? I really need to do some preparation for tomorrow's Parliamentary meeting.'

'Ah,' said Ian. 'I thought someone had spoken to you.'

'About what? The meeting is still going ahead?'

'Yes, absolutely. We've all invested a lot of time and

effort in making sure of that! But we remain a little concerned for your safety, Professor, so we've arranged for you to spend the night at a safe house. We're not sure that going back to your own place is a good idea right now. We'll keep a couple of Police Scotland officers with you at all times, then give you an escort into the Parliament building tomorrow.'

'Is that really necessary?'

'Professor!' Mona turned round to face him. 'We spent last night hiding in the trees at the back of a service station because a car full of persons unknown were trying to shoot you. You've been lured to London in an attempt to get you to miss a Health Check, and someone, for reasons we don't yet know, chose to inject you with a sedative. Do you not think this highlights a need for you to have some protection?'

'Oh, I suppose you are right.' He sighed. 'I was just so looking forward to a shower, change of clothes and a night in my own bed.'

'It's just one more night, sir,' said Ian. 'If it helps, we can try to locate Mrs Kilsyth and she can fetch whatever you need.'

The idea seemed to cheer the professor up. 'Yes, that's true. Tess will know what I need.'

'And I have a request for you both. We would rather you didn't mention the events of last night to anyone.'

'Who do you mean by "we", Ian?'

'You work for the HET, Mona, just consider yourself told.'

'That's right, Ian. I work for the HET, you don't. You work for Police Scotland, and last time I looked you were nowhere in my line management structure.'

He looked furious. 'I risked my fucking life last night

280

rescuing you two from a man with a gun, remember?'

'And the mysterious group of people you call "we" put the professor and I in that position. I answer to John Paterson and Cameron Stuttle on this, and no one else.'

'Just keep your mouth shut.' Any remaining camaraderie from the earlier part of the trip had vanished. 'And believe me, Paterson and Stuttle will have been told the same.'

'So Stuttle's not in charge of this operation?'

Ian shot her a look of absolute fury. She grinned in return. 'Said something you shouldn't have, Ian?'

'And I'll only tell Tess,' said a voice from the back seat.

'No, Professor! You can't speak to anyone, not even Mrs Kilsyth.'

'He's a civilian ...' began Mona.

'Shut it!'

'Please don't shout at Mona, I'm extremely grateful to her. But I can assure you I am deeply embarrassed about the events of the past few days, and I will be drawing no further attention to them if I can help it.'

'That's great, Professor,' said Bob, in a tone of voice that aimed to be soothing. 'So, Mona, are we all on the same page here?'

She folded her arms and returned to staring out of the window. She heard Bob sigh from the back seat, and resolved if he tried to pat her shoulder again, she'd break his fingers.

They drove in silence through streets that got steadily more urban. Mona's thoughts turned back to the night's events. She didn't buy the Twitter crazies theory, but who else was out there that would be so concerned about the professor's speech that they'd be willing to risk killing him? And all just to avoid a couple of weeks' quarantine?

'Mona, where can we drop you?' Ian shot her a conciliatory smile.

She realised how tired she was. 'Somewhere near my home. I need to sleep for a couple of hours before going in to work. In fact, if you pull in here I can leap out. I'm only about ten minutes from home.'

She undid her seat belt. 'Good luck tomorrow, Professor.'

To her surprise, he opened his door as well.

'Professor, you're staying here,' said Bob, alarmed.

'Yes, yes, I just want to say goodbye to Mona.'

He bounded over to her, and swept her up in a big bear hug.

She seized the opportunity to ask him a question. 'Professor,' she whispered. 'Are you really talking about the quarantine tomorrow, or is it something else?'

'You are a very clever woman, Mona.' He pressed something into her hand. 'Please take my card. I'd very much like to meet you properly, under less stressful circumstances.'

Bob was out of the car now, watching them.

'Thank you again for everything, Mona,' said the professor, and climbed back in without looking at her.

'Mona,' said Bob, 'we need to …'

She walked off, and was brought up short as he grabbed her arm. She tried to pull away, but he held firm. He stepped toward her and brought his mouth close to her ear. 'I get that you are pissed off that there are things here you don't know. But have you ever considered the possibility we are trying to keep *you* safe too?'

He released his grip and she ran, and didn't stop running until she was back in her flat, door safely locked behind her. She paced up and down her living room, wondering how to channel the fury that was coursing through her. Lied to. Manhandled. What the hell were Police Scotland playing at? That is, if the two of them really were just working for Police Scotland. *Sleep.* She needed to sleep, but was so wound up that it seemed a distant possibility.

She sat down on the edge of her bed and looked at the professor's contact details. Rather than handing her a single card, he'd given her a small bundle of them, held together with a rubber band. Mona smiled. The professor needed Theresa to organise him. She *would* phone him, in a couple of weeks or so, when all this was over. Maybe she'd take Bernard to meet him. That would be a meeting of minds.

She stuck the cards in the top drawer of her desk and yawned. *Bed.*

8

Bernard ran until he was about six streets away from the house, then pulled out his phone. The phone's log showed there were half a dozen missed calls from Maitland, and an equal number of text messages rising in temperament from mildly annoyed to frantic. He wasn't surprised that his colleagues were worried; after all he'd just popped out for some milk over two hours ago. He absolutely needed to phone Maitland back, not least because his colleagues might phone the police, but he really didn't want to answer any questions about the conversation he'd just had. The one thing he wanted right now was time to think about what had just happened. There had to be a way to deal with all this, there must be, if only he could get his brain into gear. He missed Mona more than he would have thought possible. Mona would know what to do.

He braced himself and pressed dial. 'Maitland?'

'Bernard, thank God.' His colleague sounded genuinely relieved. 'Where have you been?'

'I …' He wondered what to say to buy himself some breathing space. 'I got a lead on my Defaulter.'

'What? And you didn't think to mention it?' Maitland was sounding less relieved, and more back onto his usual home ground of irritation. 'We were about to phone the police, for Christ's sake. We've already phoned your landlady and your ex-wife in case they'd seen you.'

'Were they both OK?' He couldn't stop the tone of anxiety in his voice.

'They were fine. Why wouldn't they be? Bernard, what's going on?'

He didn't say anything.

'Bernard, listen to me. This is not the time to be a go-it-alone asshole. Tell us what the problem is and let us help.'

'No, I'll be fine,' he said quickly, and ended the call before Maitland could protest.

His phone immediately rang again. He turned it to silent mode and shoved it in his pocket. He had a lot of things to do. He needed to speak to Carole – well away from Maitland or anyone else from the office – and warn her about her son's activities. He needed to speak to Megan, and warn her that her troubles may not be over. He needed to speak to his wife and persuade her that she needed to relocate, at least temporarily, to a place of safety, ideally in a different hemisphere. And he needed to track down Alessandra Barr and warn her ... although he was pretty sure she'd already got the idea that she was in danger. Then, all of that groundwork done, he needed to walk into a police station, probably the one where PC McGovern worked, and explain exactly what had happened over the past day.

It would be the appropriate response. He would be covering his own back. He couldn't be held responsible for any of the day's events, not if he brought all this information directly to the proper authorities. And yet ... the police were stretched thin since the Virus. Even if he could get them to take the threats to Megan and Carrie

285

as seriously as he would like, there wasn't the manpower to provide them with round-the-clock cover. It went without saying, too, that Carole would never speak to him again if he brought Michael into all this. Maybe the police would see him as a victim, a naïve fifteen-year-old who was caught up in something he didn't understand. Maybe the whole experience would put the fear of God into him, and he'd be back to being a straight A student, who never gave his mum and dad a moment's worry. Or maybe he'd get a criminal record and end up tied more closely to the kinds of people he was already involved with.

Then there was the one final victim of all this, the woman he was looking for. The woman whose voice he had never heard, whom he wasn't sure he would recognise if he ever actually met her. If he found her, and delivered her to Kerr, would it buy some security for Megan and Carrie? A quick tip-off to Kerr and his wife would be safe. Chances were, Bernard would never know what happened to resolve the problem. But then he'd have to live for the rest of his life knowing that he'd possibly sent a woman to her death, and he knew he couldn't bear that. So, if he couldn't do what Kerr asked, and he couldn't involve the police, there was only one thing he could do. He would have to find Alessandra Barr himself, and, one way or another, keep her safe.

A taxi appeared in the distance, and he stuck his hand out. Kerr had been right about one thing. Alessandra Barr had probably gone crying to someone – and he had a pretty good idea who. The woman who had been providing a shoulder to cry on to girls in trouble for more years than anyone could remember. If only she was prepared to talk to him.

'Where to?'

'Leith, please.'

Bernard had the taxi drop him off at the Shore. It would be easier to walk the last few yards to the Women's Centre rather than let a taxi manoeuvre through the narrow streets. He ran the last few metres, and pulled up short at the sight of a police car parked outside the building. Was he too late?

He crossed the road and walked cautiously toward the centre.

'You can't go in there, sir.' A very young-looking PC stopped him, stepping in between him and the front door.

'Why? What's happened here?'

'There was a fire here yesterday evening, sir. It's all under control now though.'

'Oh my God.' Bernard's stomach flipped. 'Was anyone hurt?'

'I suggest you wait for the evening news, sir. I'm sure all the details will be in there.'

Bernard pulled out his ID. 'I'm from the HET. One of our Defaulters was last seen here.'

'Sorry.' The PC relaxed a little. 'I was worried you were the press nosing around. There were a couple of the tabloids here earlier trying to make something of it. You know how much they love a good story about prossies. Probably make their day if one of the girls set fire to the place while high on drugs.'

'So, *was* anyone hurt?'

'No fatalities, thank God, but the project manager hurt herself trying to escape.'

'Do you know how badly?'

'Walking wounded – I think she hit her head, and obviously she'd inhaled some smoke.'

'Do you know where she is now? I need to speak to her quite urgently.'

'I think they took her to the Royal. She might still be there, but I don't know that she'll be fit for visitors.'

Bernard nodded. 'Sorry, one last question. Was the fire set deliberately?'

'That's what we're trying to establish. Between you and me,' he lowered his voice, 'I reckon the girls got caught in the middle of this drugs thing. Hope you guys are treading carefully.'

He wished he could say that they had been. 'Thanks for your help.'

He walked round the corner and hailed his second taxi of the day.

'I'd like to know which ward Annemarie McDougall is on please.' He held up his HET ID in one hand, and his Green Card in the other.

The receptionist, a middle-aged woman with a dour expression, glanced from one card to the other, and failed to look impressed at either of them. 'Are you family?'

'No, I'm—'

'Then I can't give that information out.' She looked past him to the next person in the queue.

He took a sideways step, back into her line of vision. 'I'm from the Health Enforcement Team. I am seeking a Health Defaulter, and this woman is a witness. You are obliged by law to give me that information.'

'I'm not sure that I am.'

'Oh, for goodness' sake. It's the law! Do none of you people go on training courses?'

'Don't raise your voice at me, young man, or I'll have security remove you.'

Bernard tried to put a lid on his anger. 'I'm sorry. Can you please phone your boss or someone to authorise it?'

She sighed, and looked pointedly at the queue that was forming behind him.

'The quicker you phone, the quicker I'm out of here.'

His persistence seemed to have worked because she picked up the phone. Keeping her eyes firmly on him, she repeated his apparently ludicrous suggestion that he was entitled to know the whereabouts of a patient merely because he had a HET ID card...

'I'm a Health Enforcement Team officer!' he said loudly in the direction of the phone.

She waved away his intervention, and continued to listen to the person on the other end of the phone, before replacing the receiver rather more heavily than was necessary. 'Ward 73,' she said, sourly.

'Thank you so much for your help,' said Bernard, trying to make up for his earlier assertiveness. The woman did not return his smile, deliberately looking over his shoulder at the first person in the very long queue that had formed behind him. He sighed and set off to look for the ward.

There was another police officer standing outside one of the single rooms. He flashed his ID at the officer. 'I need to speak to Annemarie McDougall about a Health Defaulter.'

The policeman gave his ID the once-over, and fortunately, seemed better informed than the receptionist. 'HET? No chance it can wait? She's not looking too clever in there.'

'Sorry – you know our work is pretty urgent.'

'Well, it's all right by me, if you can get a nurse to OK it. 'Scuse me.' He waved over Bernard's shoulder at a passing nurse. 'My colleague here needs a quick word with Annemarie. Is that OK?'

'Yes, as long as it is quick.' She fixed her eye on him. 'Ten minutes, tops.'

'Best of luck,' said the policeman, opening the door for him. 'Every time we asked her a question she didn't like she had a fit of coughing.'

Annemarie was tucked up in bed, leafing through a magazine. One side of her face was swollen, a greyish-purple bruise blossoming on her temple. He wondered what other bruising wasn't visible.

'Thought I heard my name being mentioned out there.' Her voice was raspy and hoarse from the smoke. 'I know you, don't I?' She peered at him, then her face contorted as recognition hit her. 'Jesus, have I not suffered enough without the HET coming to arrest me?'

'We don't arrest people, we only have powers to detain them.'

'I'm pretty much detained already, seeing as I can't walk the length of myself.'

He sat down next to the bed. 'Did you really do all this to yourself trying to escape the fire?'

She sighed, and flung her magazine down on the bed. 'What do you think, son?'

'Do the police know what happened?'

'They have their suspicions. I tried to tell them it was a toaster fire, but they know my reputation for pissing off the wrong people, so I don't think they entirely believed me.'

'Is Alessandra, or whatever her real name is, OK?'

She shrugged. 'I'd imagine she's in better shape than me at this precise moment.'

290

'Where is she?'

Annemarie looked up at the ceiling of her room and laughed. 'Remind me what your name is, son?'

'Bernard.'

'And are you married, Bernard? Got any kids?'

'Married, no kids.'

'Now you just let me guess what happened since I last saw you. Scott Kerr and his pals paid you a visit, and threatened your wife if you didn't tell them where to find Alessandra.'

He nodded. 'You're out on a few of the details, but your general thrust is correct.'

'Aye, son, I'm seldom wrong.' She stared at him, one eye big and bright, the other swollen half-shut. 'So, now you're here, looking for her last known address so you can get him off your back.'

'No!' Bernard was horrified. 'I want to know she's safe. I'm not about to offer her up as a sacrifice.'

'Aye, son, of course not.' She looked sceptical.

'I give you my word. I'm here to try to help Alessandra.'

'I wouldn't entirely blame you if you were, son. As my current state of health shows, Kerr's a nasty bastard. So was his grandfather, mind you, but I could work with old Og. I kept his girls healthy and out of the way of the police as much as I could, which was good for him because it kept them earning. Young Scottie doesn't see it like that though. Too busy throwing his weight around to try and impress that Glaswegian lot.'

'The Barrs.'

'Aye.' She started coughing. 'Oh dear. The lot that gave poor Alessandra a kicking. You know, all these lassies think they are coming over here to be hairdressers or nannies. They don't have a clue.'

291

'Where is Alessandra actually from?'

'Couldn't tell you, son. One of them unpronounceable ones that used to be the USSR. If you want to help, can you not do the lassie a favour, and just quietly stop looking for her?'

'We can't. Once she's on the Defaulter List, we have to keep looking for her until she's found, alive or dead. And it's not us that you have to worry about finding her.'

'I know. Scottie is like a dog with a bone. He'll not give up until he finds her.'

'So how do we stop him?'

'We? Not me, son. I'm done. One kicking too many, I'm afraid. If the Women's Centre does reopen, it'll not be with me running it.'

'So how do I stop him?'

'No offence, son, but you're not cut out for this. Take your wife and get out of town until all this dies down.'

'But you do know where Alessandra is? You can tell me?'

She started to cough. 'That's me poorly here, son. You'd better get the nurse for me. And close the door on your way out.'

9

Mona ran up the last few stairs to the office. She'd had two hours of beautiful, dreamless sleep at the flat, and now felt ready to take on the world.

'Wow, it looks tidy in here.' She surveyed the office. 'Was it so quiet while we were away you decided to have a clear-out?'

'Hardly. And don't move that partition over there or you'll be crushed by an avalanche of crap.' Maitland's lack of smile suggested that this wasn't a joke. 'When is Paterson back?'

'I'm not sure. Soon – today or maybe tomorrow at the latest.' There was something strangely subdued about Maitland. He hadn't been rude to her once and she'd been in the office for nearly three minutes. 'Is everything OK?'

'Nope, it's all pretty far from OK ...' His explanation was interrupted by the arrival of Carole.

'Bloody hell, what happened to you?'

'Hi, 'ona.'

'She got kicked in the face during a search for a Defaulter.'

'I've 'ust 'een at the dentist. 'Eed two 'eeth out.'

'That's awful. It wasn't that Alessandra girl that Bernard and I were looking for, was it?'

'No, not Alessandra, but part of that investigation,' said Maitland.

'Well, I hope it's on hold until it's been risk assessed?'

'Yeah, that's under control, but—'

'And the Guv will be in soon and things can get back to normal.' She walked over to her desk, and realised that her colleagues were still staring at her. 'What?'

'There's more. Some bloke turned up at Bernard's new flat looking for him, and assaulted his flatmate. Now he's stormed out of here and won't answer his phone.'

'Oh good God.'

'And...'

'And? You mean there's yet more? Jesus Christ, Maitland, we were only gone two days.'

'Just shut up and listen. Carlotta Carmichael paid us a visit...'

'Here?' Suddenly the unusual tidiness of the office made sense. 'What did she want?'

'She's got a bee in her bonnet about both you and the Guv being on leave at the same time, and she seems to think the Guv is up to something, and, by the way, I agree with her. I'd really like to know what was so important you and Paterson had to rush off and leave me here with all this mess...'

She glared at him, and he moved on, sulkily. 'Anyway, she was in here this morning complaining about every single thing we do and, well, the upshot of her visit is that she's decided we need to have our own inspectorate.'

'Christ, Maitland. Two days. Two bloody days. How on earth are you going to explain all this to the Guv?' She stood up. 'Right, until the Guv is back in his office, I'm in charge. And the first thing we're going to do is track down Bernard.' She pulled out her mobile, and pressed on Bernard's name. The faint sound of ringing could be heard.

'Where's it coming from?'

'It's getting louder.'

'Hello.' Bernard appeared in the doorway.

'Where have you been?'

''E 'ere 'orried.' Carole gave him a rather cautious hug, which involved making contact with her arms, but keeping her face as far away as possible.

'I'm sorry, I know you were. Mona, I'm really glad you are back, but I've got some bad news. We're in trouble.'

'I know,' said Mona. 'Maitland told me.'

'No, this is new stuff. We're in even more bother than we thought.'

'Seriously?' said Maitland. 'How can we possibly be in more trouble?'

'I am never, ever leaving you two alone again,' said Mona. 'OK, Bernard, what now?'

Having been given the floor, Bernard suddenly looked nervous. 'Actually, I need to talk to Carole in private.'

From the look on Carole's face she was as surprised as Mona by this. She made a sound that was probably 'why'.

Bernard continued to look worried. 'In private?'

''Ust 'ay it.'

'OK. All right.' He leaned against the edge of a desk. 'Now, where to begin?'

'For fuck's sake, Bernard, get on with it!'

'OK, when I left here to go to the corner shop for milk, I was grabbed by two guys who pulled me into a car and took me to Scott Kerr's house. For those of you not up to speed with the latest memos on drug dealing,' he shot a look at Maitland, 'he's an Edinburgh-based drug

295

dealer, who is in the middle of a feud with the Barrs, who are drug dealers traditionally based in the west, but are looking to move on to his territory.'

'Oh, God, are you OK?'

'Completely physically unharmed, yes. So, Stephen McNiven is Scott Kerr's cousin, and it was McNiven's girlfriend that booted you in the mouth, Carole. Kerr seems to think it's all a bit inconvenient to have this assault charge hanging over his family, so he wants Carole and me to have a bit of a memory lapse about what actually happened, and to say that with hindsight we think we didn't handle the situation well, because the woman in question was obviously a vulnerable drug user.'

'Vulnerable?!' said Maitland. 'Vulnerable enough to give Carole a kick in the jaw that's going to keep her in dentist's visits for the next six months! No way are you two spouting that guff. The bitch is going down for what she did, isn't that right, Carole?'

Throughout the whole discussion, Carole hadn't taken her eyes off Bernard. She looked like a woman waiting to hear bad news, though what that news could possibly be was beyond Mona.

'Carole, I'm so sorry,' said Bernard.

''S Michael?'

He nodded.

'What's going on?' asked Mona.

'You guys remember Carole's son, Michael, who had the Virus a few months ago? Well, Kerr set Carole's son up. He's had him dealing drugs.'

Carole's head was in her hands. ''O 'tupid.'

'It wasn't his fault,' said Bernard, hastily. 'They've deliberately targeted him because Carole is a HET officer.'

'Are you sure about this, Bernard?' asked Mona.

296

'I've seen pictures. There was a girl that he liked ...'

'Addison,' said Carole, a weary tone to her voice.

'Yes. Maddison. Kerr's sister-in-law.'

Carole started to cry. In between sobs there was a stream of largely undecipherable ranting, although the words 'hate' and 'job' were clearly to be heard. She lifted up her head, and with a great effort enunciated two words. 'I resign.'

'It's not that easy to resign from the HET,' said Mona. 'I've tried.'

'It also may not be enough. We're all going to be worried about the impact of our actions on Michael, whether you're here or not. And, unfortunately, that's not all that Kerr wants from us. He also wants Alessandra Barr handed to him on a plate.'

'Why?'

'Because "Alessandra Barr" is the name of a daughter of the Barr clan who died as a young child. The McNivens foolishly used this name to get a Green Card for a prostitute they'd trafficked into the country.'

'I bet that went down well with the Barrs.'

'It went down every bit as well as you might expect. The Barrs gave "Alessandra" a beating, then she disappeared. She's an embarrassment now to Kerr, so he's got to get rid of her somehow. Now, maybe his business empire can facilitate the relocation of a prostitute from one city to another, or maybe he's planning to buy her a plane ticket back to her country of origin, but there remains a very good chance ...'

'That he's planning to kill her,' said Mona.

'Yes, but discreetly, before the Barrs kill her and dump her on his turf as a great big message to the world that Kerr is no match for the Barrs.'

'But we don't know where she is?'

'We don't, but Annemarie McDougall does.'

'So, what do we do?' asked Mona.

'Well, I think Carole and her family need to take an enforced break from Edinburgh.'

She stood up, and without a word to anyone picked up her bag and walked out.

'Poor Carole,' said Maitland. 'This whole thing sucks.'

'I know,' said Mona. 'And what do we do about Alessandra Barr?'

Bernard shifted from foot to foot. 'I have a plan.'

'Which is?'

'We kill her ourselves.'

10

'You're leaving?'

Annemarie looked up from tying her shoes. 'You again?' She broke into a chorus of coughing. 'I don't know what you're trying to achieve here, son, but I'd be happier if you just left me in peace.'

'Where's the policeman on the door?'

'They stood him down. Couldn't find anything to suggest that the fire was caused by anything other than a faulty toaster, which I could have told them.'

'But you know that it was started deliberately.'

'I don't know anything, son, other than now that PC Plod has been removed I'm free to make a run for it.'

'You can't leave!' Bernard's inner health professional asserted himself. 'You've had a very traumatic experience, not to mention the physical effects of smoke inhalation. You are really in no fit state to go home. Has a doctor signed you out?'

'I'm leaving, and that's all there is to it.'

Bernard stepped in front of the door. 'Why?'

Annemarie stood up and, wheezing as she went, came to stand in front of him. 'Two reasons, son. Number one, I'm worried that my dog is starving to death while I'm in here. And, number two, if I don't get a fag soon, I'm going to kill someone.'

'A cigarette?' said Bernard, with all the disgust of Lady

Bracknell discussing accessories. 'In your condition? Are you trying to kill yourself?'

'Well, son, call me one of life's risk-takers. So, here is the way it is.' She held on to the bed, while she struggled to get her breath. 'If you want to keep talking to me, you can give me a lift home, and you can stop on the way so that I can buy some fags.'

'Buying you cigarettes in your current condition would be tantamount to committing culpable homicide!'

'No fags, no chat.'

Bernard knew when he was beaten. 'This goes against every principle in my body.'

'Stick your head out, son, and see if the coast's clear.'

'Menthol? You really are trying to kill me, son. I asked for Benson and Hedges.'

Bernard ignored her complaint, and tried very hard not to complain in return when she immediately lit up. He failed. 'We'll be at your street in literally two minutes. Could you not have waited?'

She blew smoke in his direction. 'Apparently not. Anyhow, time to grab a parking space if you see one.'

He did as he was told. 'Which of these flats is yours?'

'The ground floor one on the corner.'

Bernard scanned up and down the street. 'OK, we better be a bit careful here. We don't know if anyone will be vigilantly awaiting your return.'

'"Vigilantly awaiting my return." I love the way you talk, it's like you're a walking poem. You should be on at the Festival, you and Pam Ayres. But relax, son. Kerr and his pals have made their point to me; they're not going to be here. Now, let's get in and check on Sheba.'

Annemarie took his arm as they crossed this road.

300

Her gait was slow, and she stopped for a fit of coughing halfway across, bringing traffic to a stop in both directions. Bernard was vaguely aware of some angry hand signals from the motorists.

'Nicotine patches are really very good these days.'

'Shut up.'

The intercom was broken, so Bernard pushed open the stair door and ushered Annemarie inside. She grabbed his arm. 'The door to my flat is open.'

'What do we do?'

'It's probably just my brother.'

'I thought you lived on your own? You were worried about your dog?'

'I am worried. Alec has a habit of going off on benders so I can't rely on him to feed Sheba. He's maybe just left the door open.'

'Do you want me to go in first and check it's OK?' said Bernard, a tad reluctantly.

'Obviously, son, I'm a lady in need of your protection.' She started to laugh at what appeared to have been a joke, then the giggles turned into a fit of coughing. Despite this, she pushed past him into the flat. There was an immediate cacophony of barking. He followed her in and found her kneeling with her arms round a large Doberman. 'Thank God she's all right. I thought the bastards might have killed her to stop her barking.'

'Have they been here?'

'They will have been, to look for Alessandra. Come into the living room.'

'I hope your brother's OK.'

'Aye, well.' Her tone suggested that she was a lot less concerned about his well-being than she had been about Sheba's. 'Take a seat.'

301

The room stank of stale smoke and essence of dog. He gingerly picked a pile of *Daily Records* off an armchair and sat down.

Annemarie caught his expression. 'Try living with an alcoholic, son. It kills your motivation for housework.'

'Sorry.'

She curled up on the sofa, the dog lying happily across her lap. 'Right, son, you've done your bit. Now say your piece and get out.'

'OK. My team can't stop looking for Alessandra, unless we are authorised to do so by someone extremely senior. We never actually close a file; it will remain open until she has a Health Check, or until we have evidence that she has died. We'll de-prioritise it after a while, but I can't guarantee that my team, or someone else, won't start looking for her again.'

'I think your team is a big waste of taxpayers' money, if you don't mind me saying so, son.'

'I don't. I don't agree with you, but you are entitled to your opinion. Anyway, Kerr wants Alessandra off his patch. Now at the HET, we have procedures for dealing with people who are, for example, experiencing domestic violence ...'

'That'll not be enough to stop Kerr looking for her. Alessandra's a tough cookie; she's had run-ins with Kerr before when she's tried to stand up for herself. As long as she's in some programme with you guys there's a danger that she'll shout her mouth off about her experiences.'

Bernard nodded. 'That's what we thought. But what if we can arrange for her to die?'

'You can fake her death?'

'We thought perhaps a suicide, somewhere well out of

302

Edinburgh. We'll have all the official paperwork, and I'll keep Kerr updated as our "investigation" unfolds.'

'And your bosses are going to OK this, are they?' She looked sceptical.

'My colleague is speaking to our superior right now. We can help you get Alessandra to a place of safety, but obviously we will need you to take us to her.'

Annemarie thought this over, momentarily stopping petting Sheba, who gave a soft growl of annoyance. 'And why should I trust you?'

'Carrie McDonald, 14d St Matthew Court, Edinburgh.'

'And who's that, son?'

'That's the name and address of my wife. We're separated, but she remains the person that I love most in the whole world. She's the person I would least like to have a visit from Scott Kerr. And now you know where she lives.'

They stared at each other. 'I need to talk to Alessandra.'

'Of course. I'll be outside in my car. With all the windows wound down.'

11

'Does he have anyone in with him?'

Stuttle's PA leapt to her feet to try to get to the door before Mona. She failed. 'No he hasn't but ...'

'Good,' said Mona, throwing open the door.

Stuttle jumped at the noise, then gave a further guilty start as he realised who it was.

'She doesn't have an appointment, Mr Stuttle.'

'It's OK, really.' He flashed his assistant a reassuring smile. 'Just close the door on the way out.'

The PA left, with a final curious glance at Mona.

'So, you're back then, safe and sound?'

'No thanks to you, sir. You nearly got us killed.'

'Come now, Mona, that's a bit of an exaggeration. Anyway, police officers expect a bit of rough and tumble.'

'Rough and tumble? You nearly got me shot!'

He conceded the point with a small nod.

'And, sir, it seems to have slipped your mind that I'm not a serving police officer. I work for the HET, not the Armed Response Team. You sent us off to London without any warning of the dangers we were likely to encounter, or any way to defend ourselves.'

'Yes, I'm afraid our intelligence did rather let us down on this one.'

'Damn right it did! And even if it was all in a day's work for me, you and your intelligence nearly got

304

Scotland's leading Virus academic killed. Have you told the First Minister that?'

'Now, Mona ...'

'Or the Chair of the Parliamentary Virus Committee?'

Stuttle sat back in his chair and sighed. 'Ian warned me that you were being less than co-operative. Sit down, Mona.'

'I'd rather stand.'

'I was under the impression that you wanted an in-depth discussion about recent events. You might want to take the weight off your feet while we talk.'

She considered this proposition, and sat.

'As you have already discussed with Ian and Bob, I was rather hoping for some discretion about all this. And now that you appear to be done shouting at your superior officer, can I ask what you want from me? Can I expect you back here tomorrow with a union rep or would a heartfelt apology from me be enough?' He folded his hands behind his head. 'Or are you looking for a big fat pay rise and a promoted post back at CID?'

'Neither of those things is of interest to me,' she lied. 'What I'm looking for is for you to listen to the dangers that you put HET staff in, day in, day out.'

'HET staff are well aware that it is their own responsibility not to put themselves in positions where they may be at risk. Staff are trained on all this at their induction; we supply them with appropriate equipment ...'

'There is a limit, sir, to how much we can protect ourselves and still get the job done. We go knocking on the doors of some very unsavoury people.'

As quickly as she could, she ran through the events of the past two days, with a particular emphasis on where the HET's systems had failed to work. Stuttle listened impassively until she sat back in her chair.

'This Carole woman – is she likely to sue?'

'I think she's more worried about her son at the moment. Six weeks' paid leave might help to head any legal action off.'

'Consider that done. And the two assault charges can be made to disappear, without any HET staff having to get involved. But I'm not stepping into the middle of a drugs war. I think we just have to accept that the prostitute is collateral damage.'

'I'm not so sure, sir.'

He raised an eyebrow.

'The HET has a process for supporting Defaulters whose identity might be compromised by attending a Health Check. It usually gets used for victims of domestic violence, or people in witness protection. We want Alessandra flagged on our system as Not to Be Pursued. And in return for that one small favour, I'll keep my mouth well and truly shut.'

'That's doable, but it's not going to get Kerr off her back.'

'Leave that to us, sir.'

'Why? What are you … On second thoughts the less I know the better. Here.' He opened one of his desk drawers and pulled out a wad of notes. 'Get her on a train. I don't care where she goes, just make sure it's out of Scotland.'

'And out of your jurisdiction, sir?'

'Yes, out of my jurisdiction.' He sighed. 'I know you think that I'm some kind of monster, Mona, but the reality is we are dealing with an unprecedented situation. This Virus thing was supposed to be over months ago, and with every day that passes there's some new threat to public health or public safety. We're basically making things up as we go. If the HET is going to cry over every sad case it comes across we're not going to be able to fulfil our primary purpose, which is protecting the well-being of the citizens of Scotland. Sometimes you have to see the big picture. Anyway, get out of here, and remember, if this all goes tits up, you are on your own.'

'Thanks for the support.'

He smiled. 'Despite your bleeding heart tendencies, Mona, you've a good grasp of how things work. Ever thought that your skills are wasted at the HET?'

'Every moment of every day, sir.' She stood up, but didn't leave. 'He knew my name, sir, the man that shot at me. I know Ian and Bob didn't believe me, or chose not to. But I distinctly heard him address me as Ms Whyte.'

His face registered neither surprise nor concern. 'You are in no personal danger, Mona. I'm sure of that.'

'Did your intelligence tell you that, sir?' She shoved the bundle of notes into her inside pocket. 'I'll close the door behind me.'

12

'Did you have to bring Sheba?' Between the cigarettes and the dog Bernard was worried his car was beginning to smell like Annemarie's flat.

'I'm not leaving her. She was traumatised. I'm sure that Kerr and his pals gave her a booting when they were at my flat.' She flicked a thumb in the direction of the backseat. 'And did *you* have to bring Speccy back there? He's not stopped for breath since we got in.'

'Sorry,' said Marcus. 'Just excited to be "in the field" again.'

Without looking round, Bernard could sense Mona rolling her eyes.

'Actually, Annemarie, we're very grateful to Marcus for helping us out with the paperwork. Why don't you talk us through what you've done?'

'Delighted to, Bernard. Now what I've done here is tried to create a workable timeline of Alessandra's sad demise. Firstly, I have a fake e-mail to Bernard from one of the Aberdeen HETs, saying that someone meeting Alessandra's description had been traced to a hostel in the town, but the staff were worried about her as she'd left quite abruptly. Then, dated a week later, we have a formal letter from one of the Highland HETs saying that Alessandra had been found dead on a remote hillside, with a death certificate appended backing up their theory of suicide. The letter helpfully notes that there has been a ban on any press coverage of the death until they've traced her relatives. And on both sets of correspondence I've given a number for you to ring if you want more information which will ring through to me. I will, of course, back up my own story if anyone purporting to be Bernard calls me.'

He passed a folder over to Annemarie. The paperwork was laid out each in its own plastic sheath. She leafed through them. 'This is dead clever. I take it back, Speccy. You rabbit on as much as you like.'

'Now all Bernard has to do is stick these through Kerr's door at the appropriate time.' Mona started to cough. 'Do you have to smoke in here, Annemarie?'

'Sorry, doll, but I'm trying to use up these menthol ones that Bernard bought me.'

'Bernard bought you cigarettes?'

'It wasn't like that.' He swerved off the main road and into a car park, rather more swiftly than was strictly necessary. 'And here we are, Newcastle railway station.'

Mona sighed, happily. 'It gives me immense pleasure to think that Stuttle gave us the money to get her off his turf, when she was already in England.'

'Aye, well that money's not going to be wasted,' said Annemarie. 'She's not far enough away from Scotland to be safe yet.'

'I only hope they let the hound on the train,' said Bernard.

'I'll have her on the leash. She's good protection for the pair of us.' As if to prove the point, Sheba started barking at a dog on the other side of the road. Annemarie reined her in. 'Woah, girl. But if they say no, son, she'll have to go back to Edinburgh with you.'

'Great.' His upholstery was never going to recover. 'Marcus, can you stay with the car?'

He gave them a cheery thumbs-up from the backseat.

'We're never going to get him back to the office now,' said Mona.

'Nope, not now he's had a taste for "field work".'

'Right, you pair, time to go.' Annemarie set off into the station.

'It feels kind of weird to finally be meeting Alessandra,' said Mona.

'I know!' The days that he had spent looking for Alessandra had given him plenty of time to wonder what she was like. He didn't usually have the luxury of this imagination time. Most of the Defaulters they chased lived small triangular lives. *Home–dealer–job centre. Pub–bookies–park bench.* They were not generally difficult to track down, and in most cases bore a strong resemblance to other Defaulters they had found. In some cases they *were* actually Defaulters they had already found, going through the system for a second or third time.

But Alessandra was much more complex. They didn't even know what she looked like; he assumed she would now look nothing like the picture in her file. What was her real name? Where was she from: Georgia? Ukraine? Turkmenistan? Were there parents waiting for her back home? Siblings? A husband and children? And when she finally opened her mouth, what would she sound like?

'It's like I know everything and nothing about her both at the same time.'

'In here,' said Annemarie, and went into the café on the forecourt. She waved to a middle-aged woman sat at a corner table. In hairstyle, size and general attitude she

310

bore a remarkable resemblance to Annemarie. As they approached, the young woman she was with looked up at them. *Alessandra.* Bernard couldn't help but stare at her. She looked horribly young. The word 'prostitute' had conjured up for him an older woman, world-weary, the troubled blonde from Alessandra's Green Card photo. But the girl with the very short brown hair and big dark eyes sitting before him barely looked twenty.

'Hiya, Annemarie. We've got a problem.' The accent was pure Geordie. 'This one's saying she doesn't want to go.'

'Doesn't want to go? Ali, doll, what's all this about?' Annemarie bent down and gave her a hug. Alessandra held her close and started to cry.

'I go and it very bad for my family back home.'

'I don't think Scottie Kerr will go looking for your family all the way over there. He's got enough on his plate with the Glaswegians without him setting out for your bit of the world. Anyway, that wee runt couldn't find his arse with both hands, never mind find your home on a map.'

Alessandra shook her head. 'Is not him. Is more peoples.'

The other woman helped out. 'She's worried about the people her parents paid to get her a "nanny's" job over here. They sold her on to Scott Kerr once she got here but her parents still owe on the debt.'

'I think I must go back.'

'Doll, you go back to Edinburgh and you're going to end up dead. Bernard, son, you talk to her.'

With a slightly worried look at Mona, Bernard sat down at the table. 'Hello, Alessandra. I'm Bernard, and I have this for you.' He placed the Green Card on the

311

table. 'We've arranged for somewhere for you to stay in London. A lovely man called Elijah and his friends will look after you.'

Her hand went to her throat and she started playing nervously with her necklace. Bernard noticed that it was a St Christopher. He pointed at it.

'Elijah is a Christian, just like you. He's not like the men you met in Edinburgh. He has somewhere for you to stay, and he will help you to find a job. And a friend of ours in the local police will make sure that you are safe. You'll be able to wire money home so that they can pay the debts. You just can't tell them where you are, and they can't tell them that the money is really from you.'

Alessandra looked desperately undecided. 'Annamaria, what I do?'

Annemarie took her arm and stood up, coughing as she did so. 'You, me and Sheba here are getting on a train.' She picked up the Green Card. 'I'll give this Elijah bloke the once-over. And if I'm not happy, we're coming straight back.' She winked at Bernard behind Alessandra's back.

'And we've got friends in London that'll come and check on you,' said the Geordie woman. 'You won't be all alone.'

Bernard had a vision of an international sisterhood of squat, grey-haired women who dedicated their lives to helping women like Alessandra escape the clutches of men like Kerr. He was both cheered, and slightly scared, at the thought.

'Come on, doll. You can't stay here, and you can't go back. The only way to go is forward. Let's get our tickets.'

312

Annemarie shepherded Alessandra away from them and into the glass-fronted ticket booth. After a minute's conversation with the man behind the counter, Annemarie turned and gave them a thumbs-up, which he took to mean that the dog wasn't coming back to Edinburgh. Alessandra stopped and gave them a shy wave, before the two of them disappeared through the ticket barriers.

'Right, that's me done.' The Geordie woman gave them a curt nod. 'Safe journey back.'

'We'd better get back to Marcus,' said Mona.

'Do you think she's going to be OK?' he asked.

'Hard to say. She's starting over in a new city, with pretty limited English. We can't guarantee that Kerr is going to believe our story and stop looking for her. And she's probably right to worry about her folks back home. But given the limited number of options open to her, I think we've given her the best possible chance. And she's going to have some good people looking out for her in London.' She gave him a gentle nudge. 'You did well, Bernard. Really well.'

He smiled. This was the first time he could remember Mona giving him praise that wasn't qualified by a statement like, 'for a civilian', or 'for someone who doesn't actually know what he's doing'. 'Are we going to tell Mr Paterson about any of this?'

'Hmmm.' Mona thought this over. 'Probably best not to worry him. We'll have to tell him that Stuttle agreed some time off for Carole, but otherwise let's keep quiet. He'll have enough on his plate with Carlotta Carmichael's plan.'

'Yup, I'm looking forward to Maitland updating him on all that.' He knocked on the car window, and Marcus

313

grinned back at him. 'But right now, let's just go home.'

'Yup. And on the way, you can tell us how a health Nazi like yourself came to be buying cigarettes for a woman who's only just got out of hospital.'

FRIDAY

SHOCK

'Good morning, all!'

Paterson swept into the office carrying a huge bunch of flowers.

'Guv, you shouldn't have.'

'They're not from me. They are addressed to the North Edinburgh HET, and I had the pleasure of plucking them out of Marguerite's clutches before she could bring them up here herself. Her nose was very out of joint.'

Mona grabbed the envelope attached to the flowers and opened it. '"With our most grateful thanks, Tess and Sandy."' She grinned. 'How nice.'

'Is that a bruise, Guv?' asked Maitland.

'This little thing?'

Mona regarded Paterson's visage. Her bet would be on a swift right hook in a darkened service station car park.

'A minor shaving cut. And,' he held up his right hand, which had two of his fingers bandaged and splinted together, 'shut my hand in a drawer.' He winked at Maitland, who looked annoyed something was going on that no one was sharing with him. 'Mona, a word in my office.'

'You seem in a very good mood, Guv.' She shut the door firmly behind her, giving Maitland a cheery smile as she did so.

'Yes, it turns out that the best way to get over several years of a dysfunctional father–son relationship is to have a really big rammy outside a service station. Absolutely nothing bonds you like the joint endeavour of attempting to beat the crap out of a couple of goons. Greg and I got on great after that. Laughed all the way to A&E. And, you were right.'

'About what?'

'Him and Liz *are* an item. Thinks she might actually be "the one".'

'Fantastic, Guv.'

'So.' He indicated that she should sit down. 'What happened on your side of things? Did the HET liaison folk get to you before anyone else did?'

'Sort of. Ian Jacobsen found us, but not until after someone had tried to shoot us.'

His eyes bulged. 'Shoot you? As in men with guns?'

'Yup. Well, one man, anyway. Shouted at us to come out, and when we didn't he started firing.' She wanted to go on, to tell him about the man calling her by name, but couldn't bring herself to do it. If he didn't believe her, or even worse, pretended not to, like the HET liaison guys had done, she didn't think she could bear it.

'That's taking things to a whole new level. What was Stuttle thinking, sending us off into that kind of situation?'

'Apparently the turn of events took him by surprise. He soon wised up though; Ian Jacobsen and his pal were both armed.'

'And did they say who these guys were that were after the professor?'

'Nope. I'm pretty sure they had their suspicions, but they definitely weren't for sharing.'

'Figures. Anyway, goes without saying that everything that happened over the past couple of days is top secret. Stuttle's not going to want word of all this getting out.'

'Oh, yeah, he made that crystal clear.'

'You've seen him?' Paterson looked surprised, and she kicked herself for her lack of discretion.

'Yes, I had a debrief yesterday.'

'Oh, right. I thought he'd wait until we were both back. Still, I suppose he wants to be on top of things. You know what the likes of Carlotta Carmichael are for ferreting out information. God knows we don't want her finding out about our little jaunt down south.'

'I think Maitland needs to update you ...'

'I'll hear all about the Parliamentary Committee later. But the other thing I wanted to say to you is that I ...' He paused and drummed his fingers on the desk. 'I may have overheard something that I wasn't supposed to on our drive back. You know, when you and Greg were discussing your ...' He paused, looking for a word.

'Sexuality, Guv?'

'That would be the word, yes, thank you, Mona. I didn't realise until that point that you are actually, ehm ...'

'Gay, Guv?'

'Yes. Again, thank you. Were you planning to share this information with your colleagues at any point?'

She sighed. 'I don't know. I'm not sure I can bear Carole and Bernard fawning over me, saying how proud they are. And Maitland will make endless jokes about me wearing dungarees.'

'Mona – you underestimate your colleagues. The lesbian-wearing-dungarees thing is old hat. Maitland

319

will be able to come up with some far more modern and cutting way to disparage your life choices.'

She smiled. 'You may be right.'

'You could have told me, you know.'

'Sorry, Guv. I would have but, well … I'm glad you know now though.'

'Yeah, well. Anyway, get out of my office while I find out what's been happening while I was gone.' He flung open the door. 'So, what did I miss?'

Mona and Bernard looked expectantly at Maitland, who remained schtum.

Bernard decided to help out. 'Maitland has some news for you, Mr Paterson.'

'Right, spit it out.'

Maitland glared at Bernard. 'Well, actually …' There was a pause with the gestation period of an elephant. 'I'm thinking of getting married.'

Paterson looked surprised. 'Fantastic news. Although I thought you'd only been going out five minutes. Anyway, that kind of news deserves bacon rolls all round, and I'm buying. Just let me do a quick check of my e-mails and we'll head out.'

They waited until the door closed again on Paterson.

'You're going to have to tell him sometime,' said Bernard, in a whisper that was both fierce and not particularly quiet. 'Preferably before Carlotta Carmichael's office gets in touch.'

'Yes, but I was thinking of doing it somewhere public where he can't kill me. And I need to speak to Kate, really soon.'

Mona laughed. 'Why? To tell her she's getting married?'

'Shut up.'

Paterson reappeared in the doorway. 'Will Bircham-Fowler's speech be on Parliament TV? It should be on any minute.'

'I'll get it.' Bernard sat down at his PC and called up the Parliament site. 'That's odd – they're just showing an empty chamber.'

They gathered round his screen.

'Flick over to the news, Bernard.' He clicked on the live news feed.

A presenter was speaking without making a sound. 'Don't you have speakers?'

'It must be on mute.' He tried to remember what button to press. 'How do I get the sound to turn on?'

'There's an icon that you have to press.'

'There's Theresa in the background.' Mona pointed at the screen. 'What is she … Is she crying?'

Bernard, at last, found the mute button and deselected it.

' …*and Professor Bircham-Fowler's heart attack has come as a great shock to his friends and colleagues.*'

'Heart attack?'

'Is he dead?'

'How was he when you left him, Mona?'

Their questions all came at once, everyone talking over everyone else as they tried to work out what was happening. 'He was fine when I left him with Ian Jacobsen. He was tired, but he wasn't complaining about feeling ill or anything. I suppose it was a pretty upsetting few days for him, and he is in his sixties … What's going on, Guv?'

'I don't know.' Paterson was still staring at the screen with an expression on his face that she couldn't quite place. 'I thought they'd take him to a safe house …'

'So you don't think this was a heart attack? You think someone did this to him?'

'I'm not saying that,' said Paterson quickly. 'People like the professor do have heart attacks, Mona. He was no spring chicken.' He blinked and looked away, uncomfortable under her gaze. 'I think, Mona, we have to accept that the professor was just put under too much stress.'

Paterson was moving onto acceptance of this far too quickly for her liking. She was reminded of Bob's overly soothing tones on the drive back to Edinburgh. She decided to try something. 'When the professor and I were shot at, Guv...'

'You were shot at?' said Maitland. 'When were you going to mention that?'

She ignored him. 'The gunman knew my name. I tried to tell the Police Scotland guys that, but they refused to believe me. Said I was over-tired, imagining things.'

There was a silence, and Paterson's face contorted through several expressions before he responded. 'It was a difficult few days, Mona, you could have been—'

'He knew my name!'

Out of the corner of her eye she could see Bernard and Maitland exchanging glances.

'Everyone get on with your work.' Paterson turned on his heel, and retreated into his office, slamming the door behind him, hard.

'What was...?'

'Not now, Maitland.'

She picked up her bag and walked out, a quieter but no less furious exit than Paterson's. She was sure this wasn't just a random event, a stress-induced heart attack. But the Guv was going to toe the party line on all this. Paterson's first instinct was to think about his job, to think – as always – about keeping Stuttle happy.

'Mona.'

'Bernard, this isn't a good time.'

'I just thought you'd like to know that the professor is still alive. According to the BBC website he's in a critical condition in hospital.'

'Until someone else gets to him and finishes off the job.'

What did this mean for her? The man who had pointed a gun at them last night knew her by name. Was she in danger?

'Mona, wait.'

She could hear Bernard hurrying after her.

'You're not going to do anything stupid, are you?'

She didn't answer.

'Because the professor isn't your responsibility now. There are other people looking after him.'

She thought about the events of the previous night. The professor had been quick to protect her, sheltering her body from the gunfire.

'I think he is my responsibility. And I'm not sure that Stuttle and his pals can actually protect him.'

'And you can?'

'I can try.'

He was looking at her with his usual annoying expression that was part doubt and part confusion.

'Go back to the office, Bernard, and I'll see you on Monday. I've just had a really shitty …'

'Let me help.'

'What?'

'Professor Bircham-Fowler says a lot of things that people don't like, but I think he is honest and open, and makes a lot of sense. I don't really understand what's going on, but if you say he's in danger I believe you. I want to help. We need the professor and people like him. Their voices need to be heard.'

She stared at him, then a slow smile spread across her face. 'That's good. That's really, really good, Bernard. Because I think I've got a plan ...'

ACKNOWLEDGEMENTS

Huge thanks are due to everyone at Sandstone Press for all their support in producing this book, particularly Moira Forsyth.

I'm extremely grateful to everyone who has supported my books so far, whether that is turning up to launches and events, helping publicise it, or providing events to promote crime writing. A special thank you to the Murder and Mayhem folk – it's been a blast!

Thanks to friends, both old and new, for putting up with me.

And finally, thanks to Gordon for his love and support. And to my sons; I remain convinced that one day they will finally put down the X-box controller and actually read something I've written.

Turn the page for an exclusive first look at *Death at the Plague Museum*, the third book in the *Health of Strangers* series.

I

The man fell, his hands clutching wildly at the air, grabbing at imaginary handholds like a desperate climber
reverse-mountaineering his way to the earth. The jacket
of his suit flapped as he fell, an ineffective parachute that
did nothing to slow his inexorable journey toward the
ground.

As he passed the second-floor balcony the screen
went hazy for a second, before another shot of the body
appeared.

Cameron Stuttle, Chief Executive of the Scottish
Health Enforcement Partnership, paused the recording.
'The boys from IT edited the whole thing together. The
museum's got CCTV on each floor, apart from the very
top one. We thought it would be useful if the four of
you from the Health Enforcement Team saw his entire
downward journey.'

From this angle, the camera was pointing at the man's
face. Mona winced at his horrified expression, fear and
confusion writ large. She'd be replaying that image in
her head, she knew, probably just as she was falling off
to sleep tonight. At least she'd be able to put tonight's
insomnia down to work rather than her usual concerns
about her love life, or her mother's health.

The screen went fuzzy again, and a third camera angle
kicked in. This time, the screen was empty apart from a

plastic model of something large and scientific. A foot appeared in the corner of the picture, rapidly followed by the rest of the body, which crashed at speed into the sculpture.

'Ooh,' said Maitland. 'That's got to hurt. What was the thing that he landed on?'

'It's a 3-D model of the H1N1 virus,' said Bernard, his eyes tightly closed. 'It's part of their standing exhibition.'

'How come you know so much about it?'

'I'm a member.' Still without fully opening his eyes, Bernard dug into his wallet and produced a small card. Mona took it from him and examined it, Maitland peering over her shoulder. It proclaimed the bearer of the card to be a full member of the Edinburgh Museum of Plagues and Pandemics. The flip side highlighted the benefits of this, which included free access to all the exhibitions, and a 10% discount in the café and shop.

'Can we see it again?' John Paterson, the HET team leader, was staring thoughtfully at the blank TV screen.

'OK,' Stuttle pressed a button and the recording started again. 'Once more with feeling. You might want to look away now, Bernard.'

Mona watched again as the man fell fearfully to his death through the central internal stairwell of the museum. Something about the whole recording unsettled her. 'Is it just me, or does he look mighty panicked for a man that's opted to end it all?'

Paterson nodded. 'Yeah, he's flailing about a lot for a suicide. Don't jumpers just let themselves fall?' He frowned. 'What makes you so sure this was intentional, Cameron? How do you know someone didn't tip him over the top?'

'A couple of things. First of all, as far as we can make

330

out he was completely alone in the building. There's no evidence on any of the CCTV cameras of any movement other than his, and, like everywhere else these days, this building has secure Green Card technology. Nobody gets into the building without entering their Green Card in the machine.' He paused, as if waiting for someone to challenge him. Satisfied that they were all in agreement on this, he carried on. 'And secondly, he left a note, of sorts.'

'Of sorts?' Maitland looked intrigued.

'It's a little bit ambiguous. Could be suicide note, or it could be a resignation letter.'

'From what? What was his job?'

'I'll come back to that in a minute. Bernard, did you have a question?'

Bernard was sitting patiently with his hand raised. Maitland nudged Mona in the ribs. 'Probably wants to know what was going on while he was too scared to look.'

'Shut up.' She tried not to smile.

Bernard looked put out but kept going. 'It's more of a comment really. I think it's a strange place to choose to commit suicide.'

'Jumpers often choose somewhere significant to them ...' said Mona.

'Yeah, maybe he was also a member.' Maitland smirked. 'Probably wanted one last 10% off at the shop. Check his bag for souvenirs.'

Bernard's cheeks were scarlet. 'That wasn't what I meant. I was trying to say that it was an odd place to choose to jump, because there is no guarantee that you would actually die. You'd end up horribly injured, but depending on where you landed you might survive.'

'A very valid point, Bernard.' Stuttle nodded.

If possible, it appeared that Bernard's cheeks turned even redder.

Stuttle continued. 'Particularly as in this case, the fall didn't immediately kill him. He'd probably have splattered if he'd landed on the marble floor at reception, but the plastic model thingy cushioned his fall.'

'So was it the fall that killed him?' Paterson raised an eyebrow.

'We're not sure yet. The pathologists are running some tests even as we speak, but the initial indications are that there was something in his bloodstream that shouldn't have been.'

'Like poison?' asked Mona.

Cameron shrugged. 'Possibly.'

There was a small ripple of interest, which Paterson raised his hand to quell. 'Fascinating as this is, I don't see what it has to do with the HET. We search for people who have missed their monthly health check. If this guy is overdue for a health check he's got a really, really good excuse.'

'I'm aware of all that.'

Paterson continued to look suspicious. 'This isn't one of those scenarios when you need some dirty work doing, and you are going to pressgang us into helping you?'

Mona's mind went back to her recent trip to London with Paterson to search for a missing professor. The words 'pressgang' and 'dirty work' had all been entirely applicable to it.

'I'm hurt that you would think that of me, John,' said Cameron, smiling. 'Let me explain ...'

His justification was interrupted by a knock on the office door. Their heads all swivelled round to see Ian

Jacobsen from Police Scotland appear. Mona felt a wave of fury rising up from her feet. She tutted loudly, and turned back to glare at Stuttle, who was busy not catching her eye.

'Ian, perfect timing. I was just explaining to our HET colleagues about the unfortunate incident at the pandemics museum.'

'Morning all.' Ian smiled at the company. Only Bernard smiled back, then looked slightly alarmed when he realised none of his colleagues was extending similar pleasantries. 'I'm hoping that the HET and Police Scotland can work jointly on this.'

'No way.' Mona couldn't believe what she was hearing.

'Mona ...'

'No, I'm sorry Mr Stuttle, but I'd rather resign than work with Ian and his colleagues.'

A look passed between Stuttle and Paterson that she didn't understand.

'Seriously, Guv, last time we worked together I nearly got shot.'

It was Ian's turn to tut. 'Last time we worked together I was under the impression I saved your life ...'

Mona's jaw fell open at this flagrant rewriting of history.

'Mona,' Stuttle's tone was at its most conciliatory, 'just listen to what Ian has to say. I'm sure we can accommodate everyone.'

She was torn between continuing to make her point, and having her curiosity satisfied about the body. She ended up not saying anything, which Ian took as a signal to start talking.

'I have to stress to you all that everything from today's meeting is confidential ...'

'Of course.' Paterson responded for all of them.

'The gentleman that you just watched take a tumble was called Nathan McVie.'

'I recognise that name,' said Bernard.

'You should. He is – was – Director of Pandemic Policy for the Scottish Government. Which made him probably the second most important civil servant with regards to the Virus. Not, it has to be said, a particular fan of the HETs. He regarded them as largely window-dressing, with limited actual impact on the Virus.'

'Always nice to meet a fan,' said Paterson. 'But I still fail to see what this has to do with us. He's dead, not missing.'

'True. And if that's all there was to it I wouldn't be imposing on your time. But let me tell you about Mr McVie's last day. At 10am last Friday, he turned up here for a meeting–'

'With the museum staff?'

'No, they'd no involvement in the meeting at all. The museum rents out conference spaces on the top floor, and McVie had booked one late on Thursday. Although we are wondering why Mr McVie couldn't find a meeting room anywhere in Victoria Quay, St Andrews House or any of the other Edinburgh buildings owned by the Government. Anyway, four people attended the meeting; Mr McVie, Carlotta Carmichael MSP—' he broke off in response to the low growl of dismay that was coming collectively from the HET staff '—the same Ms Carmichael who was recently spotted at the North Edinburgh HET office, complaining about the standards of housekeeping and threatening to establish an Inspector of HETs post, if my sources are correct.' Ian grinned.

'Shut up and get on with it.'

'So McVie, Ms Carmichael, and two other civil servants were at the meeting: Jasper Connington, who is Director-General Health for the Scottish Government, and Helen Sopel, Director of the Virus Operational Response team.'

'Still not seeing what it has to do with us.'

'At 8.30 this morning, Helen Sopel failed to turn up for her monthly scheduled health check. As you can imagine for someone in her position, missing a Health Check is unthinkable. She didn't turn up for work this morning, and her colleagues couldn't get any answer from her mobile. While her staff were wondering what they should do about her unexpected absence, her sister phoned up looking for her. Apparently she was worried as Helen stood her up for a cinema trip on Sunday night.'

'That's not good.'

'Quite so.' Stuttle nodded. 'The four most important people in Virus policy in Scotland had a meeting here on Friday morning. At 11.30pm on Friday night, one of them kills himself, and at some point over the weekend, another one goes missing.'

'Carlotta Car ....'

'Carlotta Carmichael was absolutely alive and well as of an hour ago, so don't get your hopes up, John.'

'Do we know what the meeting was about?' asked Bernard.

'No, we don't. But we need to get Helen Sopel found and into a health check before anyone notices that she's gone. Because these are the people at the very top of Virus policy, these are the people who are continually popping up on the TV telling us that everything is under control, these are the people who are supposed to be making everything all right. If word gets out that they are going crazy, there's going to be panic on the streets.' He looked round at them all. 'There's going to be bloodshed.'

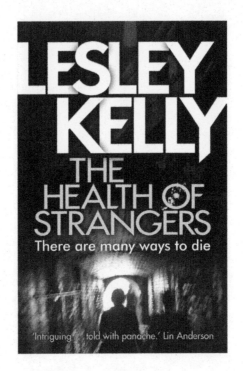

LESLEY KELLY

THE HEALTH OF STRANGERS

There are many ways to die

'Intriguing... told with panache.' Lin Anderson

In an Edinburgh reeling from a deadly Virus, two students go missing. Mona and Bernard have to tackle cults, late night raves and the mysterious involvement of overseas governments, to reach the girls before anyone else does...

Pages which virtually turned themselves. I bloody loved it.

GRAB THIS BOOK